NEVER LET ME GO

by the same author

A PALE VIEW OF HILLS
AN ARTIST OF THE FLOATING WORLD
THE REMAINS OF THE DAY
THE UNCONSOLED
WHEN WE WERE ORPHANS

Never Let Me Go

KAZUO ISHIGURO

faber and faber

First published in 2005
by Faber and Faber Limited
3 Queen Square London WC1N 3AU

Typeset by Faber and Faber Limited
Printed in England by Mackays of Chatham plc,
Chatham, Kent

A CIP record for this book
is available from the British Library

ISBN 0–571–22411–3

2 4 6 8 10 9 7 5 3

To Lorna and Naomi

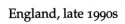

England, late 1990s

PART ONE

CHAPTER ONE

My name is Kathy H. I'm thirty-one years old, and I've been a carer now for over eleven years. That sounds long enough, I know, but actually they want me to go on for another eight months, until the end of this year. That'll make it almost exactly twelve years. Now I know my being a carer so long isn't necessarily because they think I'm fantastic at what I do. There are some really good carers who've been told to stop after just two or three years. And I can think of one carer at least who went on for all of fourteen years despite being a complete waste of space. So I'm not trying to boast. But then I do know for a fact they've been pleased with my work, and by and large, I have too. My donors have always tended to do much better than expected. Their recovery times have been impressive, and hardly any of them have been classified as 'agitated', even before fourth donation. Okay, maybe I *am* boasting now. But it means a lot to me, being able to do my work well, especially that bit about my donors staying 'calm'. I've developed a kind of instinct around donors. I know when to hang around and comfort them, when to leave them to themselves; when to listen to everything they have to say, and when just to shrug and tell them to snap out of it.

Anyway, I'm not making any big claims for myself. I know carers, working now, who are just as good and don't get half the credit. If you're one of them, I can understand how you might get resentful – about my bedsit, my car, above all, the way I get to pick and choose who I look after. And I'm a Hailsham student – which is enough by itself sometimes to get people's backs up. Kathy H., they say, she gets to pick and choose, and she always chooses her own kind: people from Hailsham, or one of the other privileged estates. No wonder she has a great record. I've heard it said enough, so I'm sure you've heard it plenty more, and maybe there's something in it. But I'm not the first to be allowed to pick and choose, and I doubt if I'll be the last. And anyway, I've done my share of looking after donors brought up in every kind of place. By the time I finish, remember, I'll have done twelve years of this, and it's only for the last six they've let me choose.

And why shouldn't they? Carers aren't machines. You try and do your best for every donor, but in the end, it wears you down. You don't have unlimited patience and energy. So when you get a chance to choose, of course, you choose your own kind. That's natural. There's no way I could have gone on for as long as I have if I'd stopped feeling for my donors every step of the way. And anyway, if I'd never started choosing, how would I ever have got close again to Ruth and Tommy after all those years?

But these days, of course, there are fewer and fewer donors left who I remember, and so in practice, I haven't been choosing that much. As I say, the work gets a lot harder when you don't have that deeper link with the donor, and though I'll miss being a carer, it feels just about right to be finishing at last come the end of the year.

Ruth, incidentally, was only the third or fourth donor I got to choose. She already had a carer assigned to her at the time, and I remember it taking a bit of nerve on my part. But in the end I managed it, and the instant I saw her again, at that recovery centre in Dover, all our differences – while they didn't exactly vanish – seemed not nearly as important as all the other things: like the fact that we'd grown up together at Hailsham, the fact that we knew and remembered things no one else did. It's ever since then, I suppose, I started seeking out for my donors people from the past, and whenever I could, people from Hailsham.

There have been times over the years when I've tried to leave Hailsham behind, when I've told myself I shouldn't look back so much. But then there came a point when I just stopped resisting. It had to do with this particular donor I had once, in my third year as a carer; it was his reaction when I mentioned I was from Hailsham. He'd just come through his third donation, it hadn't gone well, and he must have known he wasn't going to make it.

He could hardly breathe, but he looked towards me and said: 'Hailsham. I bet that was a beautiful place.' Then the next morning, when I was making conversation to keep his mind off it all, and I asked where *he'd* grown up, he mentioned some place in Dorset and his face beneath the blotches went into a completely new kind of grimace. And I realised then how desperately he didn't want reminded. Instead, he wanted to hear about Hailsham.

So over the next five or six days, I told him whatever he wanted to know, and he'd lie there, all hooked up, a gentle smile breaking through. He'd ask me about the big things and the little things. About our guardians, about how we each had our own collection chests under our beds, the football, the rounders, the little path that took you all round the outside of the main house, round all its nooks and crannies, the duck pond, the food, the view from the Art Room over the fields on a foggy morning. Sometimes he'd make me say things over and over; things I'd told him only the day before, he'd ask about like I'd never told him. 'Did you have a sports pavilion?' 'Which guardian was your special favourite?' At first I thought this was just the drugs, but then I realised his mind was clear enough. What he wanted was not just to hear about Hailsham, but to *remember* Hailsham, just like it had been his own childhood. He knew he was close to completing and so that's what he was doing: getting me to describe things to him, so they'd really sink in, so that maybe during those sleepless nights, with the drugs and the pain and the exhaustion, the line would blur between what were my memories and what were his. That was when I first understood, really understood, just how lucky we'd been – Tommy, Ruth, me, all the rest of us.

Driving around the country now, I still see things that will remind me of Hailsham. I might pass the corner of a misty field, or see part of a large house in the distance as I come down the side of a valley, even a particular arrangement of poplar trees up on a hillside, and I'll think: 'Maybe that's it! I've found it! This actually *is* Hailsham!' Then I see it's impossible and I go on driving, my thoughts drifting on elsewhere. In particular, there are those pavilions. I spot them all over the country, standing on the far side of playing fields, little white prefab buildings with a row of windows unnaturally high up, tucked almost under the eaves. I think they built a whole lot like that in the fifties and sixties, which is probably when ours was put up. If I drive past one I keep looking over to it for as long as possible, and one day I'll crash the car like that, but I keep doing it. Not long ago I was driving through an empty stretch of Worcestershire and saw one beside a cricket ground so like ours at Hailsham I actually turned the car and went back for a second look.

We loved our sports pavilion, maybe because it reminded us of those sweet little cottages people always had in picture books when we were young. I can remember us back in the Juniors, pleading with guardians to hold the next lesson in the pavilion instead of the usual room. Then by the time we were in Senior 2 – when we were twelve, going on thirteen – the pavilion had become the place to hide out with your best friends when you wanted to get away from the rest of Hailsham.

The pavilion was big enough to take two separate groups without them bothering each other – in the summer, a third group could hang about out on the veranda. But ideally you and your friends wanted the place just to yourselves, so there was often jockeying and arguing. The guardians were always telling us to be civilised about it, but in practice, you needed to have some strong personalities in your group to stand a chance of getting the pavilion during a break or free period. I wasn't exactly the wilting type myself, but I suppose it was really because of Ruth we got in there as often as we did.

Usually we just spread ourselves around the chairs and benches – there'd be five of us, six if Jenny B. came along – and had a good gossip. There was a kind of conversation that could only happen when you were hidden away in the pavilion; we might discuss something that was worrying us, or we might end up screaming with laughter, or in a furious row. Mostly, it was a way to unwind for a while with your closest friends.

On the particular afternoon I'm now thinking of, we were standing up on stools and benches, crowding around the high windows. That gave us a clear view of the North Playing Field where about a dozen boys from our year and Senior 3 had gathered to play football. There was bright sunshine, but it must have been raining earlier that day because I can remember how the sun was glinting on the muddy surface of the grass.

Someone said we shouldn't be so obvious about watching, but we hardly moved back at all. Then Ruth said: 'He doesn't suspect a thing. Look at him. He really doesn't suspect a thing.'

When she said this, I looked at her and searched for signs of disapproval about what the boys were going to do to Tommy. But the next second Ruth gave a little laugh and said: 'The idiot!'

And I realised that for Ruth and the others, whatever the boys chose to do was pretty remote from us; whether we approved or not didn't come into it. We were gathered around the windows at that moment not because we relished the prospect of seeing Tommy get humiliated yet again, but just because we'd heard about this latest plot and were vaguely curious to watch it unfold. In those days, I don't think what the boys did amongst themselves went much deeper than that. For Ruth, for the others, it was that detached, and the chances are that's how it was for me too.

Or maybe I'm remembering it wrong. Maybe even then, when I saw Tommy rushing about that field, undisguised delight on his face to be accepted back in the fold again, about to play the game at which he so excelled, maybe I did feel a little stab of pain. What I do remember is that I noticed Tommy was wearing the light blue polo shirt he'd got in the Sales the previous month – the one he was so proud of. I remember thinking: 'He's really stupid, playing football in that. It'll get ruined, then how's he going to feel?' Out loud, I said, to no one in particular: 'Tommy's got his shirt on. His favourite polo shirt.'

I don't think anyone heard me, because they were all laughing at Laura – the big clown in our group – mimicking one after the other the expressions that appeared on Tommy's face as he ran, waved, called, tackled. The other boys were all moving around the field in that deliberately languorous way they have when they're warming up, but Tommy, in his excitement, seemed already to be going full pelt. I said, louder this time: 'He's going to be so sick if he ruins that shirt.' This time Ruth heard me, but she must have thought I'd meant it as some kind of joke, because she laughed half-heartedly, then made some quip of her own.

Then the boys had stopped kicking the ball about, and were standing in a pack in the mud, their chests gently rising and falling as they waited for the team picking to start. The two captains who emerged were from Senior 3, though everyone knew Tommy was a better player than any of that year. They tossed for first pick, then the one who'd won stared at the group.

'Look at him,' someone behind me said. 'He's completely convinced he's going to be first pick. Just look at him!'

There *was* something comical about Tommy at that moment, something that made you think, well, yes, if he's going to be that daft, he deserves what's coming. The other boys were all pretending to ignore the picking process, pretending they didn't care where they came in the order. Some were talking quietly to each other, some re-tying their laces, others just staring down at their feet as they trammelled the mud. But Tommy was looking eagerly at the Senior 3 boy, as though his name had already been called.

Laura kept up her performance all through the team-picking, doing all the different expressions that went across Tommy's face: the bright eager one at the start; the puzzled concern when four picks had gone by and he still hadn't been chosen; the hurt and panic as it began to dawn on him what was really going on. I didn't keep glancing round at Laura, though, because I was watching Tommy; I only knew what she was doing because the others kept laughing and egging her on. Then when Tommy was left standing alone, and the boys all began sniggering, I heard Ruth say:

'It's coming. Hold it. Seven seconds. Seven, six, five . . .'

She never got there. Tommy burst into thunderous bellowing, and the boys, now laughing openly, started to run off towards the

8

South Playing Field. Tommy took a few strides after them – it was hard to say whether his instinct was to give angry chase or if he was panicked at being left behind. In any case he soon stopped and stood there, glaring after them, his face scarlet. Then he began to scream and shout, a nonsensical jumble of swear words and insults.

We'd all seen plenty of Tommy's tantrums by then, so we came down off our stools and spread ourselves around the room. We tried to start up a conversation about something else, but there was Tommy going on and on in the background, and although at first we just rolled our eyes and tried to ignore it, in the end – probably a full ten minutes after we'd first moved away – we were back up at the windows again.

The other boys were now completely out of view, and Tommy was no longer trying to direct his comments in any particular direction. He was just raving, flinging his limbs about, at the sky, at the wind, at the nearest fence post. Laura said he was maybe 'rehearsing his Shakespeare'. Someone else pointed out how each time he screamed something he'd raise one foot off the ground, pointing it outwards, 'like a dog doing a pee'. Actually, I'd noticed the same foot movement myself, but what had struck me was that each time he stamped the foot back down again, flecks of mud flew up around his shins. I thought again about his precious shirt, but he was too far away for me to see if he'd got much mud on it.

'I suppose it is a bit cruel,' Ruth said, 'the way they always work him up like that. But it's his own fault. If he learnt to keep his cool, they'd leave him alone.'

'They'd still keep on at him,' Hannah said. 'Graham K.'s temper's just as bad, but that only makes them all the more careful with him. The reason they go for Tommy's because he's a layabout.'

Then everyone was talking at once, about how Tommy never even tried to be creative, about how he hadn't even put anything in for the Spring Exchange. I suppose the truth was, by that stage, each of us was secretly wishing a guardian would come from the house and take him away. And although we hadn't had any part

9

in this latest plan to rile Tommy, we *had* taken out ringside seats, and we were starting to feel guilty. But there was no sign of a guardian, so we just kept swapping reasons why Tommy deserved everything he got. Then when Ruth looked at her watch and said even though we still had time, we should get back to the main house, nobody argued.

Tommy was still going strong as we came out of the pavilion. The house was over to our left, and since Tommy was standing in the field straight ahead of us, there was no need to go anywhere near him. In any case, he was facing the other way and didn't seem to register us at all. All the same, as my friends set off along the edge of the field, I started to drift over towards him. I knew this would puzzle the others, but I kept going – even when I heard Ruth's urgent whisper to me to come back.

I suppose Tommy wasn't used to being disturbed during his rages, because his first response when I came up to him was to stare at me for a second, then carry on as before. It *was* like he was doing Shakespeare and I'd come up onto the stage in the middle of his performance. Even when I said: 'Tommy, your nice shirt. You'll get it all messed up,' there was no sign of him having heard me.

So I reached forward and put a hand on his arm. Afterwards, the others thought he'd meant to do it, but I was pretty sure it was unintentional. His arms were still flailing about, and he wasn't to know I was about to put out my hand. Anyway, as he threw up his arm, he knocked my hand aside and hit the side of my face. It didn't hurt at all, but I let out a gasp, and so did most of the girls behind me.

That's when at last Tommy seemed to become aware of me, of the others, of himself, of the fact that he was there in that field, behaving the way he had been, and stared at me a bit stupidly.

'Tommy,' I said, quite sternly. 'There's mud all over your shirt.'

'So what?' he mumbled. But even as he said this, he looked down and noticed the brown specks, and only just stopped himself crying out in alarm. Then I saw the surprise register on his face that I should know about his feelings for the polo shirt.

'It's nothing to worry about,' I said, before the silence got humiliating for him. 'It'll come off. If you can't get it off yourself, just take it to Miss Jody.'

He went on examining his shirt, then said grumpily: 'It's nothing to do with you anyway.'

He seemed to regret immediately this last remark and looked at me sheepishly, as though expecting me to say something comforting back to him. But I'd had enough of him by now, particularly with the girls watching – and for all I knew, any number of others from the windows of the main house. So I turned away with a shrug and rejoined my friends.

Ruth put an arm around my shoulders as we walked away. 'At least you got him to pipe down,' she said. 'Are you okay? Mad animal.'

CHAPTER TWO

This was all a long time ago so I might have some of it wrong; but my memory of it is that my approaching Tommy that afternoon was part of a phase I was going through around that time – something to do with compulsively setting myself challenges – and I'd more or less forgotten all about it when Tommy stopped me a few days later.

I don't know how it was where you were, but at Hailsham we had to have some form of medical almost every week – usually up in Room 18 at the very top of the house – with stern Nurse Trisha, or Crow Face, as we called her. That sunny morning a crowd of us was going up the central staircase to be examined by her, while another lot she'd just finished with was on its way down. So the stairwell was filled with echoing noise, and I was climbing the steps head down, just following the heels of the person in front, when a voice near me went: 'Kath!'

Tommy, who was in the stream coming down, had stopped dead on the stairs with a big open smile that immediately irritated me. A few years earlier maybe, if we ran into someone we were pleased to see, we'd put on that sort of look. But we were thirteen by then, and this was a boy running into a girl in a really public situation. I felt like saying: 'Tommy, why don't you grow up?' But I stopped myself, and said instead: 'Tommy, you're holding everyone up. And so am I.'

He glanced upwards and sure enough the flight above was already grinding to a halt. For a second he looked panicked, then he squeezed himself right into the wall next to me, so it was just about possible for people to push past. Then he said:

'Kath, I've been looking all over for you. I meant to say sorry. I mean, I'm really, really sorry. I honestly didn't mean to hit you the other day. I wouldn't dream of hitting a girl, and even if I did,

I'd never want to hit *you*. I'm really, really sorry.'

'It's okay. An accident, that's all.' I gave him a nod and made to move away. But Tommy said brightly:

'The shirt's all right now. It all washed out.'

'That's good.'

'It didn't hurt, did it? When I hit you?'

'Sure. Fractured skull. Concussion, the lot. Even Crow Face might notice it. That's if I ever get up there.'

'But seriously, Kath. No hard feelings, right? I'm awfully sorry. I am, honestly.'

At last I gave him a smile and said with no irony: 'Look, Tommy, it was an accident and it's now one hundred per cent forgotten. I don't hold it against you one tiny bit.'

He still looked unsure, but now some older students were pushing behind him, telling him to move. He gave me a quick smile and patted my shoulder, like he might do to a younger boy, and pushed his way into the flow. Then, as I began to climb, I heard him shout from below: 'See you, Kath!'

I'd found the whole thing mildly embarrassing, but it didn't lead to any teasing or gossip; and I must admit, if it hadn't been for that encounter on the stairs, I probably wouldn't have taken the interest I did in Tommy's problems over the next several weeks.

I saw a few of the incidents myself. But mostly I heard about them, and when I did, I quizzed people until I'd got a more or less full account. There were more temper tantrums, like the time Tommy was supposed to have heaved over two desks in Room 14, spilling all the contents on the floor, while the rest of the class, having escaped on to the landing, barricaded the door to stop him coming out. There was the time Mr Christopher had had to pin back his arms to stop him attacking Reggie D. during football practice. Everyone could see, too, when the Senior 2 boys went on their fields run, Tommy was the only one without a running part-ner. He was a good runner, and would quickly open up ten, fif-teen yards between him and the rest, maybe thinking this would disguise the fact that no one wanted to run with him. Then there were rumours almost every day of pranks that had been played on him. A lot of these were the usual stuff – weird things in his bed, a worm in his cereal – but some of it sounded pointlessly nasty: like the time someone cleaned a toilet with his toothbrush so it was waiting for him with shit all over the bristles. His size and strength – and I suppose that temper – meant no one tried actual physical bullying, but from what I remember, for a couple of months at least, these incidents kept coming. I thought sooner or later someone would start saying it had gone too far, but it just kept on, and no one said anything.

I tried to bring it up once myself, in the dorm after lights-out. In the Seniors, we were down to six per dorm, so it was just our little group, and we often had our most intimate conversations lying in the dark before we fell asleep. You could talk about things there you wouldn't dream of talking about any other place, not even in the pavilion. So one night I brought up Tommy. I didn't say much; I just summed up what had been happening to him and said it wasn't really very fair. When I'd finished, there was a funny sort of silence hanging in the dark, and I realised everyone was waiting for Ruth's response – which was usually what happened whenever something a bit awkward came up. I kept waiting, then I heard a sigh from Ruth's side of the room, and she said:

'You've got a point, Kathy. It's not nice. But if he wants it to stop, he's got to change his own attitude. He didn't have a thing for the Spring Exchange. And has he got anything for next month? I bet he hasn't.'

I should explain a bit here about the Exchanges we had at Hailsham. Four times a year – spring, summer, autumn, winter – we had a kind of big exhibition-cum-sale of all the things we'd been creating in the three months since the last Exchange. Paintings, drawings, pottery; all sorts of 'sculptures' made from whatever was the craze of the day – bashed-up cans, maybe, or bottle tops stuck onto cardboard. For each thing you put in, you were paid in Exchange Tokens – the guardians decided how many your particular masterpiece merited – and then on the day of the Exchange you went along with your tokens and 'bought' the stuff you liked. The rule was you could only buy work done by students in your own year, but that still gave us plenty to choose from, since most of us could get pretty prolific over a three-month period.

Looking back now, I can see why the Exchanges became so important to us. For a start, they were our only means, aside from the Sales – the Sales were something else, which I'll come to later – of building up a collection of personal possessions. If, say, you wanted to decorate the walls around your bed, or wanted something to carry around in your bag and place on your desk from room to room, then you could find it at the Exchange. I can see now, too, how the Exchanges had a more subtle effect on us all. If you think about it, being dependent on each other to produce the stuff that might become your private treasures – that's bound to do things to your relationships. The Tommy business was typical. A lot of the time, how you were regarded at Hailsham, how much you were liked and respected, had to do with how good you were at 'creating'.

Ruth and I often found ourselves remembering these things a few years ago, when I was caring for her down at the recovery centre in Dover.

'It's all part of what made Hailsham so special,' she said once. 'The way we were encouraged to value each other's work.'

'True,' I said. 'But sometimes, when I think about the Exchanges now, a lot of it seems a bit odd. The poetry, for instance. I remember we were allowed to hand in poems, instead of a drawing or a painting. And the strange thing was, we all thought that was fine, we thought that made sense.'

'Why shouldn't it? Poetry's important.'

'But we're talking about nine-year-old stuff, funny little lines, all misspelt, in exercise books. We'd spend our precious tokens on an exercise book full of that stuff rather than on something really nice for around our beds. If we were so keen on a person's poetry, why didn't we just borrow it and copy it down ourselves any old afternoon? But you remember how it was. An Exchange would come along and we'd be standing there torn between Susie K.'s poems and those giraffes Jackie used to make.'

'Jackie's giraffes,' Ruth said with a laugh. 'They were so beautiful. I used to have one.'

We were having this conversation on a fine summer evening, sitting out on the little balcony of her recovery room. It was a few months after her first donation, and now she was over the worst of it, I'd always time my evening visits so that we'd be able to spend a half hour or so out there, watching the sun go down over the rooftops. You could see lots of aerials and satellite dishes, and sometimes, right over in the distance, a glistening line that was the sea. I'd bring mineral water and biscuits, and we'd sit there talking about anything that came into our heads. The centre Ruth was in that time, it's one of my favourites, and I wouldn't mind at all if that's where I ended up. The recovery rooms are small, but they're well-designed and comfortable. Everything – the walls, the floor – has been done in gleaming white tiles, which the centre keeps so clean when you first go in it's almost like entering a hall of mirrors. Of course, you don't exactly see yourself reflected back loads of times, but you almost think you do. When you lift an arm, or when someone sits up in bed, you can feel this pale, shadowy movement all around you in the tiles. Anyway, Ruth's room at that centre, it also had these big glass sliding panels, so she could easily see the outside from her bed. Even with her head on the pillow she'd see a big lot of sky, and if it was warm enough, she could get all the fresh air she wanted by stepping out onto the balcony. I loved visiting her there, loved those meandering talks we had, through the summer to the early autumn, sitting on that balcony together, talking about Hailsham, the Cottages, whatever else drifted into our thoughts.

'What I'm saying,' I went on, 'is that when we were that age, when we were eleven, say, we really weren't interested in each other's poems at all. But remember, someone like Christy? Christy had this great reputation for poetry, and we all looked up to her for it. Even you, Ruth, you didn't dare boss Christy around. All because we thought she was great at poetry. But we didn't know a thing about poetry. We didn't care about it. It's strange.'

But Ruth didn't get my point – or maybe she was deliberately avoiding it. Maybe she was determined to remember us all as more sophisticated than we were. Or maybe she could sense where my talk was leading, and didn't want us to go that way. Anyway, she let out a long sigh and said:

'We all thought Christy's poems were so good. But I wonder how they'd look to us now. I wish we had some here, I'd love to see what we'd think.' Then she laughed and said: 'I *have* still got some poems by Peter B. But that was much later, when we were in Senior 4. I must have fancied him. I can't think why else I'd have bought his poems. They're just hysterically daft. Takes himself so seriously. But Christy, she was good, I remember she was. It's funny, she went right off poems when she started her painting. And she was nowhere near as good at that.'

But let me get back to Tommy. What Ruth said that time in our dorm after lights-out, about how Tommy had brought all his problems on himself, probably summed up what most people at Hailsham thought at that time. But it was when she said what she did that it occurred to me, as I lay there, that this whole notion of his deliberately not trying was one that had been doing the rounds from as far back as the Juniors. And it came home to me, with a kind of chill, that Tommy had been going through what he'd been going through not just for weeks or months, but for years.

Tommy and I talked about all this not so long ago, and his own account of how his troubles began confirmed what I was thinking that night. According to him, it had all started one afternoon in one of Miss Geraldine's art classes. Until that day, Tommy told me, he'd always quite enjoyed painting. But then that day in Miss Geraldine's class, Tommy had done this particular watercolour – of an elephant standing in some tall grass – and that was what started it all off. He'd done it, he claimed, as a kind of joke. I quizzed him a lot on this point and I suspect the truth was that it was like a lot of things at that age: you don't have any clear reason, you just do it. You do it because you think it might get a laugh, or because you want to see if it'll cause a stir. And when you're asked to explain it afterwards, it doesn't seem to make any sense. We've all done things like that. Tommy didn't quite put it this way, but I'm sure that's how it happened.

Anyway, he did his elephant, which was exactly the sort of picture a kid three years younger might have done. It took him no more than twenty minutes and it got a laugh, sure enough, though not quite the sort he'd expected. Even so, it might not have led to anything – and this is a big irony, I suppose – if Miss Geraldine hadn't been taking the class that day.

Miss Geraldine was everyone's favourite guardian when we were that age. She was gentle, soft-spoken, and always comforted you when you needed it, even when you'd done something bad, or been told off by another guardian. If she ever had to tell you off herself, then for days afterwards she'd give you lots of extra attention, like she owed you something. It was unlucky for Tommy that it was Miss Geraldine taking art that day and not, say, Mr Robert or Miss Emily herself – the head guardian – who often took art. Had it been either of those two, Tommy would have got a bit of a telling off, he could have done his smirk, and the worst the others would have thought was that it was a feeble joke. He might even have had some students think him a right clown. But Miss Geraldine being Miss Geraldine, it didn't go that way. Instead, she did her best to look at the picture with kindness and understanding. And probably guessing Tommy was in danger of getting stick from the others, she went too far the other way, actually finding things to praise, pointing them out to the class. That was how the resentment started.

'After we left the room,' Tommy remembered, 'that's when I first heard them talking. And they didn't care I could hear.'

My guess is that from some time before he did that elephant, Tommy had had the feeling he wasn't keeping up – that his painting in particular was like that of students much younger than him – and he'd been covering up the best he could by doing deliberately childish pictures. But after the elephant painting, the whole thing had been brought into the open, and now everyone was watching to see what he did next. It seems he did make an effort for a while, but he'd no sooner have started on something, there'd be sneers and giggles all around him. In fact, the harder he tried, the more laughable his efforts turned out. So before long Tommy had gone back to his original defence, producing work that seemed deliberately childish, work that said he couldn't care less. From there, the thing had got deeper and deeper.

For a while he'd only had to suffer during art lessons – though that was often enough, because we did a lot of art in the Juniors. But then it grew bigger. He got left out of games, boys refused to sit next to him at dinner, or pretended not to hear if he said anything in his dorm after lights-out. At first it wasn't so relentless. Months could go by without incident, he'd think the whole thing was behind him, then something he did – or one of his enemies, like Arthur H. – would get it all going again.

I'm not sure when the big temper tantrums started. My own memory of it is that Tommy was always known for his temper, even in the Infants, but he claimed to me they only began after the teasing got bad. Anyway, it was those temper tantrums that really got people going, escalating everything, and around the time I'm talking about – the summer of our Senior 2, when we were thirteen – that was when the persecution reached its peak.

Then it all stopped, not overnight, but rapidly enough. I was, as I say, watching the situation closely around then, so I saw the signs before most of the others. It started with a period – it might have been a month, maybe longer – when the pranks went on pretty steadily, but Tommy failed to lose his temper. Sometimes I could see he was close to it, but he somehow controlled himself; other times, he'd quietly shrug, or react like he hadn't noticed a thing. At first these responses caused disappointment; maybe people were resentful, even, like he'd let them down. Then gradually, people got bored and the pranks became more half-hearted, until one day it struck me there hadn't been any for over a week.

This wouldn't necessarily have been so significant by itself, but I'd spotted other changes. Little things, like Alexander J. and Peter N. walking across the courtyard with him towards the fields, the three of them chatting quite naturally; a subtle but clear difference in people's voices when his name got mentioned. Then once, towards the end of an afternoon break, a group of us were sitting on the grass quite close to the South Playing Field where the boys, as usual, were playing their football. I was joining in our conversation, but keeping an eye on Tommy, who I noticed was right at the heart of the game. At one point he got tripped, and picking himself up, placed the ball on the ground to take the free kick himself. As the boys spread out in anticipation, I saw Arthur H. – one of his biggest tormentors – a few yards behind Tommy's back, begin mimicking him, doing a daft version of the way Tommy was standing over the ball, hands on hips. I watched carefully, but none of the others took up Arthur's cue. They must all have seen, because all eyes were looking towards Tommy, waiting for his kick, and Arthur was right behind him – but no one was interested. Tommy floated the ball across the grass, the game went on, and Arthur H. didn't try anything else.

I was pleased about all these developments, but also mystified. There'd been no real change in Tommy's work – his reputation for 'creativity' was as low as ever. I could see that an end to the tantrums was a big help, but what seemed to be the key factor was harder to put your finger on. There was something about Tommy himself – the way he carried himself, the way he looked people in the face and talked in his open, good-natured way – that was different from before, and which had in turn changed the attitudes of those around him. But what had brought all this on wasn't clear.

I was mystified, and decided to probe him a bit the next time we could talk in private. The chance came along before long, when I was lining up for lunch and spotted him a few places ahead in the queue.

I suppose this might sound odd, but at Hailsham, the lunch queue *was* one of the better places to have a private talk. It was something to do with the acoustics in the Great Hall; all the hub-bub and the high ceilings meant that so long as you lowered your voices, stood quite close, and made sure your neighbours were deep in their own chat, you had a fair chance of not being over-heard. In any case, we weren't exactly spoilt for choice. 'Quiet' places were often the worst, because there was always someone likely to be passing within earshot. And as soon as you looked like you were trying to sneak off for a secret talk, the whole place seemed to sense it within minutes, and you'd have no chance.

So when I saw Tommy a few places ahead of me, I waved him over – the rule being that though you couldn't jump the queue going forwards it was fine to go back. He came over with a delighted smile, and we stood together for a moment without saying much – not out of awkwardness, but because we were waiting for any interest aroused by Tommy's moving back to fade. Then I said to him:

'You seem much happier these days, Tommy. Things seem to be going much better for you.'

'You notice everything, don't you, Kath?' He said this completely without sarcasm. 'Yeah, everything's all right. I'm getting on all right.'

'So what's happened? Did you find God or something?'

'God?' Tommy was lost for a second. Then he laughed and said: 'Oh, I see. You're talking about me not . . . getting so angry.'

'Not just that, Tommy. You've turned things around for yourself. I've been watching. So that's why I was asking.'

Tommy shrugged. 'I've grown up a bit, I suppose. And maybe everyone else has too. Can't keep on with the same stuff all the time. Gets boring.'

I said nothing, but just kept looking right at him, until he gave another little laugh and said: 'Kath, you're so nosy. Okay, I suppose there is something. Something that happened. If you want, I'll tell you.'

'Well, go on then.'

'I'll tell you, Kath, but you mustn't spread it, all right? A couple of months back, I had this talk with Miss Lucy. And I felt much better afterwards. It's hard to explain. But she said something, and it all felt much better.'

'So what did she say?'

'Well . . . The thing is, it might sound strange. It did to me at first. What she said was that if I didn't want to be creative, if I really didn't feel like it, that was perfectly all right. Nothing wrong with it, she said.'

'That's what she told you?'

Tommy nodded, but I was already turning away.

'That's just rubbish, Tommy. If you're going to play stupid games, I can't be bothered.'

I was genuinely angry, because I thought he was lying to me, just when I deserved to be taken into his confidence. Spotting a girl I knew a few places back, I went over to her, leaving Tommy standing. I could see he was bewildered and crestfallen, but after the months I'd spent worrying about him, I felt betrayed, and didn't care how he felt. I chatted with my friend – I think it was Matilda – as cheerfully as possible, and hardly looked his way for the rest of the time we were in the queue.

But as I was carrying my plate to the tables, Tommy came up behind me and said quickly:

'Kath, I wasn't trying to pull your leg, if that's what you think. It's what happened. I'll tell you about it if you give me half a chance.'

'Don't talk rubbish, Tommy.'

'Kath, I'll tell you about it. I'll be down at the pond after lunch. If you come down there, I'll tell you.'

I gave him a reproachful look and walked off without responding, but already, I suppose, I'd begun to entertain the possibility that he wasn't, after all, making it up about Miss Lucy. And by the time I sat down with my friends, I was trying to figure out how I could sneak off afterwards down to the pond without getting everyone curious.

CHAPTER THREE

The pond lay to the south of the house. To get there you went out the back entrance, and down the narrow twisting path, pushing past the overgrown bracken that, in the early autumn, would still be blocking your way. Or if there were no guardians around, you could take a short cut through the rhubarb patch. Anyway, once you came out to the pond, you'd find a tranquil atmosphere waiting, with ducks and bulrushes and pond-weed. It wasn't, though, a good place for a discreet conversation – not nearly as good as the lunch queue. For a start you could be clearly seen from the house. And the way the sound travelled across the water was hard to predict; if people wanted to eavesdrop, it was the easiest thing to walk down the outer path and crouch in the bushes on the other side of the pond. But since it had been me that had cut him off in the lunch queue, I supposed I had to make the best of it. It was well into October by then, but the sun was out that day and I decided I could just about make out I'd gone strolling aimlessly down there and happened to come across Tommy.

Maybe because I was keen to keep up this impression – though I'd no idea if anyone was actually watching – I didn't try and sit down when I eventually found him seated on a large flat rock not far from the water's edge. It must have been a Friday or a weekend, because I remember we had on our own clothes. I don't remember exactly what Tommy was wearing – probably one of the raggy football shirts he wore even when the weather was chilly – but I definitely had on the maroon track suit top that zipped up the front, which I'd got at a Sale in Senior 1. I walked round him and stood with my back to the water, facing the house, so that I'd see if people started gathering at the windows. Then for a few minutes we talked about nothing in particular, just like the lunch-queue business hadn't happened. I'm not sure if it was for Tommy's benefit, or for any onlookers', but I'd kept my posture looking very provisional, and at one point made a move to carry on with my stroll. I saw a kind of panic cross Tommy's face then, and I immediately felt sorry to have teased him, even though I hadn't meant to. So I said, like I'd just remembered:

'By the way, what was that you were saying earlier on? About Miss Lucy telling you something?'

'Oh . . .' Tommy gazed past me to the pond, pretending too this was a topic he'd forgotten all about. 'Miss Lucy. Oh that.'

Miss Lucy was the most sporting of the guardians at Hailsham, though you might not have guessed it from her appearance. She had a squat, almost bulldoggy figure, and her odd black hair, when it grew, grew upwards so it never covered her ears or chunky neck. But she was really strong and fit, and even when we were older, most of us – even the boys – couldn't keep up with her on a fields run. She was superb at hockey, and could even hold her own with the Senior boys on the football pitch. I remember watching once when James B. tried to trip her as she went past him with the ball, and he was the one sent flying instead. When we'd been in the Juniors, she'd never been someone like Miss Geraldine who you turned to when you were upset. In fact, she didn't tend to speak much to us when we were younger. It was only in the Seniors, really, we'd started to appreciate her brisk style.

'You were saying something,' I said to Tommy. 'Something about Miss Lucy telling you it was all right not to be creative.'

'She did say something like that. She said I shouldn't worry. Not mind what other people were saying. A couple of months ago now. Maybe longer.'

Over at the house, a few Juniors had stopped at one of the upstairs windows and were watching us. But I now crouched down in front of Tommy, no longer pretending anything.

'Tommy, that's a funny thing for her to say. Are you sure you got it right?'

'Of course I got it right.' His voice lowered suddenly. 'She didn't just say it once. We were in her room and she gave me a whole talk about it.'

When she'd first asked him to come to h.
Appreciation, Tommy explained, he'd expected ,
ture about how he should try harder – the sort of th.
already from various guardians, including Miss Emi.
But as they were walking from the house towards the Oran
where the guardians had their living quarters – Tommy bega.
get an inkling this was something different. Then, once he was
seated in Miss Lucy's easy chair – she'd remained standing by the
window – she asked him to tell her the whole story, as he saw it,
of what had been happening to him. So Tommy had begun going
through it all. But before he was even half way she'd suddenly
broken in and started to talk herself. She'd known a lot of students, she'd said, who'd for a long time found it very difficult to
be creative: painting, drawing, poetry, none of it going right for
years. Then one day they'd turned a corner and blossomed. It was
quite possible Tommy was one of these.

Tommy had heard all of this before, but there was something
about Miss Lucy's manner that made him keep listening hard.

'I could tell,' he told me, 'she was leading up to something.
Something different.'

Sure enough, she was soon saying things Tommy found difficult to follow. But she kept repeating it until eventually he began
to understand. If Tommy had genuinely tried, she was saying,
but he just couldn't be very creative, then that was quite all right,
he wasn't to worry about it. It was wrong for anyone, whether
they were students or guardians, to punish him for it, or put pressure on him in any way. It simply wasn't his fault. And when
Tommy had protested it was all very well Miss Lucy saying this,
but everyone *did* think it was his fault, she'd given a sigh and
looked out of her window. Then she'd said:

'It may not help you much. But just you remember this. There's
at least one person here at Hailsham who believes otherwise. At
least one person who believes you're a very good student, as good
as any she's ever come across, never mind how creative you are.'

'She wasn't having you on, was she?' I asked Tommy. 'It wasn't
some clever way of telling you off?'

.t definitely wasn't anything like that. Anyway . . .' For the first time he seemed worried about being overheard and glanced over his shoulder towards the house. The Juniors at the window had lost interest and gone; some girls from our year were walking towards the pavilion, but they were still a good way off. Tommy turned back to me and said almost in a whisper:

'Anyway, when she said all this, she was *shaking*.'

'What do you mean, shaking?'

'Shaking. With rage. I could see her. She was furious. But furious deep inside.'

'Who at?'

'I wasn't sure. Not at me anyway, that was the most important thing!' He gave a laugh, then became serious again. 'I don't know who she was angry with. But she was angry all right.'

I stood up again because my calves were aching. 'It's pretty weird, Tommy.'

'Funny thing is, this talk with her, it did help. Helped a lot. When you were saying earlier on, about how things seemed better for me now. Well, it's because of that. Because afterwards, thinking about what she'd said, I realised she was right, that it wasn't my fault. Okay, I hadn't handled it well. But deep down, it wasn't my fault. That's what made the difference. And whenever I felt rocky about it, I'd catch sight of her walking about, or I'd be in one of her lessons, and she wouldn't say anything about our talk, but I'd look at her, and she'd sometimes see me and give me a little nod. And that's all I needed. You were asking earlier if something had happened. Well, that's what happened. But Kath, listen, don't breathe a word to anyone about this, right?'

I nodded, but asked: 'Did she make you promise that?'

'No, no, she didn't make me promise anything. But you're not to breathe a word. You've got to really promise.'

'All right.' The girls heading for the pavilion had spotted me and were waving and calling. I waved back and said to Tommy: 'I'd better go. We can talk more about it soon.'

But Tommy ignored this. 'There's something else,' he went on. 'Something else she said I can't quite figure out. I was going to ask you about it. She said we weren't being taught enough, something like that.'

'Taught enough? You mean she thinks we should be studying even harder than we are?'

'No, I don't think she meant that. What she was talking about was, you know, about *us*. What's going to happen to us one day. Donations and all that.'

'But we *have* been taught about all that,' I said. 'I wonder what she meant. Does she think there are things we haven't been told yet?'

Tommy thought for a moment, then shook his head. 'I don't think she meant it like that. She just thinks we aren't taught about it enough. Because she said she'd a good mind to talk to us about it herself.'

'About what exactly?'

'I'm not sure. Maybe I got it all wrong, Kath, I don't know. Maybe she was meaning something else completely, something else to do with me not being creative. I don't really understand it.'

Tommy was looking at me as though he expected me to come up with an answer. I went on thinking for a few seconds, then said:

'Tommy, think back carefully. You said she got angry . . .'

'Well, that's what it looked like. She was quiet, but she was shaking.'

'All right, whatever. Let's say she got angry. Was it when she got angry she started to say this other stuff? About how we weren't taught enough about donations and the rest of it?'

'I suppose so . . .'

'Now, Tommy, think. Why did she bring it up? She's talking about you and you not creating. Then suddenly she starts up about this other stuff. What's the link? Why did she bring up donations? What's that got to do with you being creative?'

'I don't know. There must have been some reason, I suppose. Maybe one thing reminded her of the other. Kath, you're getting really worked up about this yourself now.'

I laughed, because he was right: I'd been frowning, completely lost in my thoughts. The fact was, my mind was going in various directions at once. And Tommy's account of his talk with Miss Lucy had reminded me of something, perhaps a whole series of things, little incidents from the past to do with Miss Lucy that had puzzled me at the time.

'It's just that . . .' I stopped and sighed. 'I can't quite put it right, not even to myself. But all this, what you're saying, it sort of fits with a lot of other things that are puzzling. I keep thinking about all these things. Like why Madame comes and takes away our best pictures. What's that for exactly?'

'It's for the Gallery.'

'But what *is* her gallery? She keeps coming here and taking away our best work. She must have stacks of it by now. I asked Miss Geraldine once how long Madame's been coming here, and she said for as long as Hailsham's been here. What *is* this gallery? Why should she have a gallery of things done by us?'

'Maybe she sells them. Outside, out there, they sell everything.'

I shook my head. 'That can't be it. It's got something to do with what Miss Lucy said to you. About us, about how one day we'll start giving donations. I don't know why, but I've had this feeling for some time now, that it's all linked in, though I can't figure out how. I'll have to go now, Tommy. Let's not tell anyone yet, about what we've been saying.'

'No. And don't tell anyone about Miss Lucy.'

'But will you tell me if she says anything else to you like that?'

Tommy nodded, then glanced around him again. 'Like you say, you'd better go, Kath. Someone's going to hear us soon.'

The gallery Tommy and I were discussing was something we'd all of us grown up with. Everyone talked about it as though it existed, though in truth none of us knew for sure that it did. I'm sure I was pretty typical in not being able to remember how or when I'd first heard about it. Certainly, it hadn't been from the guardians: they never mentioned the Gallery, and there was an unspoken rule that we should never even raise the subject in their presence.

I'd suppose now it was something passed down through the different generations of Hailsham students. I remember a time when I could only have been five or six, sitting at a low table beside Amanda C., our hands clammy with modelling clay. I can't remember if there were other children with us, or which guardian was in charge. All I remember is Amanda C. – who was a year older than me – looking at what I was making and exclaiming: 'That's really, really good, Kathy! That's *so* good! I bet that'll get in the Gallery!'

I must by then have already known about the Gallery, because I remember the excitement and pride when she said that – and then the next moment, thinking to myself: 'That's ridiculous. None of us are good enough for the Gallery yet.'

As we got older, we went on talking about the Gallery. If you wanted to praise someone's work, you'd say: 'That's good enough for the Gallery.' And after we discovered irony, whenever we came across any laughably bad work, we'd go: 'Oh yes! Straight to the Gallery with that one!'

But did we really believe in the Gallery? Today, I'm not sure. As I've said, we never mentioned it to the guardians and looking back, it seems to me this was a rule we imposed on ourselves, as much as anything the guardians had decided. There's an instance I can remember from when we were about eleven. We were in Room 7 on a sunny winter's morning. We'd just finished Mr Roger's class, and a few of us had stayed on to chat with him. We were sitting up on our desks, and I can't remember exactly what we were talking about, but Mr Roger, as usual, was making us laugh and laugh. Then Carole H. had said, through her giggles: 'You might even get it picked for the Gallery!' She immediately put her hand over her mouth with an 'oops!' and the atmosphere remained light-hearted; but we all knew, Mr Roger included, that she'd made a mistake. Not a disaster, exactly: it would have been much the same had one of us let slip a rude word, or used a guardian's nickname to his or her face. Mr Roger smiled indulgently, as though to say: 'Let it pass, we'll pretend you never said that,' and we carried on as before.

If for us the Gallery remained in a hazy realm, what was solid enough fact was Madame's turning up usually twice – sometimes three or four times – each year to select from our best work. We called her 'Madame' because she was French or Belgian – there was a dispute as to which – and that was what the guardians always called her. She was a tall, narrow woman with short hair, probably quite young still, though at the time we wouldn't have thought of her as such. She always wore a sharp grey suit, and unlike the gardeners, unlike the drivers who brought in our supplies – unlike virtually anyone else who came in from outside – she wouldn't talk to us and kept us at a distance with her chilly look. For years we thought of her as 'snooty', but then one night, around when we were eight, Ruth came up with another theory.

'She's scared of us,' she declared.

We were lying in the dark in our dorm. In the Juniors, we were fifteen to a dorm, so didn't tend to have the sort of long intimate conversations we did once we got to the Senior dorms. But most of what became our 'group' had beds close together by then, and we were already getting the habit of talking into the night.

'What do you mean, scared of us?' someone asked. 'How can she be scared of us? What could we do to her?'

'I don't know,' Ruth said. 'I don't know, but I'm sure she is. I used to think she was just snooty, but it's something else, I'm sure of it now. Madame's scared of us.'

We argued about this on and off for the next few days. Most of us didn't agree with Ruth, but then that just made her all the more determined to prove she was right. So in the end we settled on a plan to put her theory to the test the next time Madame came to Hailsham.

Although Madame's visits were never announced, it was always pretty obvious when she was due. The lead-up to her arrival began weeks before, with the guardians sifting through all our work – our paintings, sketches, pottery, all our essays and poems. This usually went on for at least a fortnight, by the end of which four or five items from each Junior and Senior year would have ended up in the billiards room. The billiards room would get closed during this period, but if you stood on the low wall of the terrace outside, you'd be able to see through the windows the haul of stuff getting larger and larger. Once the guardians started laying it out neatly, on tables and easels, like a miniature version of one of our Exchanges, then you knew Madame would be coming within a day or two.

That autumn I'm now talking about, we needed to know not just the day, but the precise moment Madame turned up, since she often stayed no longer than an hour or two. So as soon as we saw the stuff getting displayed in the billiards room, we decided to take turns keeping look-out.

This was a task made much easier by the way the grounds were laid out. Hailsham stood in a smooth hollow with fields rising on all sides. That meant that from almost any of the classroom windows in the main house – and even from the pavilion – you had a good view of the long narrow road that came down across the fields and arrived at the main gate. The gate itself was still a fair distance off, and any vehicle would then have to take the gravelled drive, going past shrubs and flowerbeds, before at last reaching the courtyard in front of the main house. Days could sometimes go by without us seeing a vehicle coming down that narrow road, and the ones that did were usually vans or lorries bringing supplies, gardeners or workmen. A car was a rarity, and the sight of one in the distance was sometimes enough to cause bedlam during a class.

The afternoon Madame's car was spotted coming across the fields, it was windy and sunny, with a few storm clouds starting to gather. We were in Room 9 – on the first floor at the front of the house – and when the whisper went around, poor Mr Frank, who was trying to teach us spelling, couldn't understand why we'd suddenly got so restless.

The plan we'd come up with to test Ruth's theory was very simple: we – the six of us in on it – would lie in wait for Madame somewhere, then 'swarm out' all around her, all at once. We'd all remain perfectly civilised and just go on our way, but if we timed it right, and she was taken off-guard, we'd see – Ruth insisted – that she really was afraid of us.

Our main worry was that we just wouldn't get an opportunity

31

during the short time she was at Hailsham. But as Mr Frank's class drew to an end, we could see Madame, directly below in the courtyard, parking her car. We had a hurried conference out on the landing, then followed the rest of the class down the stairs and loitered just inside the main doorway. We could see out into the bright courtyard, where Madame was still sitting behind the wheel, rummaging in her briefcase. Eventually she emerged from the car and came towards us, dressed in her usual grey suit, her briefcase held tightly to herself in both arms. At a signal from Ruth we all sauntered out, moving straight for her, but like we were all in a dream. Only when she came to a stiff halt did we each murmur: 'Excuse me, Miss,' and separate.

I'll never forget the strange change that came over us the next instant. Until that point, this whole thing about Madame had been, if not a joke exactly, very much a private thing we'd wanted to settle among ourselves. We hadn't thought much about how Madame herself, or anyone else, would come into it. What I mean is, until then, it had been a pretty light-hearted matter, with a bit of a dare element to it. And it wasn't even as though Madame did anything other than what we predicted she'd do: she just froze and waited for us to pass by. She didn't shriek, or even let out a gasp. But we were all so keenly tuned in to picking up her response, and that's probably why it had such an effect on us. As she came to a halt, I glanced quickly at her face – as did the others, I'm sure. And I can still see it now, the shudder she seemed to be suppressing, the real dread that one of us would accidentally brush against her. And though we just kept on walking, we all felt it; it was like we'd walked from the sun right into chilly shade. Ruth had been right: Madame *was* afraid of us. But she was afraid of us in the same way someone might be afraid of spiders. We hadn't been ready for that. It had never occurred to us to wonder how *we* would feel, being seen like that, being the spiders.

By the time we'd crossed the courtyard and reached the grass, we were a very different group from the one that had stood about excitedly waiting for Madame to get out of her car. Hannah looked ready to burst into tears. Even Ruth looked really shaken. Then one of us – I think it was Laura – said:

'If she doesn't like us, why does she want our work? Why doesn't she just leave us alone? Who asks her to come here anyway?'

No one answered, and we carried on over to the pavilion, not saying anything more about what had happened.

Thinking back now, I can see we were just at that age when we knew a few things about ourselves – about who we were, how we were different from our guardians, from the people outside – but hadn't yet understood what any of it meant. I'm sure somewhere in your childhood, you too had an experience like ours that day; similar if not in the actual details, then inside, in the feelings. Because it doesn't really matter how well your guardians try to prepare you: all the talks, videos, discussions, warnings, none of that can really bring it home. Not when you're eight years old, and you're all together in a place like Hailsham; when you've got guardians like the ones we had; when the gardeners and the delivery men joke and laugh with you and call you 'sweetheart'.

All the same, some of it must go in somewhere. It must go in, because by the time a moment like that comes along, there's a part of you that's been waiting. Maybe from as early as when you're five or six, there's been a whisper going at the back of your head, saying: 'One day, maybe not so long from now, you'll get to know how it feels.' So you're waiting, even if you don't quite know it, waiting for the moment when you realise that you really are different to them; that there are people out there, like Madame, who don't hate you or wish you any harm, but who nevertheless shudder at the very thought of you – of how you were brought into this world and why – and who dread the idea of your hand brushing against theirs. The first time you glimpse yourself through the eyes of a person like that, it's a cold moment. It's like walking past a mirror you've walked past every day of your life, and suddenly it shows you something else, something troubling and strange.

CHAPTER FOUR

I won't be a carer any more come the end of the year, and though I've got a lot out of it, I have to admit I'll welcome the chance to rest – to stop and think and remember. I'm sure it's at least partly to do with that, to do with preparing for the change of pace, that I've been getting this urge to order all these old memories. What I really wanted, I suppose, was to get straight all the things that happened between me and Tommy and Ruth after we grew up and left Hailsham. But I realise now just how much of what occurred later came out of our time at Hailsham, and that's why I want first to go over these earlier memories quite carefully. Take all this curiosity about Madame, for instance. At one level, it was just us kids larking about. But at another, as you'll see, it was the start of a process that kept growing and growing over the years until it came to dominate our lives.

After that day, mention of Madame became, while not taboo exactly, pretty rare among us. And this was something that soon spread beyond our little group to just about all the students in our year. We were, I'd say, as curious as ever about her, but we all sensed that to probe any further – about what she did with our work, whether there really was a gallery – would get us into territory we weren't ready for yet.

The topic of the Gallery, though, still cropped up every once in a while, so that when a few years later Tommy started telling me beside the pond about his odd talk with Miss Lucy, I found something tugging away at my memory. It was only afterwards, when I'd left him sitting on his rock and was hurrying towards the fields to catch up with my friends, that it came back to me.

It was something Miss Lucy had once said to us during a class. I'd remembered it because it had puzzled me at the time, and also because it was one of the few occasions when the Gallery had been mentioned so deliberately in front of a guardian.

We'd been in the middle of what we later came to call the 'tokens controversy'. Tommy and I discussed the tokens controversy a few years ago, and we couldn't at first agree when it had happened. I said we'd been ten at the time; he thought it was later, but in the end came round to agreeing with me. I'm pretty sure I got it right: we were in Junior 4 – a while after that incident with Madame, but still three years before our talk by the pond.

The tokens controversy was, I suppose, all part of our getting more acquisitive as we grew older. For years – I think I've said already – we'd thought that having work chosen for the billiards room, never mind taken away by Madame, was a huge triumph. But by the time we were ten, we'd grown more ambivalent about it. The Exchanges, with their system of tokens as currency, had given us a keen eye for pricing up anything we produced. We'd become preoccupied with T-shirts, with decorating around our beds, with personalising our desks. And of course, we had our 'collections' to think of.

I don't know if you had 'collections' where you were. When you come across old students from Hailsham, you always find them, sooner or later, getting nostalgic about their collections. At the time, of course, we took it all for granted. You each had a wooden chest with your name on it, which you kept under your bed and filled with your possessions – the stuff you acquired from the Sales or the Exchanges. I can remember one or two students not bothering much with their collections, but most of us took enormous care, bringing things out to display, putting other things away carefully.

The point is, by the time we were ten, this whole notion that it was a great honour to have something taken by Madame collided with a feeling that we were losing our most marketable stuff. This all came to a head in the tokens controversy.

It began with a number of students, mainly boys, muttering that we should get tokens to compensate when Madame took something away. A lot of students agreed with this, but others were outraged by the idea. Arguments went on between us for some time, and then one day Roy J. – who was a year above us, and had had a number of things taken by Madame – decided to go and see Miss Emily about it.

Miss Emily, our head guardian, was older than the others. She wasn't especially tall, but something about the way she carried herself, always very straight with her head right up, made you think she was. She wore her silvery hair tied back, but strands were always coming loose and floating around her. They would have driven me mad, but Miss Emily always ignored them, like they were beneath her contempt. By the evening, she was a pretty strange sight, with bits of loose hair everywhere which she wouldn't bother to push away off her face when she talked to you in her quiet, deliberate voice. We were all pretty scared of her and didn't think of her in the way we did the other guardians. But we considered her to be fair and respected her decisions; and even in the Juniors, we probably recognised that it was her presence, intimidating though it was, that made us all feel so safe at Hailsham.

It took some nerve to go and see her without being summoned; to go with the sort of demands Roy was making seemed suicidal. But Roy didn't get the terrible telling-off we were expecting, and in the days that followed, there were reports of guardians talking – even arguing – about the tokens question. In the end, it was announced that we *would* get tokens, but not many because it was a 'most distinguished honour' to have work selected by Madame. This didn't really go down well with either camp, and the arguments rumbled on.

It was against this background that Polly T. asked Miss Lucy her question that morning. We were in the library, sitting around the big oak table. I remember there was a log burning in the fireplace, and that we were doing a play-reading. At some point, a line in the play had led to Laura making some wisecrack about the tokens business, and we'd all laughed, Miss Lucy included. Then Miss Lucy had said that since everyone at Hailsham was talking about little else, we should forget the play-reading and spend the rest of the lesson exchanging our views about the tokens. And that's what we were doing when Polly asked, completely out of the blue: 'Miss, why does Madame take our things anyway?'

We all went silent. Miss Lucy didn't often get cross, but when she did, you certainly knew about it, and we thought for a second Polly was for it. But then we saw Miss Lucy wasn't angry, just deep in thought. I remember feeling furious at Polly for so stupidly breaking the unwritten rule, but at the same time, being terribly excited about what answer Miss Lucy might give. And clearly I wasn't the only one with these mixed emotions: virtually everybody shot daggers at Polly, before turning eagerly to Miss Lucy – which was, I suppose, pretty unfair on poor Polly. After what seemed a very long while, Miss Lucy said:

'All I can tell you today is that it's for a good reason. A very important reason. But if I tried to explain it to you now, I don't think you'd understand. One day, I hope, it'll be explained to you.'

We didn't press her. The atmosphere around the table had become one of deep embarrassment, and curious as we were to hear more, we wanted most for the talk to get away from this dodgy territory. The next moment, then, we were all relieved to be arguing again – a bit artificially perhaps – about the tokens. But Miss Lucy's words had puzzled me and I kept thinking about them on and off for the next few days. That's why that afternoon by the pond, when Tommy was telling me about his talk with Miss Lucy, about how she'd said to him we weren't being 'taught enough' about some things, the memory of that time in the library – along with maybe one or two other little episodes like that – started tugging at my mind.

While we're on the subject of the tokens, I want just to say a bit about our Sales, which I've mentioned a few times already. The Sales were important to us because that was how we got hold of things from outside. Tommy's polo-shirt, for instance, came from a Sale. That's where we got our clothes, our toys, the special things that hadn't been made by another student.

Once every month, a big white van would come down that long road and you'd feel the excitement all through the house and grounds. By the time it pulled up in the courtyard there'd be a crowd waiting – mainly Juniors, because once you were past twelve or thirteen it wasn't the thing to be getting so obviously excited. But the truth was we all were.

Looking back now, it's funny to think we got so worked up, because usually the Sales were a big disappointment. There'd be nothing remotely special and we'd spend our tokens just renewing stuff that was wearing out or broken with more of the same. But the point was, I suppose, we'd all of us in the past found something at a Sale, something that had become special: a jacket, a watch, a pair of craft scissors never used but kept proudly next to a bed. We'd all found something like that at one time, and so however much we tried to pretend otherwise, we couldn't ever shake off the old feelings of hope and excitement.

Actually there was some point in hanging about the van as it was being unloaded. What you did – if you were one of these Juniors – was to follow back and forth from the storeroom the two men in overalls carrying the big cardboard boxes, asking them what was inside. 'A lot of goodies, sweetheart,' was the usual reply. Then if you kept asking: 'But is it a *bumper crop*?' they'd sooner or later smile and say: 'Oh, I'd say so, sweetheart. A real bumper crop,' bringing a thrilled cheer.

The boxes were often open at the top, so you'd catch glimpses of all kinds of things, and sometimes, though they weren't really supposed to, the men would let you move a few items about for a better look. And that was why, by the time of the actual Sale a week or so later, all sorts of rumours would be going around, maybe about a particular track-suit or a music cassette, and if there was trouble, it was almost always because a few students had set their hearts on the same item.

The Sales were a complete contrast to the hushed atmosphere of the Exchanges. They were held in the Dining Hall, and were crowded and noisy. In fact the pushing and shouting was all part of the fun, and they stayed for the most part pretty good-humoured. Except, as I say, every now and then, things would get out of hand, with students grabbing and tugging, sometimes fighting. Then the monitors would threaten to close the whole thing down, and we'd all of us have to face a talking to from Miss Emily at assembly the next morning.

Our day at Hailsham always began with an assembly, which was usually pretty brief – a few announcements, maybe a poem read out by a student. Miss Emily didn't often say much; she'd just sit very straight on the stage, nodding at whatever was being said, occasionally turning a frosty eye towards any whispering in the crowd. But on a morning after a rowdy Sale, everything was different. She'd order us to sit down on the floor – we usually stood at assemblies – and there'd be no announcements or performances, just Miss Emily talking to us for twenty, thirty minutes, sometimes even longer. She'd rarely raise her voice, but there was something steely about her on these occasions and none of us, not even the Senior 5s, dared make a sound.

There was a real sense of feeling bad that we had, in some collective way, let down Miss Emily, but try as we might, we couldn't really follow these lectures. It was partly her language. 'Unworthy of privilege' and 'misuse of opportunity': these were two regular phrases Ruth and I came up with when we were reminiscing in her room at the centre in Dover. Her general drift was clear enough: we were all very special, being Hailsham students, and so it was all the more disappointing when we behaved badly. Beyond that though, things became a fog. Sometimes she'd be going on very intensely then come to a sudden stop with something like: 'What is it? What is it? What can it be that thwarts us?' Then she'd stand there, eyes closed, a frown on her face like she was trying to puzzle out the answer. And although we felt bewildered and awkward, we'd sit there willing her on to make whatever discovery was needed in her head. She might then resume with a gentle sigh – a signal that we were going to be forgiven – or just as easily explode out of her silence with: 'But I will not be coerced! Oh no! And neither will Hailsham!'

When we were remembering these long speeches, Ruth

remarked how odd it was they should have been so unfathomable, since Miss Emily, in a classroom, could be as clear as anything. When I mentioned how I'd sometimes seen the head wandering around Hailsham in a dream, talking to herself, Ruth took offence, saying:

'She was never like that! How could Hailsham have been the way it was if the person in charge had been potty? Miss Emily had an intellect you could slice logs with.'

I didn't argue. Certainly, Miss Emily could be uncannily sharp. If, say, you were somewhere you shouldn't be in the main house or the grounds, and you heard a guardian coming, you could often hide somewhere. Hailsham was full of hiding places, indoors and out: cupboards, nooks, bushes, hedges. But if you saw Miss Emily coming, your heart sank because she'd always know you were there hiding. It was like she had some extra sense. You could go into a cupboard, close the door tight and not move a muscle, you just knew Miss Emily's footsteps would stop outside and her voice would say: 'All right. Out you come.'

That was what had happened to Sylvie C. once on the second-floor landing, and on that occasion Miss Emily had gone into one of her rages. She never shouted like, say, Miss Lucy did when she got mad at you, but if anything Miss Emily getting angry was scarier. Her eyes narrowed and she'd whisper furiously to herself, like she was discussing with an invisible colleague what punishment was awful enough for you. The way she did it meant half of you was dying to hear and the other half completely not wanting to. But usually with Miss Emily nothing too awful would come out of it. She hardly ever put you in detention, made you do chores or withdrew privileges. All the same, you felt dreadful, just knowing you'd fallen in her estimation, and you wanted to do something straight away to redeem yourself.

But the thing was, there was no predicting with Miss Emily. Sylvie may have got a full portion that time, but when Laura got caught running through the rhubarb patch, Miss Emily just snapped: 'Shouldn't be here, girl. Off you go,' and walked on.

And then there was the time I thought I was in hot water with her. The little footpath that went all round the back of the main house was a real favourite of mine. It followed all the nooks, all the extensions; you had to squeeze past shrubs, you went under two ivy-covered arches and through a rusted gate. And all the time you could peer in through the windows, one after the other. I suppose part of the reason I liked the path so much was because I was never sure if it was out of bounds. Certainly, when classes were going on, you weren't supposed to walk past. But at the weekends or in the evenings – that was never clear. Most students avoided it anyway, and maybe the feeling of getting away from everyone else was another part of the appeal.

In any case, I was doing this little walk one sunny evening. I think I was in Senior 3. As usual I was glancing into the empty rooms as I went past, and then suddenly I was looking into a classroom with Miss Emily in it. She was alone, pacing slowly, talking under her breath, pointing and directing remarks to an invisible audience in the room. I assumed she was rehearsing a lesson or maybe one of her assembly talks, and I was about to hurry past before she spotted me, but just then she turned and looked straight at me. I froze, thinking I was for it, but then noticed she was carrying on as before, except now she was mouthing her address at me. Then, natural as you like, she turned away to fix her gaze on some other imaginary student in another part of the room. I crept away along the path, and for the next day or so kept dreading what Miss Emily would say when she saw me. But she never mentioned it at all.

But that's not really what I want to talk about just now. What I want to do now is get a few things down about Ruth, about how we met and became friends, about our early days together. Because more and more these days, I'll be driving past fields on a long afternoon, or maybe drinking my coffee in front of a huge window in a motorway service station, and I'll catch myself thinking about her again.

She wasn't someone I was friends with from the start. I can

remember, at five or six, doing things with Hannah and with Laura, but not with Ruth. I only have the one vague memory of Ruth from that early part of our lives.

I'm playing in a sandpit. There are a number of others in the sand with me, it's too crowded and we're getting irritated with each other. We're in the open, under a warm sun, so it's probably the sandpit in the Infants' play area, just possibly it's the sand at the end of the long jump in the North Playing Field. Anyway it's hot and I'm feeling thirsty and I'm not pleased there are so many of us in the sandpit. Then Ruth is standing there, not in the sand with the rest of us, but a few feet away. She's very angry with two of the girls somewhere behind me, about something that must have happened before, and she's standing there glaring at them. My guess is that I knew Ruth only very slightly at that point. But she must already have made some impression on me, because I remember carrying on busily with whatever I was doing in the sand, absolutely dreading the idea of her turning her gaze on me. I didn't say a word, but I was desperate for her to realise I wasn't with the girls behind me, and had had no part in whatever it was that had made her cross.

And that's all I remember of Ruth from that early time. We were the same year so we must have run into each other enough, but aside from the sandpit incident, I don't remember having anything to do with her until the Juniors a couple of years later, when we were seven, going on eight.

The South Playing Field was the one used most by the Juniors and it was there, in the corner by the poplars, that Ruth came up to me one lunchtime, looked me up and down, then asked:

'Do you want to ride my horse?'

I was in the midst of playing with two or three others at that point, but it was clear Ruth was addressing only me. This absolutely delighted me, but I made a show of weighing her up before giving a reply.

'Well, what's your horse's name?'

Ruth came a step closer. 'My *best* horse,' she said, 'is Thunder. I can't let you ride on *him*. He's much too dangerous. But you can ride Bramble, as long as you don't use your crop on him. Or if you like, you could have any of the others.' She reeled off several more names I don't now remember. Then she asked: 'Have you got any horses of your own?'

I looked at her and thought carefully before replying: 'No. I don't have any horses.'

'Not even one?'

'No.'

'All right. You can ride Bramble, and if you like him, you can have him to keep. But you're not to use your crop on him. And you've got to come *now*.'

My friends had, in any case, turned away and were carrying on with what they'd been doing. So I gave a shrug and went off with Ruth.

The field was filled with playing children, some a lot bigger than us, but Ruth led the way through them very purposefully, always a pace or two in front. When we were almost at the wire mesh boundary with the garden, she turned and said:

'Okay, we'll ride them here. You take Bramble.'

I accepted the invisible rein she was holding out, and then we were off, riding up and down the fence, sometimes cantering, sometimes at a gallop. I'd been correct in my decision to tell Ruth I didn't have any horses of my own, because after a while with Bramble, she let me try her various other horses one by one, shouting all sorts of instructions about how to handle each animal's foibles.

'I told you! You've got to really lean back on Daffodil! Much more than that! She doesn't like it unless you're *right back*!'

I must have done well enough, because eventually she let me have a go on Thunder, her favourite. I don't know how long we spent with her horses that day: it felt a substantial time, and I think we both lost ourselves completely in our game. But then suddenly, for no reason I could see, Ruth brought it all to an end, claiming I was deliberately tiring out her horses, and that I'd have to put each of them back in its stable. She pointed to a section of the fence, and I began leading the horses to it, while Ruth seemed to get crosser and crosser with me, saying I was doing everything wrong. Then she asked:

'Do you like Miss Geraldine?'

It might have been the first time I'd actually thought about whether I liked a guardian. In the end I said: 'Of course I like her.'

'But do you *really* like her? Like she's special? Like she's your favourite?'

'Yes, I do. She's my favourite.'

Ruth went on looking at me for a long time. Then finally she said: 'All right. In that case, I'll let you be one of her secret guards.'

We started to walk back towards the main house then and I waited for her to explain what she meant, but she didn't. I found out though over the next several days.

CHAPTER FIVE

I'm not sure for how long the 'secret guard' business carried on. When Ruth and I discussed it while I was caring for her down in Dover, she claimed it had been just a matter of two or three weeks – but that was almost certainly wrong. She was probably embarrassed about it and so the whole thing had shrunk in her memory. My guess is that it went on for about nine months, a year even, around when we were seven, going on eight.

I was never sure if Ruth had actually invented the secret guard herself, but there was no doubt she was the leader. There were between six and ten of us, the figure changing whenever Ruth allowed in a new member or expelled someone. We believed Miss Geraldine was the best guardian in Hailsham, and we worked on presents to give her – a large sheet with pressed flowers glued over it comes to mind. But our main reason for existing, of course, was to protect her.

By the time I joined the guard, Ruth and the others had already known for ages about the plot to kidnap Miss Geraldine. We were never quite sure who was behind it. We sometimes suspected certain of the Senior boys, sometimes boys in our own year. There was a guardian we didn't like much – a Miss Eileen – who we thought for a while might be the brains behind it. We didn't know when the abduction would take place, but one thing we felt convinced about was that the woods would come into it.

The woods were at the top of the hill that rose behind Hailsham House. All we could see really was a dark fringe of trees, but I certainly wasn't the only one of my age to feel their presence day and night. When it got bad, it was like they cast a shadow over the whole of Hailsham; all you had to do was turn your head or move towards a window and there they'd be, looming in the distance. Safest was the front of the main house, because you couldn't see them from any of the windows. Even so, you never really got away from them.

There were all kinds of horrible stories about the woods. Once, not so long before we all got to Hailsham, a boy had had a big row with his friends and run off beyond the Hailsham boundaries. His body had been found two days later, up in those woods, tied to a tree with the hands and feet chopped off. Another rumour had it that a girl's ghost wandered through those trees. She'd been a Hailsham student until one day she'd climbed over a fence just to see what it was like outside. This was a long time before us, when the guardians were much stricter, cruel even, and when she tried to get back in, she wasn't allowed. She kept hanging around outside the fences, pleading to be let back in, but no one let her. Eventually, she'd gone off somewhere out there, something had happened and she'd died. But her ghost was always wandering about the woods, gazing over Hailsham, pining to be let back in.

The guardians always insisted these stories were nonsense. But then the older students would tell us that was exactly what the guardians had told *them* when they were younger, and that we'd be told the ghastly truth soon enough, just as they were.

The woods played on our imaginations the most after dark, in our dorms as we were trying to fall asleep. You almost thought then you could hear the wind rustling the branches, and talking about it seemed to only make things worse. I remember one night, when we were furious with Marge K. – she'd done something really embarrassing to us during the day – we chose to punish her by hauling her out of bed, holding her face against the window pane and ordering her to look up at the woods. At first she kept her eyes screwed shut, but we twisted her arms and forced open her eyelids until she saw the distant outline against the moonlit sky, and that was enough to ensure for her a sobbing night of terror.

I'm not saying we necessarily went around the whole time at that age worrying about the woods. I for one could go weeks hardly thinking about them, and there were even days when a defiant surge of courage would make me think: 'How could we believe rubbish like that?' But then all it took would be one little thing – someone retelling one of those stories, a scary passage in a book, even just a chance remark reminding you of the woods – and that would mean another period of being under that shadow. It was hardly surprising then that we assumed the woods would be central in the plot to abduct Miss Geraldine.

When it came down to it, though, I don't recall our taking many practical steps towards defending Miss Geraldine; our activities always revolved around gathering more and more evidence concerning the plot itself. For some reason, we were satisfied this would keep any immediate danger at bay.

Most of our 'evidence' came from witnessing the conspirators at work. One morning, for instance, we watched from a second-floor classroom Miss Eileen and Mr Roger talking to Miss Geraldine down in the courtyard. After a while Miss Geraldine said goodbye and went off towards the Orangery, but we kept on watching, and saw Miss Eileen and Mr Roger put their heads closer together to confer furtively, their gazes fixed on Miss Geraldine's receding figure.

'Mr Roger,' Ruth sighed on that occasion, shaking her head. 'Who'd have guessed he was in it too?'

In this way we built up a list of people we knew to be in on the plot – guardians and students whom we declared our sworn enemies. And yet, all the time, I think we must have had an idea of how precarious the foundations of our fantasy were, because we always avoided any confrontation. We could decide, after intense discussions, that a particular student was a plotter, but then we'd always find a reason not to challenge him just yet – to wait until 'we had in all the evidence'. Similarly, we always agreed Miss Geraldine herself shouldn't hear a word of what we'd found out, since she'd get alarmed to no good purpose.

It would be too easy to claim it was just Ruth who kept the secret guard going long after we'd naturally outgrown it. Sure enough, the guard was important to her. She'd known about the plot for much longer than the rest of us, and this gave her enormous authority; by hinting that the *real* evidence came from a time before people like me had joined – that there were things she'd yet to reveal even to us – she could justify almost any decision she made on behalf of the group. If she decided someone should be expelled, for example, and she sensed opposition, she'd just allude darkly to stuff she knew 'from before'. There's no question Ruth was keen to keep the whole thing going. But the truth was, those of us who'd grown close to her, we each played our part in preserving the fantasy and making it last for as long as possible. What happened after that row over the chess illustrates pretty well the point I'm making.

I'd assumed Ruth was something of a chess expert and that she'd be able to teach me the game. This wasn't so crazy: we'd pass older students bent over chess sets, in window seats or on the grassy slopes, and Ruth would often pause to study a game. And as we walked off again, she'd tell me about some move she'd spotted that neither player had seen. 'Amazingly dim,' she'd murmur, shaking her head. This had all helped get me fascinated, and I was soon longing to become engrossed myself in those ornate pieces. So when I'd found a chess set at a Sale and decided to buy it – despite it costing an awful lot of tokens – I was counting on Ruth's help.

For the next several days, though, she sighed whenever I brought the subject up, or pretended she had something else really urgent to do. When I finally cornered her one rainy afternoon, and we set out the board in the billiards room, she proceeded to show me a game that was a vague variant on draughts. The distinguishing feature of chess, according to her, was that each piece moved in an L-shape – I suppose she'd got this from watching the knight – rather than in the leap-frogging way of draughts. I didn't believe this, and I was really disappointed, but I made sure to say nothing and went along with her for a while. We spent several minutes knocking each other's pieces off the board, always sliding the attacking piece in an 'L'. This continued until the time I tried to take her and she claimed it wouldn't count because I'd slid my piece up to hers in too straight a line.

At this, I stood up, packed up the set and walked off. I never said out loud that she didn't know how to play – disappointed as I was, I knew not to go that far – but my storming off was, I suppose, statement enough for her.

It was maybe a day later, I came into Room 20 at the top of the house, where Mr George had his poetry class. I don't remember if it was before or after the class, or how full the room was. I remember having books in my hands, and that as I moved towards where Ruth and the others were talking, there was a strong patch of sun across the desk-lids they were sitting on.

I could see from the way they had their heads together they were discussing secret guard stuff, and although, as I say, the row with Ruth had been only the day before, for some reason I went up to them without a second thought. It was only when I was virtually right up to them – maybe there was a look exchanged between them – that it suddenly hit me what was about to happen. It was like the split second before you step into a puddle, you realise it's there, but there's nothing you can do about it. I felt the hurt even before they went silent and stared at me, even before Ruth said: 'Oh, Kathy, how are you? If you don't mind, we've got something to discuss just now. We'll be finished in just a minute. Sorry.'

She'd hardly finished her sentence before I'd turned and was on my way out, angry more at myself for having walked into it than at Ruth and the others. I was upset, no doubt about it, though I don't know if I actually cried. And for the next few days, whenever I saw the secret guard conferring in a corner or as they walked across a field, I'd feel a flush rising to my cheeks.

Then about two days after this snub in Room 20, I was coming down the stairs of the main house when I found Moira B. just behind me. We started talking – about nothing special – and wandered out of the house together. It must have been the lunch break because as we stepped into the courtyard there were about twenty students loitering around chatting in little groups. My eyes went immediately to the far side of the courtyard, where Ruth and three of the secret guard were standing together, their backs to us, gazing intently towards the South Playing Field. I was trying to see what it was they were so interested in, when I became aware of Moira beside me also watching them. And then it occurred to me that only a month before she too had been a member of the secret guard, and had been expelled. For the next few seconds I felt something like acute embarrassment that the two of us should now be standing side by side, linked by our recent humiliations, actually staring our rejection in the face, as it were. Maybe Moira was experiencing something similar; anyway, she was the one who broke the silence, saying:

'It's so stupid, this whole secret guard thing. How can they still believe in something like that? It's like they're still in the Infants.'

Even today, I'm puzzled by the sheer force of the emotion that overtook me when I heard Moira say this. I turned to her, completely furious:

'What do *you* know about it? You just don't know anything, because you've been out of it for ages now! If you knew everything we'd found out, you wouldn't dare say anything so daft!'

'Don't talk rubbish.' Moira was never one to back down easily. 'It's just another of Ruth's made-up things, that's all.'

'Then how come I've *personally* heard them talking about it? Talking about how they're going to take Miss Geraldine to the woods in the milk van? How come I heard them planning it myself, nothing to do with Ruth or anyone else?'

Moira looked at me, unsure now. 'You heard it yourself? How? Where?'

'I heard them talking, clear as anything, heard every word, they didn't know I was there. Down by the pond, they didn't know I could hear. So that just shows how much you know!'

I pushed past her and as I made my way across the crowded courtyard, I glanced back to the figures of Ruth and the others, still gazing out towards the South Playing Field, unaware of what had just happened between me and Moira. And I noticed I didn't feel angry at all with them any more; just hugely irritated with Moira.

Even now, if I'm driving on a long grey road and my thoughts have nowhere special to go, I might find myself turning all of this over. Why was I so hostile to Moira B. that day when she was, really, a natural ally? What it was, I suppose, is that Moira was suggesting she and I cross some line together, and I wasn't prepared for that yet. I think I sensed how beyond that line, there was something harder and darker and I didn't want that. Not for me, not for any of us.

But at other times, I think that's wrong – that it was just to do with me and Ruth, and the sort of loyalty she inspired in me in those days. And maybe that's why, even though I really wanted to on several occasions, I never brought it up – about what had happened that day with Moira – the whole time I was caring for Ruth down at the centre in Dover.

All of this about Miss Geraldine reminds me of something that happened about three years later, long after the secret guard idea had faded away.

We were in Room 5 on the ground floor at the back of the house, waiting for a class to start. Room 5 was the smallest room, and especially on a winter morning like that one, when the big radiators came on and steamed up the windows, it would get really stuffy. Maybe I'm exaggerating it, but my memory is that for a whole class to fit into that room, students literally had to pile on top of each other.

That morning Ruth had got a chair behind a desk, and I was sitting up on its lid, with two or three others of our group perched or leaning in nearby. In fact, I think it was when I was squeezing up to let someone else in beside me that I first noticed the pencil case.

I can see the thing now like it's here in front of me. It was shiny, like a polished shoe; a deep tan colour with circled red dots drifting all over it. The zip across the top edge had a furry pom-pom to pull it. I'd almost sat on the pencil case when I'd shifted and

Ruth quickly moved it out of my way. But I'd seen it, as she'd intended me to, and I said:

'Oh! Where did you get that? Was it in the Sale?'

It was noisy in the room, but the girls nearby had heard, so there were soon four or five of us staring admiringly at the pencil case. Ruth said nothing for a few seconds while she checked carefully the faces around her. Finally she said very deliberately:

'Let's just agree. Let's *agree* I got it in the Sale.' Then she gave us all a knowing smile.

This might sound a pretty innocuous sort of response, but actually it was like she'd suddenly got up and hit me, and for the next few moments I felt hot and chilly at the same time. I knew exactly what she'd meant by her answer and smile: she was claiming the pencil case was a gift from Miss Geraldine.

There could be no mistake about this because it had been building up for weeks. There was a certain smile, a certain voice Ruth would use – sometimes accompanied by a finger to the lips or a hand raised stage-whisper style – whenever she wanted to hint about some little mark of favour Miss Geraldine had shown her: Miss Geraldine had allowed Ruth to play a music tape in the billiards room before four o'clock on a weekday; Miss Geraldine had ordered silence on a fields walk, but when Ruth had drawn up beside her, she'd started to talk to her, then let the rest of the group talk. It was always stuff like that, and never explicitly claimed, just implied by her smile and 'let's say no more' expression.

Of course, officially, guardians weren't supposed to show favouritism, but there were little displays of affection all the time within certain parameters; and most of what Ruth suggested fell easily within them. Still, I hated it when Ruth hinted in this way. I was never sure, of course, if she was telling the truth, but since she wasn't actually 'telling' it, only hinting, it was never possible to challenge her. So each time it happened, I'd have to let it go, biting my lip and hoping the moment would pass quickly.

Sometimes I'd see from the way a conversation was moving that one of these moments was coming, and I'd brace myself. Even then, it would always hit me with some force, so that for several minutes I wouldn't be able to concentrate on anything going on around me. But on that winter morning in Room 5, it had come at me straight out of the blue. Even after I'd seen the pencil case, the idea of a guardian giving a present like that was so beyond the bounds, I hadn't seen it coming at all. So once Ruth had said what she'd said, I wasn't able, in my usual way, to let the emotional flurry just pass. I just stared at her, making no attempt to disguise my anger. Ruth, perhaps seeing danger, said to me quickly in a stage whisper: 'Not a word!' and smiled again. But I couldn't return the smile and went on glaring at her. Then luckily the guardian arrived and the class started.

I was never the sort of kid who brooded over things for hours on end. I've got that way a bit these days, but that's the work I do and the long hours of quiet when I'm driving across these empty fields. I wasn't like, say, Laura, who for all her clowning around could worry for days, weeks even, about some little thing someone said to her. But after that morning in Room 5, I did go around in a bit of a trance. I'd drift off in the middle of conversations; whole lessons went by with me not knowing what was going on. I was determined Ruth shouldn't get away with it this time, but for a long while I wasn't doing anything constructive about it; just playing fantastic scenes in my head where I'd expose her and force her to admit she'd made it up. I even had one hazy fantasy where Miss Geraldine herself heard about it and gave Ruth a complete dressing-down in front of everyone.

After days of this I started to think more solidly. If the pencil case hadn't come from Miss Geraldine, where had it come from? She might have got it from another student, but that was unlikely. If it had belonged to anyone else first, even someone years above us, a gorgeous item like that wouldn't have gone unnoticed. Ruth would never risk a story like hers knowing the pencil case had already knocked around Hailsham. Almost certainly she'd found it at a Sale. Here, too, Ruth ran the risk of others having seen it before she'd bought it. But if – as sometimes happened, though it wasn't really allowed – she'd heard about the pencil case coming in and reserved it with one of the monitors before the

Sale opened, she could then be reasonably confident hardly anyone had seen it.

Unfortunately for Ruth, though, there were registers kept of everything bought at the Sales, along with a record of who'd done the buying. While these registers weren't easily obtainable – the monitors took them back to Miss Emily's office after each Sale – they weren't top secret either. If I hung around a monitor at the next Sale, it wouldn't be difficult to browse through the pages.

So I had the outlines of a plan, and I think I went on refining it for several days before it occurred to me it wasn't actually necessary to carry out all the steps. Provided I was right about the pencil case coming from a Sale, all I had to do was bluff.

That was how Ruth and I came to have our conversation under the eaves. There was fog and drizzle that day. The two of us were walking from the dorm huts perhaps towards the pavilion, I'm not sure. Anyway, as we were crossing the courtyard, the rain suddenly got heavier and since we were in no hurry, we tucked ourselves in under the eaves of the main house, a little to one side of the front entrance.

We sheltered there for a while, and every so often a student would come running out of the fog and in through the doors of the house, but the rain didn't ease. And the longer we continued to stand there, the more tense I grew because I could see this was the opportunity I'd been waiting for. Ruth too, I'm sure, sensed something was coming up. In the end, I decided to come straight out with it.

'At the Sale last Tuesday,' I said. 'I was just looking through the book. You know, the register thing.'

'Why were you looking at the register?' Ruth asked quickly. 'Why were you doing something like that?'

'Oh, no reason. Christopher C. was one of the monitors, so I was just talking to him. He's the best Senior boy, definitely. And I was just turning over the pages of the register, just for something to do.'

Ruth's mind, I could tell, had raced on, and she now knew

exactly what this was about. But she said calmly: 'Boring sort of thing to look at.'

'No, it was quite interesting really. You can see all the things people have bought.'

I'd said this staring out at the rain. Then I glanced at Ruth and got a real shock. I don't know what I'd expected; for all my fantasies of the past month, I'd never really considered what it would be like in a real situation like the one unfolding at that moment. Now I saw how upset Ruth was; how for once she was at a complete loss for words, and had turned away on the verge of tears. And suddenly my behaviour seemed to me utterly baffling. All this effort, all this planning, just to upset my dearest friend. So what if she'd fibbed a little about her pencil case? Didn't we all dream from time to time about one guardian or other bending the rules and doing something special for us? A spontaneous hug, a secret letter, a gift? All Ruth had done was to take one of these harmless daydreams a step further; she hadn't even mentioned Miss Geraldine by name.

I now felt awful, and I was confused. But as we stood there together staring at the fog and rain, I could think of no way now to repair the damage I'd done. I think I said something pathetic like: 'It's all right, I didn't see anything much,' which hung stupidly in the air. Then after a few further seconds of silence, Ruth walked off into the rain.

CHAPTER SIX

I think I'd have felt better about what had happened if Ruth had held it against me in some obvious way. But this was one instance when she seemed just to cave in. It was like she was too ashamed of the matter – too *crushed* by it – even to be angry or to want to get me back. The first few times I saw her after the conversation under the eaves, I was ready for at least a bit of huffiness, but no, she was completely civil, if a little flat. It occurred to me she was scared I'd expose her – the pencil case, sure enough, vanished from view – and I wanted to tell her she'd nothing to fear from me. The trouble was, because none of this had actually been talked about in the open, I couldn't find a way of bringing it all up with her.

I did my best, meanwhile, to take any opportunity to imply to Ruth she had a special place in Miss Geraldine's heart. There was the time, for example, when a bunch of us were desperate to go out and practise rounders during break, because we'd been challenged by a group from the year above. Our problem was that it was raining, and it looked unlikely we'd be allowed outside. I noticed though that Miss Geraldine was one of the guardians on duty, and so I said:

'If *Ruth* goes and asks Miss Geraldine, then we'd stand a chance.'

As far as I remember, this suggestion wasn't taken up; maybe hardly anyone heard it, because a lot of us were talking all at once. But the point is, I said it standing right behind Ruth, and I could see she was pleased.

Then another time a few of us were leaving a classroom with Miss Geraldine, and I happened to find myself about to go out the door right after Miss Geraldine herself. What I did was to slow right down so that Ruth, coming behind me, could instead pass through the door beside Miss Geraldine. I did this without any fuss, as though this were the natural and proper thing and what Miss Geraldine would like – just the way I'd have done if, say, I'd accidentally got myself between two best friends. On that occasion, as far as I remember, Ruth looked puzzled and surprised for a split second, then gave me a quick nod and went past.

Little things like these might well have pleased Ruth, but they were still far removed from what had actually happened between us under the eaves that foggy day, and the sense that I'd never be able to sort things just continued to grow. There's a particular memory I have of sitting by myself one evening on one of the benches outside the pavilion, trying over and over to think of some way out, while a heavy mix of remorse and frustration brought me virtually to tears. If things had stayed that way, I'm not sure what would have happened. Maybe it would all have got forgotten eventually; or maybe Ruth and I would have drifted apart. As it was, right out of the blue, a chance came along for me to put things right.

We were in the middle of one of Mr Roger's art lessons, except for some reason he'd gone out half way. So we were all just drifting about among the easels, chatting and looking at each other's work. Then at one point a girl called Midge A. came over to where we were and said to Ruth, in a perfectly friendly way:

'Where's your pencil case? It's so luscious.'

Ruth tensed and glanced quickly about to see who was present. It was our usual gang with perhaps a couple of outsiders loitering nearby. I hadn't mentioned to a soul anything about the Sales Register business, but I suppose Ruth wasn't to know that. Her voice was softer than usual when she replied to Midge:

'I haven't got it here. I keep it in my collection chest.'

'It's so luscious. Where did you get it?'

Midge was quizzing her completely innocently, that was now obvious. But almost all of us who'd been in Room 5 the time Ruth had first brought out the pencil case were here now, looking on, and I saw Ruth hesitate. It was only later, when I replayed it all, that I appreciated how perfectly shaped a chance it was for me.

At the time I didn't really think. I just came in before Midge or anyone else had the chance to notice Ruth was in a curious quandary.

'We can't say where it came from.'

Ruth, Midge, the rest of them, they all looked at me, maybe a little surprised. But I kept my cool and went on, addressing only Midge.

'There are some very good reasons why we can't tell you where it came from.'

Midge shrugged. 'So it's a mystery.'

'A *big* mystery,' I said, then gave her a smile to show her I wasn't trying to be nasty to her.

The others were nodding to back me up, though Ruth herself had on a vague expression, like she'd suddenly become preoccupied with something else entirely. Midge shrugged again, and as far as I remember that was the end of it. Either she walked off, or else she started talking about something different.

Now, for much the same reasons I'd not been able to talk openly to Ruth about what I'd done to her over the Sales Register business, she of course wasn't able to thank me for the way I'd intervened with Midge. But it was obvious from her manner towards me, not just over the next few days, but over the weeks that followed, how pleased she was with me. And having recently been in much the same position, it was easy to recognise the signs of her looking around for some opportunity to do something nice, something really special for me. It was a good feeling, and I remember even thinking once or twice how it would be better if she didn't get a chance for ages, just so the good feeling between us could go on and on. As it was, an opportunity did come along for her, about a month after the Midge episode, the time I lost my favourite tape.

I still have a copy of that tape and until recently I'd listen to it occasionally driving out in the open country on a drizzly day. But now the tape machine in my car's got so dodgy, I don't dare play it in that. And there never seems enough time to play it when I'm back in my bedsit. Even so, it's one of my most precious possessions. Maybe come the end of the year, when I'm no longer a carer, I'll be able to listen to it more often.

The album's called *Songs After Dark* and it's by Judy Bridgewater. What I've got today isn't the actual cassette, the one I had back then at Hailsham, the one I lost. It's the one Tommy and I found in Norfolk years afterwards – but that's another story I'll come to later. What I want to talk about is the first tape, the one that disappeared.

I should explain before I go any further this whole thing we had in those days about Norfolk. We kept it going for years and years – it became a sort of in-joke, I suppose – and it all started from one particular lesson we had when we were pretty young.

It was Miss Emily herself who taught us about the different counties of England. She'd pin up a big map over the blackboard, and next to it, set up an easel. And if she was talking about, say, Oxfordshire, she'd place on the easel a large calendar with photos of the county. She had quite a collection of these picture calendars, and we got through most of the counties this way. She'd tap a spot on the map with her pointer, turn to the easel and reveal another picture. There'd be little villages with streams going through them, white monuments on hillsides, old churches beside fields; if she was telling us about a coastal place, there'd be beaches crowded with people, cliffs with seagulls. I suppose she wanted us to have a grasp of what was out there surrounding us, and it's amazing, even now, after all these miles I've covered as a carer, the extent to which my idea of the various counties is still set by these pictures Miss Emily put up on her easel. I'd be driving through Derbyshire, say, and catch myself looking for a particular village green with a mock-Tudor pub and a war memorial – and realise it's the image Miss Emily showed us the first time I ever heard of Derbyshire.

Anyway, the point is, there was a gap in Miss Emily's calendar collection: none of them had a single picture of Norfolk. We had these same lectures repeated a number of times, and I'd always wonder if this time she'd found a picture of Norfolk, but it was always the same. She'd wave her pointer over the map and say, as a sort of afterthought: 'And over here, we've got Norfolk. Very nice there.'

Then, that particular time, I remember how she paused and drifted off into thought, maybe because she hadn't planned what should happen next instead of a picture. Eventually she came out of her dream and tapped the map again.

'You see, because it's stuck out here on the east, on this hump jutting into the sea, it's not on the way to anywhere. People going north and south' – she moved the pointer up and down – 'they bypass it altogether. For that reason, it's a peaceful corner of England, rather nice. But it's also something of a lost corner.'

A *lost corner*. That's what she called it, and that was what started it. Because at Hailsham, we had our own 'Lost Corner' up on the third floor, where the lost property was kept; if you lost or found anything, that's where you went. Someone – I can't remember who it was – claimed after the lesson that what Miss Emily had said was that Norfolk was England's 'lost corner', where all the lost property found in the country ended up. Somehow this idea caught on and soon had become accepted fact virtually throughout our entire year.

Not long ago, when Tommy and I were reminiscing about all of this, he thought we'd never really believed in the notion, that it was a joke right from the start. But I'm pretty certain he was wrong there. Sure enough, by the time we were twelve or thirteen, the Norfolk thing *had* become a big joke. But my memory of it – and Ruth remembered it the same way – is that at the beginning, we believed in Norfolk in the most literal way; that just as lorries came to Hailsham with our food and stuff for our Sales, there was some similar operation going on, except on a grander scale, with vehicles moving all over England, delivering anything left behind in fields and trains to this place called Norfolk. The fact that we'd never seen a picture of the place only added to its mystique.

This might all sound daft, but you have to remember that to us, at that stage in our lives, any place beyond Hailsham was like a fantasy land; we had only the haziest notions of the world out-side and about what was and wasn't possible there. Besides, we never bothered to examine our Norfolk theory in any detail. What was important to us, as Ruth said one evening when we were sitting in that tiled room in Dover, looking out at the sunset, was that 'when we lost something precious, and we'd looked and looked and still couldn't find it, then we didn't have to be com-pletely heartbroken. We still had that last bit of comfort, thinking one day, when we were grown up, and we were free to travel around the country, we could always go and find it again in Norfolk.'

I'm sure Ruth was right about that. Norfolk came to be a real source of comfort for us, probably much more than we admitted at the time, and that was why we were still talking about it – albeit as a sort of joke – when we were much older. And that's why, years and years later, that day Tommy and I found another copy of that lost tape of mine in a town on the Norfolk coast, we didn't just think it pretty funny; we both felt deep down some tug, some old wish to believe again in something that was once close to our hearts.

But I wanted to talk about my tape, *Songs After Dark* by Judy Bridgewater. I suppose it was originally an LP – the recording date's 1956 – but what I had was the cassette, and the cover pic-ture was what must have been a scaled-down version of the record sleeve. Judy Bridgewater is wearing a purple satin dress, one of those off-the-shoulder ones popular in those days, and you can see her from just above the waist because she's sitting on a bar-stool. I think it's supposed to be South America, because there are palms behind her and swarthy waiters in white tuxedos. You're looking at Judy from exactly where the barman would be when he's serving her drinks. She's looking back in a friendly, not too sexy way, like she might be flirting just a tiny bit, but you're someone she knows from way back. Now the other thing about this cover is that Judy's got her elbows up on the bar and there's a cigarette burning in her hand. And it was because of this cigarette that I got so secretive about the tape, right from the moment I found it at the Sale.

I don't know how it was where you were, but at Hailsham the guardians were really strict about smoking. I'm sure they'd have preferred it if we never found out smoking even existed; but since this wasn't possible, they made sure to give us some sort of lecture each time any reference to cigarettes came along. Even if we were being shown a picture of a famous writer or world leader, and they happened to have a cigarette in their hand, then the whole lesson would grind to a halt. There was even a rumour that some classic books – like the Sherlock Holmes ones – weren't in our library because the main characters smoked too much, and when you came across a page torn out of an illustrated book or magazine, this was because there'd been a picture on it of someone smoking. And then there were the actual lessons where they showed us horrible pictures of what smoking did to the insides of your body. That's why it was such a shock that time Marge K. asked Miss Lucy her question.

We were sitting on the grass after a rounders match and Miss Lucy had been giving us a typical talk on smoking when Marge suddenly asked if Miss Lucy had herself ever had a cigarette. Miss Lucy went quiet for a few seconds. Then she said:

'I'd like to be able to say no. But to be honest, I did smoke for a little while. For about two years, when I was younger.'

You can imagine what a shock this was. Before Miss Lucy's reply, we'd all been glaring at Marge, really furious she'd asked such a rude question – to us, she might as well have asked if Miss Lucy had ever attacked anyone with an axe. And for days afterwards I remember how we made Marge's life an utter misery; in fact, that incident I mentioned before, the night we held Marge's face to the dorm window to make her look at the woods, that was all part of what came afterwards. But at the time, the moment Miss Lucy said what she did, we were too confused to think any more about Marge. I think we all just stared at Miss Lucy in horror, waiting for what she'd say next.

When she did speak, Miss Lucy seemed to be weighing up each

word carefully. 'It's not good that I smoked. It wasn't good for me so I stopped it. But what you must understand is that for you, all of you, it's much, much worse to smoke than it ever was for me.'

Then she paused and went quiet. Someone said later she'd gone off into a daydream, but I was pretty sure, as was Ruth, that she was thinking hard about what to say next. Finally she said:

'You've been told about it. You're students. You're . . . *special*. So keeping yourselves well, keeping yourselves very healthy inside, that's much more important for each of you than it is for me.'

She stopped again and looked at us in a strange way. Afterwards, when we discussed it, some of us were sure she was dying for someone to ask: 'Why? Why is it so much worse for us?' But no one did. I've often thought about that day, and I'm sure now, in the light of what happened later, that we only needed to ask and Miss Lucy would have told us all kinds of things. All it would have taken was just one more question about smoking.

So why had we stayed silent that day? I suppose it was because even at that age – we were nine or ten – we knew just enough to make us wary of that whole territory. It's hard now to remember just how much we knew by then. We certainly knew – though not in any deep sense – that we were different from our guardians, and also from the normal people outside; we perhaps even knew that a long way down the line there were donations waiting for us. But we didn't really know what that meant. If we were keen to avoid certain topics, it was probably more because it *embar-rassed* us. We hated the way our guardians, usually so on top of everything, became so awkward whenever we came near this ter-ritory. It unnerved us to see them change like that. I think that's why we never asked that one further question, and why we pun-ished Marge K. so cruelly for bringing it all up that day after the rounders match.

Anyway, that's why I was so secretive about my tape. I even turned the cover inside out so you'd only see Judy and her cigarette if you opened up the plastic case. But the reason the tape meant so much to me had nothing to do with the cigarette, or even with the way Judy Bridgewater sang – she's one of those singers from her time, cocktail-bar stuff, not the sort of thing any of us at Hailsham liked. What made the tape so special for me was this one particular song: track number three, 'Never Let Me Go'.

It's slow and late night and American, and there's a bit that keeps coming round when Judy sings: 'Never let me go . . . Oh baby, baby . . . Never let me go . . .' I was eleven then, and hadn't listened to much music, but this one song, it really got to me. I always tried to keep the tape wound to just that spot so I could play the song whenever a chance came by.

I didn't have so many opportunities, mind you, this being a few years before Walkmans started appearing at the Sales. There was a big machine in the billiards room, but I hardly ever played the tape in there because it was always full of people. The Art Room also had a player, but that was usually just as noisy. The only place I could listen properly was in our dorm.

By then we'd gone into the small six-bed dorms over in the separate huts, and in ours we had a portable cassette player up on the shelf above the radiator. So that's where I used to go, in the day when no one else was likely to be about, to play my song over and over.

What was so special about this song? Well, the thing was, I didn't used to listen properly to the words; I just waited for that bit that went: 'Baby, baby, never let me go . . .' And what I'd imagine was a woman who'd been told she couldn't have babies, who'd really, really wanted them all her life. Then there's a sort of miracle and she has a baby, and she holds this baby very close to her and walks around singing: 'Baby, never let me go . . .' partly because she's so happy, but also because she's so afraid something will happen, that the baby will get ill or be taken away from her. Even at the time, I realised this couldn't be right, that this interpretation didn't fit with the rest of the lyrics. But that wasn't an issue with me. The song was about what I said, and I used to listen to it again and again, on my own, whenever I got the chance.

64

There was one strange incident around this time I should tell you about here. It really unsettled me, and although I wasn't to find out its real meaning until years later, I think I sensed, even then, some deeper significance to it.

It was a sunny afternoon and I'd gone to our dorm to get something. I remember how bright it was because the curtains in our room hadn't been pulled back properly, and you could see the sun coming in in big shafts and see all the dust in the air. I hadn't meant to play the tape, but since I was there all by myself, an impulse made me get the cassette out of my collection box and put it into the player.

Maybe the volume had been turned right up by whoever had been using it last, I don't know. But it was much louder than I usually had it and that was probably why I didn't hear her before I did. Or maybe I'd just got complacent by then. Anyway, what I was doing was swaying about slowly in time to the song, holding an imaginary baby to my breast. In fact, to make it all the more embarrassing, it was one of those times I'd grabbed a pillow to stand in for the baby, and I was doing this slow dance, my eyes closed, singing along softly each time those lines came around again:

'Oh baby, *baby*, never let me go . . .'

The song was almost over when something made me realise I wasn't alone, and I opened my eyes to find myself staring at Madame framed in the doorway.

I froze in shock. Then within a second or two, I began to feel a new kind of alarm, because I could see there was something strange about the situation. The door was almost half open – it was a sort of rule we couldn't close dorm doors completely except for when we were sleeping – but Madame hadn't nearly come up to the threshold. She was out in the corridor, standing very still, her head angled to one side to give her a view of what I was doing inside. And the odd thing was she was crying. It might even have been one of her sobs that had come through the song to jerk me out of my dream.

When I think about this now, it seems to me, even if she wasn't a guardian, she was the adult, and she should have said or done something, even if it was just to tell me off. Then I'd have known how to behave. But she just went on standing out there, sobbing and sobbing, staring at me through the doorway with that same look in her eyes she always had when she looked at us, like she was seeing something that gave her the creeps. Except this time there was something else, something extra in that look I couldn't fathom.

I didn't know what to do or say, or what to expect next. Perhaps she would come into the room, shout at me, hit me even, I didn't have a clue. As it was, she turned and the next moment I could hear her footsteps leaving the hut. I realised the tape had gone onto the next track, and I turned it off and sat down on the nearest bed. And as I did so, I saw through the window in front of me her figure hurrying off towards the main house. She didn't glance back, but I could tell from the way her back was hunched up she was still sobbing.

When I got back to my friends a few minutes later, I didn't tell them anything about what had happened. Someone noticed I wasn't right and said something, but I just shrugged and kept quiet. I wasn't ashamed exactly: but it was a bit like that earlier time, when we'd all waylaid Madame in the courtyard as she got out of her car. What I wished more than anything was that the thing hadn't happened at all, and I thought that by not mentioning it I'd be doing myself and everyone else a favour.

I did, though, talk to Tommy about it a couple of years later. This was in those days following our conversation by the pond when he'd first confided in me about Miss Lucy; the days during which – as I see it – we started off our whole thing of wondering and asking questions about ourselves that we kept going between us through the years. When I told Tommy about what had happened with Madame in the dorm, he came up with a fairly simple explanation. By then, of course, we all knew something I hadn't known back then, which was that none of us could have babies. It's just possible I'd somehow picked up the idea when I was younger without fully registering it, and that's why I heard what I did when I listened to that song. But there was no way I'd known properly back then. As I say, by the time Tommy and I were discussing it, we'd all been told clearly enough. None of us, incidentally, was particularly bothered about it; in fact, I remember some people being pleased we could have sex without worrying about all of that – though proper sex was still some way off for most of us at that stage. Anyway, when I told Tommy about what had happened, he said:

'Madame's probably not a bad person, even though she's creepy. So when she saw you dancing like that, holding your baby, she thought it was really tragic, how you couldn't have babies. That's why she started crying.'

'But Tommy,' I pointed out, 'how could she have known the song had anything to do with people having babies? How could she have known the pillow I was holding was supposed to be a baby? That was only in my head.'

Tommy thought about this, then said only half jokingly: 'Maybe Madame can read minds. She's strange. Maybe she can see right inside you. It wouldn't surprise me.'

This gave us both a little chill, and though we giggled, we didn't say any more about it.

The tape disappeared a couple of months after the incident with Madame. I never linked the two events at the time and I've no reason to link them now. I was in the dorm one night, just before lights-out, and was rummaging through my collection chest to pass the time until the others came back from the bathroom. It's odd but when it first dawned on me the tape wasn't there any more, my main thought was that I mustn't give away how panicked I was. I can remember actually making a point of humming absent-mindedly while I went on searching. I've thought about it a lot and I still don't know how to explain it: these were my closest friends in that room with me and yet I didn't want them to know how upset I was about my tape going missing.

I suppose it had something to do with it being a secret, just how much it had meant to me. Maybe all of us at Hailsham had little secrets like that – little private nooks created out of thin air where we could go off alone with our fears and longings. But the very fact that we had such needs would have felt wrong to us at the time – like somehow we were letting the side down.

Anyway, once I was quite sure the tape was gone, I asked each of the others in the dorm, very casually, if they'd seen it. I wasn't yet completely distraught because there was just the chance I'd left it in the billiards room; otherwise my hope was that someone had borrowed it and would give it back in the morning.

Well, the tape didn't turn up the next day and I've still no idea what happened to it. The truth is, I suppose, there was far more thieving going on at Hailsham than we – or the guardians – ever wanted to admit. But the reason I'm going into all this now is to explain about Ruth and how she reacted. What you have to remember is that I lost my tape less than a month after that time Midge had quizzed Ruth in the Art Room about her pencil case and I'd come to the rescue. Ever since, as I told you, Ruth had been looking out for something nice to do for me in return, and the tape disappearing gave her a real opportunity. You could even say it wasn't until after my tape vanished that things got back to normal with us – maybe for the first time since that rainy morning I'd mentioned the Sales Register to her under the eaves of the main house.

The night I first noticed the tape had gone, I'd made sure to ask everyone about it, and that of course had included Ruth. Looking back, I can see how she must have realised, then and there, exactly what losing the tape meant to me, and at the same time, how important it was for me there was no fuss. So she'd replied that night with a distracted shrug and gone on with what she was doing. But the next morning, when I was coming back from the bathroom, I could hear her – in a casual voice like it wasn't anything much – asking Hannah if she was sure she hadn't seen my tape.

Then maybe a fortnight later, when I'd long reconciled myself to having truly lost my tape, she came and found me during the lunch break. It was one of the first really good days of spring that year, and I'd been sitting on the grass talking with a couple of the older girls. When Ruth came up and asked if I wanted to go for a little stroll, it was obvious she had something particular on her mind. So I left the older girls and followed her to the edge of the North Playing Field, then up the north hill, until we were standing there by the wooden fence looking down on the sweep of green dotted with clusters of students. There was a strong breeze at the top of the hill, and I remember being surprised by it because I hadn't noticed it down on the grass. We stood there looking over the grounds for a while, then she held out a little bag to me. When I took it, I could tell there was a cassette tape inside and my heart leapt. But Ruth said immediately:

'Kathy, it's not your one. The one you lost. I tried to find it for you, but it's really gone.'

'Yeah,' I said. 'Gone to Norfolk.'

We both laughed. Then I took the tape out of the bag with a disappointed air, and I'm not sure the disappointment wasn't still there on my face while I examined it.

I was holding something called *Twenty Classic Dance Tunes*. When I played it later, I discovered it was orchestra stuff for ballroom dancing. Of course, the moment she was giving it to me, I didn't know what sort of music it was, but I did know it wasn't anything like Judy Bridgewater. Then again, almost immediately, I saw how Ruth wasn't to know that – how to Ruth, who didn't know the first thing about music, this tape might easily make up for the one I'd lost. And suddenly I felt the disappointment ebbing away and being replaced by a real happiness. We didn't do things like hug each other much at Hailsham. But I squeezed one of her hands in both mine when I thanked her. She said: 'I found it at the last Sale. I just thought it's the sort of thing you'd like.' And I said that, yes, it was exactly the sort of thing.

I still have it now. I don't play it much because the music has nothing to do with anything. It's an object, like a brooch or a ring, and especially now Ruth has gone, it's become one of my most precious possessions.

CHAPTER SEVEN

I want to move on now to our last years at Hailsham. I'm talking about the period from when we were thirteen to when we left at sixteen. In my memory my life at Hailsham falls into two distinct chunks: this last era, and everything that came before. The earlier years – the ones I've just been telling you about – they tend to blur into each other as a kind of golden time, and when I think about them at all, even the not-so-great things, I can't help feeling a sort of glow. But those last years feel different. They weren't unhappy exactly – I've got plenty of memories I treasure from them – but they were more serious, and in some ways darker. Maybe I've exaggerated it in my mind, but I've got an impression of things changing rapidly around then, like day moving into night.

That talk with Tommy beside the pond: I think of it now as a kind of marker between the two eras. Not that anything significant started to happen immediately afterwards; but for me at least, that conversation was a turning point. I definitely started to look at everything differently. Where before I'd have backed away from awkward stuff, I began instead, more and more, to ask questions, if not out loud, at least within myself.

In particular, that conversation got me looking at Miss Lucy in a new light. I watched her carefully whenever I could, not just from curiosity, but because I now saw her as the most likely source of important clues. And that's how it was, over the next year or two, I came to notice various odd little things she said or did that my friends missed altogether.

There was the time, for example, maybe a few weeks after the talk by the pond, when Miss Lucy was taking us for English. We'd been looking at some poetry, but had somehow drifted onto talking about soldiers in World War Two being kept in prison camps. One of the boys asked if the fences around the camps had been electrified, and then someone else had said how strange it must have been, living in a place like that, where you could commit suicide any time you liked just by touching a fence. This might have been intended as a serious point, but the rest of us thought it pretty funny. We were all laughing and talking at once, and then Laura – typical of her – got up on her seat and did a hysterical impersonation of someone reaching out and getting electrocuted. For a moment things got riotous, with everyone shouting and mimicking touching electric fences.

I went on watching Miss Lucy through all this and I could see, just for a second, a ghostly expression come over her face as she watched the class in front of her. Then – I kept watching carefully – she pulled herself together, smiled and said:'It's just as well the fences at Hailsham aren't electrified. You get terrible accidents sometimes.'

She said this quite softly, and because people were still shout- ing, she was more or less drowned out. But I heard her clearly enough. 'You get terrible accidents sometimes.' What accidents? Where? But no one picked her up on it, and we went back to dis- cussing our poem.

There were other little incidents like that, and before long I came to see Miss Lucy as being not quite like the other guardians. It's even possible I began to realise, right back then, the nature of her worries and frustrations. But that's probably going too far; chances are, at the time, I noticed all these things without know- ing what on earth to make of them. And if these incidents now seem full of significance and all of a piece, it's probably because I'm looking at them in the light of what came later – particularly what happened that day at the pavilion while we were sheltering from the downpour.

We were fifteen by then, already into our last year at Hailsham. We'd been in the pavilion getting ready for a game of rounders. The boys were going through a phase of 'enjoying' rounders in order to flirt with us, so there were over thirty of us that after- noon. The downpour had started while we were changing, and we found ourselves gathering on the veranda – which was sheltered by the pavilion roof – while we waited for it to stop. But the rain kept going, and when the last of us had emerged, the veranda was pretty crowded, with everyone milling around restlessly. I remember Laura was demonstrating to me an especially disgusting way of blowing your nose for when you really wanted to put off a boy.

Miss Lucy was the only guardian present. She was leaning over the rail at the front, peering into the rain like she was trying to see right across the playing field. I was watching her as carefully as ever in those days, and even as I was laughing at Laura, I was stealing glances at Miss Lucy's back. I remember wondering if there wasn't something a bit odd about her posture, the way her head was bent down just a little too far so she looked like a crouching animal waiting to pounce. And the way she was leaning forward over the rail meant drops from the overhanging gutter were only just missing her – but she seemed to show no sign of caring. I remember actually convincing myself there was nothing unusual in all this – that she was simply anxious for the rain to stop – and turning my attention back to what Laura was saying. Then a few minutes later, when I'd forgotten all about Miss Lucy and was laughing my head off at something, I suddenly realised things had gone quiet around us, and that Miss Lucy was speaking.

She was standing at the same spot as before, but she'd turned to face us now, so her back was against the rail, and the rainy sky behind her.

'No, no, I'm sorry, I'm going to have to interrupt you,' she was saying, and I could see she was talking to two boys sitting on the benches immediately in front of her. Her voice wasn't exactly strange, but she was speaking very loudly, in the sort of voice she'd use to announce something to the lot of us, and that was why we'd all gone quiet. 'No, Peter, I'm going to have to stop you. I can't listen to you any more and keep silent.'

Then she raised her gaze to include the rest of us and took a deep breath. 'All right, you can hear this, it's for all of you. It's time someone spelt it out.'

We waited while she kept staring at us. Later, some people said they'd thought she was going to give us a big telling-off; others that she was about to announce a new rule on how we played rounders. But I knew before she said another word it would be something more.

'Boys, you must forgive me for listening. But you were right behind me, so I couldn't help it. Peter, why don't you tell the others what you were saying to Gordon just now?'

Peter J. looked bewildered and I could see him getting ready his injured innocence face. But then Miss Lucy said again, this time much more gently:

'Peter, go on. Please tell the others what you were just saying.'

Peter shrugged. 'We were just talking about what it would feel like if we became actors. What sort of life it would be.'

'Yes,' Miss Lucy said, 'and you were saying to Gordon you'd have to go to America to stand the best chance.'

Peter J. shrugged again and muttered quietly: 'Yes, Miss Lucy.'

But Miss Lucy was now moving her gaze over the lot of us. 'I know you don't mean any harm. But there's just too much talk like this. I hear it all the time, it's been allowed to go on, and it's not right.' I could see more drops coming off the gutter and landing on her shoulder, but she didn't seem to notice. 'If no one else will talk to you,' she continued, 'then I will. The problem, as I see it, is that you've been told and not told. You've been told, but none of you really understand, and I dare say, some people are quite happy to leave it that way. But I'm not. If you're going to have decent lives, then you've got to know and know properly. None of you will go to America, none of you will be film stars. And none of you will be working in supermarkets as I heard some of you planning the other day. Your lives are set out for you. You'll become adults, then before you're old, before you're even middle-aged, you'll start to donate your vital organs. That's what each of you was created to do. You're not like the actors you watch on your videos, you're not even like me. You were brought into this world for a purpose, and your futures, all of them, have been decided. So you're not to talk that way any more. You'll be

73

leaving Hailsham before long, and it's not so far off, the day you'll be preparing for your first donations. You need to remember that. If you're to have decent lives, you have to know who you are and what lies ahead of you, every one of you.'

Then she went silent, but my impression was that she was continuing to say things inside her head, because for some time her gaze kept roving over us, going from face to face just as if she were still speaking to us. We were all pretty relieved when she turned to look out over the playing field again.

'It's not so bad now,' she said, even though the rain was as steady as ever. 'Let's just go out there. Then maybe the sun will come out too.'

I think that was all she said. When I was discussing it with Ruth a few years ago at the centre in Dover, she claimed Miss Lucy had told us a lot more; that she'd explained how before donations we'd all spend some time first as carers, about the usual sequence of the donations, the recovery centres and so on – but I'm pretty sure she didn't. Okay, she probably intended to when she began talking. But my guess is once she'd set off, once she'd seen the puzzled, uncomfortable faces in front of her, she realised the impossibility of completing what she'd started.

It's hard to say clearly what sort of impact Miss Lucy's outburst at the pavilion made. Word got round fast enough, but the talk mostly focused on Miss Lucy herself rather than on what she'd been trying to tell us. Some students thought she'd lost her marbles for a moment; others that she'd been asked to say what she had by Miss Emily and the other guardians; there were even some who'd actually been there and who thought Miss Lucy had been telling us off for being too rowdy on the veranda. But as I say there was surprisingly little discussion about what she'd said. If it did come up, people tended to say: 'Well so what? We already knew all that.'

But that had been Miss Lucy's point exactly. We'd been 'told and not told', as she'd put it. A few years ago, when Tommy and I were going over it all again, and I reminded him of Miss Lucy's 'told and not told' idea, he came up with a theory.

Tommy thought it possible the guardians had, throughout all our years at Hailsham, timed very carefully and deliberately everything they told us, so that we were always just too young to understand properly the latest piece of information. But of course we'd take it in at some level, so that before long all this stuff was there in our heads without us ever having examined it properly.

It's a bit too much like a conspiracy theory for me – I don't think our guardians were that crafty – but there's probably something in it. Certainly, it feels like I *always* knew about donations in some vague way, even as early as six or seven. And it's curious, when we were older and the guardians were giving us those talks, nothing came as a complete surprise. It *was* like we'd heard everything somewhere before.

One thing that occurs to me now is that when the guardians first started giving us proper lectures about sex, they tended to run them together with talk about the donations. At that age – again, I'm talking of around thirteen – we were all pretty worried and excited about sex, and naturally would have pushed the other stuff into the background. In other words, it's possible the guardians managed to smuggle into our heads a lot of the basic facts about our futures.

Now to be fair, it was probably natural to run these two subjects together. If, say, they were telling us how we'd have to be very careful to avoid diseases when we had sex, it would have been odd not to mention how much more important this was for us than for normal people outside. And that, of course, would bring us onto the donations.

Then there was the whole business about our not being able to have babies. Miss Emily used to give a lot of the sex lectures herself, and I remember once, she brought in a life-size skeleton from the biology class to demonstrate how it was done. We watched in complete astonishment as she put the skeleton through various contortions, thrusting her pointer around without the slightest self-consciousness. She was going through all the nuts and bolts of how you did it, what went in where, the different variations, like this was still Geography. Then suddenly, with the skeleton in an obscene heap on the desktop, she turned away and began telling us how we had to be careful *who* we had sex with. Not just because of the diseases, but because, she said, 'sex affects emotions in ways you'd never expect'. We had to be extremely careful about having sex in the outside world, especially with people who weren't students, because out there sex meant all sorts of things. Out there people were even fighting and killing each other over who had sex with whom. And the reason it meant so much – so much more than, say, dancing or table-tennis – was because the people out there were different from us students: they could have babies from sex. That was why it was so important to them, this question of who did it with whom. And even though, as we knew, it was completely impossible for any of us to have babies, out there, we had to behave like them. We had to respect the rules and treat sex as something pretty special.

Miss Emily's lecture that day was typical of what I'm talking about. We'd be focusing on sex, and then the other stuff would creep in. I suppose that was all part of how we came to be 'told and not told'.

I think in the end we must have absorbed quite a lot of information, because I remember, around that age, a marked change in the way we approached the whole territory surrounding the donations. Until then, as I've said, we'd done everything to avoid the subject; we'd backed off at the first sign we were entering that ground, and there'd been severe punishment for any idiot – like Marge that time – who got careless. But from when we were thirteen, like I say, things started to change. We still didn't discuss the donations and all that went with them; we still found the whole area awkward enough. But it became something we made jokes about, in much the way we joked about sex. Looking back now, I'd say the rule about not discussing the donations openly was still there, as strong as ever. But now it was okay, almost required, every now and then, to make some jokey allusion to these things that lay in front of us.

A good example is what happened the time Tommy got the gash on his elbow. It must have been just before my talk with him by the pond; a time, I suppose, when Tommy was still coming out of that phase of being teased and taunted.

It wasn't such a bad gash, and though he was sent to Crow Face to have it seen to, he was back almost straight away with a square of dressing plastered to his elbow. No one thought much about it until a couple of days later, when Tommy took off the dressing to reveal something at just that stage between sealing and still being an open wound. You could see bits of skin starting to bond, and soft red bits peeping up from underneath. We were in the middle of lunch, so everyone crowded round to go 'urgh!' Then Christopher H., from the year above, said with a dead straight face: 'Pity it's on that bit of the elbow. Just about anywhere else, it wouldn't matter.'

Tommy looked worried – Christopher being someone he looked up to in those days – and asked what he meant. Christopher went on eating, then said nonchalantly:

'Don't you know? If it's right on the elbow like that, it can *unzip*. All you have to do is bend your arm quickly. Not just that actual bit, the whole elbow, it can all unzip like a bag opening up. Thought you'd know that.'

I could hear Tommy complaining that Crow Face hadn't warned him of anything of that sort, but Christopher shrugged and said: 'She thought you knew, of course. Everyone knows.'

A number of people nearby murmured agreement. 'You've got to keep your arm dead straight,' someone else said. 'Bending it at all's really dangerous.'

The next day I could see Tommy going about with his arm held out very rigidly and looking worried. Everybody was laughing at him, and I was cross about that, but I had to admit, there was a funny side to it. Then towards the end of the afternoon as we were leaving the Art Room, he came up to me in the corridor and said: 'Kath, can I just have a quick word?'

This was maybe a couple of weeks after the time I'd gone up to him in the playing field to remind him about his polo shirt, so it had got about we were special friends of some sort. All the same, his coming up like that asking for a private talk was pretty embarrassing and threw me off balance. Maybe that partly explains why I wasn't more helpful than I was.

'I'm not too worried or anything,' he began, once he'd got me aside. 'But I wanted to play safe, that's all. We should never take chances with our health. I need someone to help, Kath.' He was, he explained, concerned about what he'd do in his sleep. He might easily bend his elbow in the night. 'I have these dreams all the time where I'm fighting loads of Roman soldiers.'

When I quizzed him a bit, it became obvious all kinds of people – people who hadn't been there that lunch-time – had been coming up to him to repeat Christopher H.'s warning. In fact, it seemed a few had carried the joke further: Tommy had been told of a student who'd gone to sleep with a cut on the elbow just like his and woken up to find his whole upper arm and hand skeletally exposed, the skin flopping about next to him 'like one of those long gloves in *My Fair Lady* '.

What Tommy was asking me now was to help tie a splint on the arm to keep it rigid through the night.

'I don't trust any of the others,' he said, holding up a thick ruler he wanted to use. 'They might deliberately do it so it comes undone in the night.'

He was looking at me in complete innocence and I didn't know what to say. A part of me wanted badly to tell him what was going on, and I suppose I knew that to do anything else would be to betray the trust we'd built up since the moment I'd reminded him about his polo shirt. And for me to strap up his arm in a splint would have meant my becoming one of the main perpetrators of the joke. I still feel ashamed I didn't tell him then. But you've got to remember I was still young, and that I only had a few seconds to decide. And when someone's asking you to do something in such a pleading way, everything goes against saying no.

I suppose the main thing was that I didn't want to upset him. Because I could see, for all his anxiety about his elbow, Tommy was touched by all the concern he believed had been shown him.

Of course, I knew he'd find out the truth sooner or later, but at that moment I just couldn't tell him. The best I could do was to ask:

'Did Crow Face tell you you had to do this?'

'No. But imagine how angry she'd be if my elbow slipped out.'

I still feel bad about it, but I promised to strap his arm for him – in Room 14 half an hour before the night bell – and watched him go off grateful and reassured.

As it happened, I didn't have to go through with it because Tommy found out first. It was around eight in the evening, I was coming down the main staircase, and heard a burst of laughter rising up the stairwell from the ground floor. My heart sank because I knew immediately it was to do with Tommy. I paused on the first-floor landing and looked over the rail just as Tommy came out of the billiards room with thunderous footsteps. I remember thinking: 'At least he's not shouting.' And he didn't, the whole time he went to the cloakroom, got his things and left the main house. And all that time, laughter kept coming from the open doorway of the billiards room, and voices yelling things like: 'If you lose your temper, your elbow will *definitely* pop out!'

I thought about following him out into the evening and catching up with him before he got to his dorm hut, but then I remembered how I'd promised to put his arm in a splint for the night, and didn't move. I just kept saying to myself: 'At least he didn't have a tantrum. At least he kept hold of that temper.'

But I've gone off a bit. The reason I was talking about all this was because the idea of things 'unzipping' carried over from Tommy's elbow to become a running joke among us about the donations. The idea was that when the time came, you'd be able just to unzip a bit of yourself, a kidney or something would slide out, and you'd hand it over. It wasn't something we found so funny in itself; it was more a way of putting each other off our food. You unzipped your liver, say, and dumped it on someone's plate, that sort of thing. I remember once Gary B., who had this unbelievable appetite, coming back with a third helping of pudding, and virtually the whole table 'unzipping' bits of themselves and piling it all over Gary's bowl, while he went on determinedly stuffing himself.

Tommy never liked it much when the unzipping stuff came up again, but by then the days of his being teased were past and no one connected the joke with him any more. It was just done to get a laugh, to put someone off their dinner – and, I suppose, as some way of acknowledging what was in front of us. And this was my original point. By that time in our lives, we no longer shrank from the subject of donations as we'd have done a year or two earlier; but neither did we think about it very seriously, or discuss it. All that business about 'unzipping', that was typical of the way the whole subject impinged on us when we were thirteen.

So I'd say Miss Lucy had it about right when she said, a couple of years later, that we'd been 'told and not told'. And what's more, now I think about it, I'd say what Miss Lucy said to us that afternoon led to a real shift in our attitudes. It was after that day, jokes about donations faded away, and we started to think properly about things. If anything, the donations went back to being a subject to be avoided, but not in the way it had been when we were younger. This time round it wasn't awkward or embarrassing any more; just sombre and serious.

'It's funny,' Tommy said to me when we were remembering it all again a few years ago. 'None of us stopped to think about how *she* felt, Miss Lucy herself. We never worried if she'd got into trouble, saying what she did to us. We were so selfish back then.'

'But you can't blame us,' I said. 'We'd been taught to think about each other, but never about the guardians. The idea the guardians had differences between them, that never occurred to us.'

'But we were old enough,' Tommy said. 'By that age, it *should* have occurred to us. But it didn't. We didn't think about poor Miss Lucy at all. Not even after that time, you know, when you saw her.'

I knew straight away what he meant. He was talking about the morning early in our last summer at Hailsham, when I'd stumbled across her up in Room 22. Thinking about it now, I'd say

Tommy had a point. After that moment it should have been clear, even to us, how troubled Miss Lucy had become. But as he said, we never considered anything from her viewpoint, and it never occurred to us to say or do anything to support her.

CHAPTER EIGHT

Many of us had turned sixteen by then. It was a morning of brilliant sunshine and we'd all just come down to the courtyard after a lesson in the main house, when I remembered something I'd left in the classroom. So I went back up to the third floor and that's how the thing with Miss Lucy happened.

In those days I had this secret game. When I found myself alone, I'd stop and look for a view – out of a window, say, or through a doorway into a room – any view so long as there were no people in it. I did this so that I could, for a few seconds at least, create the illusion the place wasn't crawling with students, but that instead Hailsham was this quiet, tranquil house where I lived with just five or six others. To make this work, you had to get yourself into a sort of dream, and shut off all the stray noises and voices. Usually you had to be pretty patient too: if, say, you were focusing from a window on one particular bit of the playing field, you could wait ages for those couple of seconds when there wasn't anyone at all in your frame. Anyway, that was what I was doing that morning after I'd fetched whatever it was I'd left in the classroom and come back out onto the third-floor landing.

I was keeping very still near a window looking down onto a section of the courtyard where I'd been standing only moments before. My friends had gone, and the courtyard was steadily emptying, so I was waiting for my trick to work, when I heard behind me what sounded like gas or steam escaping in sharp bursts.

It was a hissing noise that would go on for about ten seconds, pause, then come again. I wasn't alarmed exactly, but since I seemed to be the only person around, I thought I'd better go and investigate.

I went across the landing towards the sound, along the corridor past the room I'd just been in, and down to Room 22, second from the end. The door was partly open, and just as I came up to it, the hissing started up again with a new intensity. I don't know what I expected to discover as I cautiously pushed the door, but I was properly surprised to find Miss Lucy.

Room 22 was hardly used for classes because it was so small and, even on a day like that one, hardly any light got in. The guardians sometimes went in there to mark our work or get on with reading. That morning the room was darker than ever because the blinds had been pulled almost all the way down. There were two tables pushed together for a group to sit around, but Miss Lucy was there alone near the back. I could see several loose sheets of dark, shiny paper scattered over the table in front of her. She herself was leaning over in concentration, forehead very low, arms up on the surface, scrawling furious lines over a page with a pencil. Underneath the heavy black lines I could see neat blue handwriting. As I watched, she went on scrubbing the pencil point over the paper, almost in the way we did shading in Art, except her movements were much more angry, as if she didn't mind gouging right through the sheet. Then I realised, in the same instant, that this was the source of the odd noise, and that what I'd taken for dark shiny paper on the table had also, not long before, been pages of neat handwriting.

She was so lost in what she was doing, it took a while for her to realise I was there. When she looked up with a start, I could see her face was flushed, but there were no traces of tears. She stared at me, then put down her pencil.

'Hello, young lady,' she said, then took a deep breath. 'What can I do for you?'

I think I turned away so I didn't have to look at her or at the papers over the desk. I can't remember if I said very much – if I explained about the noise and how I'd worried about it being gas. In any case, there was no proper conversation: she didn't want me there and neither did I. I think I made some apology and went out, half expecting her to call me back. But she didn't, and what I remember now is that I went down the staircase burning with shame and resentment. At that moment I wished more than anything that I hadn't seen what I'd just seen, though if you'd asked me to define just what I was so upset about, I wouldn't have been able to explain. Shame, as I say, had a lot to do with it, and also fury, though not exactly at Miss Lucy herself. I was very confused, and that's probably why I didn't say anything about it to my friends until much later.

After that morning I became convinced something else – perhaps something awful – lay around the corner to do with Miss Lucy, and I kept my eyes and ears open for it. But the days passed and I heard nothing. What I didn't know at the time was that something pretty significant *had* happened only a few days after I'd seen her in Room 22 – something between Miss Lucy and Tommy that had left him upset and disorientated. There would have been a time not so much earlier when Tommy and I would have immediately reported to each other any news of this sort; but just around that summer, various things were going on which meant we weren't talking so freely.

That's why I didn't hear about it for so long. Afterwards I could have kicked myself for not guessing, for not seeking Tommy out and getting it out of him. But as I've said, there was a lot going on around then, between Tommy and Ruth, a whole host of other stuff, and I'd put all the changes I'd noticed in him down to that.

It's probably going too far to say Tommy's whole act fell apart that summer, but there were times when I got seriously worried he was turning back into the awkward and changeable figure from several years before. Once, for instance, a few of us were going back from the pavilion towards the dorm huts and found ourselves walking behind Tommy and a couple of other boys. They were just few paces ahead, and all of them – Tommy included – looked to be in good form, laughing and shoving each other. In fact, I'd say Laura, who was walking beside me, took her cue from the way the boys were larking about. The thing was, Tommy must have been sitting on the ground earlier, because there was a sizeable chunk of mud stuck on his rugby shirt near the small of his back. He was obviously unaware of it, and I don't think his friends had seen it either or they'd surely have made something of it. Anyway, Laura being Laura shouted out something like: 'Tommy! You got poo-poo on your back! What have you been doing?'

She'd done this in a completely friendly way, and if some of the rest of us made a few noises too, it wasn't anything more than the sort of thing students did the whole time. So it was a complete shock when Tommy came to a dead halt, wheeled round and stared at Laura with a face like thunder. We all stopped too – the boys looking as bewildered as we were – and for a few seconds I thought Tommy was going to blow for the first time in years. But then he abruptly stalked off, leaving us all swapping looks and shrugging.

Nearly as bad was the time I showed him Patricia C.'s calendar. Patricia was two years below us but everyone was in awe of her drawing skills, and her stuff was always sought after at the Art Exchanges. I'd been particularly pleased with the calendar, which I'd managed to get at the last Exchange, because word had been going round about it from weeks before. It wasn't anything like, say, Miss Emily's flappy colour calendars of the English counties. Patricia's calendar was tiny and dumpy, and for each month there was a stunning little pencil sketch of a scene from Hailsham life. I wish I still had it now, especially since in some of the pictures – like the ones for June and for September – you can make out the faces of particular students and guardians. It's one of the things I lost when I left the Cottages, when my mind was elsewhere and I wasn't being so careful what I took with me – but I'll come to all that in its place. My point now is that Patricia's calendar was a real catch, I was proud of it, and that's why I wanted to show it to Tommy.

I'd spotted him standing in the late afternoon sunshine beside the big sycamore near the South Playing Field, and since my calendar was there in my bag – I'd been showing it off during our music lesson – I'd gone over to him.

He was absorbed in a football match involving some younger boys over in the next field and at this stage his mood seemed just fine, tranquil even. He smiled when I came up to him and we chatted for a minute about nothing in particular. Then I said: 'Tommy, look what I managed to get.' I didn't try to keep the triumph out of my voice, and I may even have gone 'dah-dah!' as I brought it out and handed it to him. When he took the calendar, there was still a smile on his features, but as he flicked through I could see something closing off inside him.

'That Patricia,' I began to say, but I could hear my own voice changing. 'She's so clever . . .'

But Tommy was already handing it back to me. Then without another word he marched past me off towards the main house.

This last incident should have given me a clue. If I'd thought about it with half a brain, I should have guessed Tommy's recent moods had something to do with Miss Lucy and his old problems about 'being creative'. But with everything else going on just at that time, I didn't, as I say, think in these terms at all. I suppose I must have assumed those old problems had been left behind with our early teen years, and that only the big issues that now loomed so large could possibly preoccupy any of us.

So what had been going on? Well, for a start, Ruth and Tommy had had a serious bust-up. They'd been a couple for about six months by then; at least, that's how long they'd been 'public' about it – walking around with arms around each other, that kind of thing. They were respected as a couple because they weren't show-offs. Some others, Sylvia B. and Roger D., for example, could get stomach-churning, and you had to give them a chorus of vomiting noises just to keep them in order. But Ruth and Tommy never did anything gross in front of people, and if sometimes they cuddled or whatever, it felt like they were genuinely doing it for each other, not for an audience.

Looking back now, I can see we were pretty confused about this whole area around sex. That's hardly surprising, I suppose, given we were barely sixteen. But what added to the confusion – I can see it more clearly now – was the fact that the guardians were themselves confused. On the one hand we had, say, Miss Emily's talks, when she'd tell us how important it was not to be ashamed of our bodies, to 'respect our physical needs', how sex was 'a very beautiful gift' as long as both people really wanted it. But when it came down to it, the guardians made it more or less impossible for any of us actually to do much without breaking rules. We couldn't visit the boys' dorms after nine o'clock, they couldn't visit ours. The classrooms were all officially 'out of bounds' in the evenings, as were the areas behind the sheds and the pavilion. And you didn't want to do it in the fields even when it was warm enough, because you'd almost certainly discover afterwards you'd had an audience watching from the house passing around binoculars. In other words, for all the talk of sex being beautiful, we had the distinct impression we'd be in trouble if the guardians caught us at it.

I say this, but the only real case I personally knew of like that was when Jenny C. and Rob D. got interrupted in Room 14. They were doing it after lunch, right there over one of the desks, and Mr Jack had come in to get something. According to Jenny, Mr Jack had turned red and gone right out again, but they'd been put off and had stopped. They'd more or less dressed themselves when Mr Jack came back, just as though for the first time, and pretended to be surprised and shocked.

'It's very clear to me what you've been doing and it's not appropriate,' he'd said, and told them both to go and see Miss Emily. But once they'd got to Miss Emily's office, she'd told them she was on her way to an important meeting and didn't have time to talk to them.

'But you know you shouldn't have been doing whatever you were doing, and I don't expect you'll do it again,' she'd said, before rushing out with her folders.

Gay sex, incidentally, was something we were even more confused about. For some reason, we called it 'umbrella sex'; if you fancied someone your own sex, you were 'an umbrella'. I don't know how it was where you were, but at Hailsham we definitely weren't at all kind towards any signs of gay stuff. The boys especially could do the cruellest things. According to Ruth this was because quite a few of them had done things with each other when they'd been younger, before they'd realised what they were doing. So now they were ridiculously tense about it. I don't know if she was right, but for sure, accusing someone of 'getting all umbrella' could easily end in a fight.

When we discussed all these things – as we did endlessly back then – we couldn't decide whether or not the guardians wanted us to have sex or not. Some people thought they did, but that we kept trying to do it at all the wrong times. Hannah had the theory that it was their duty to make us have sex because otherwise we wouldn't be good donors later on. According to her, things like your kidneys and pancreas didn't work properly unless you kept having sex. Someone else said what we had to remember was that the guardians were 'normals'. That's why they were so odd about it; for them, sex was for when you wanted babies, and even though they knew, intellectually, that *we* couldn't have babies, they still felt uneasy about us doing it because deep down they couldn't quite believe we wouldn't end up with babies.

Annette B. had another theory: that the guardians were uncomfortable about us having sex with each other because *they'd* then want to have sex with us. Mr Chris in particular, she said, looked at us girls in that way. Laura said that what Annette really meant was *she* wanted to have sex with Mr Chris. We all cracked up at this because the idea of having sex with Mr Chris seemed absurd, as well as completely sick-making.

The theory I think came closest was the one put forward by Ruth. 'They're telling us about sex for after we leave Hailsham,' she said. 'They want us to do it properly, with someone we like and without getting diseases. But they really mean it for after we leave. They don't want us doing it here, because it's too much hassle for them.'

My guess, anyway, is that there wasn't nearly as much sex going on as people made out. A lot of snogging and touching up, maybe; and couples *hinting* they were having proper sex. But looking back, I wonder how much of it there really was. If everyone who claimed to be doing it really had been, then that's all you'd have seen when you walked about Hailsham – couples going at it left, right and centre.

What I remember is that there was this discreet agreement among us all not to quiz each other too much about our claims. If, say, Hannah rolled her eyes when you were discussing another girl and murmured: 'Virgin' – meaning 'Of course *we're* not, but she is, so what can you expect?' – then it definitely wasn't on to ask her: 'Who did you do it with? When? Where?' No, you just nodded knowingly. It was like there was some parallel universe we all vanished off to where we had all this sex.

I must have seen at the time how all these claims being made around me didn't add up. All the same, as that summer approached, I began to feel more and more the odd one out. In a way, sex had got like 'being creative' had been a few years earlier. It felt like if you hadn't done it yet, you ought to, and quickly. And in my case, the whole thing was made more complicated by the fact that two of the girls I was closest to definitely *had* done it. Laura with Rob D., even though they'd never been a proper couple. And Ruth with Tommy.

For all that, I'd been holding it off for ages, repeating to myself Miss Emily's advice – 'If you can't find someone with whom you truly wish to share this experience, then *don't!*' But around the spring of the year I'm talking about now, I started to think I wouldn't mind having sex with a boy. Not just to see what it was like, but also because it occurred to me I needed to get familiar with sex, and it would be just as well to practise first with a boy I didn't care about too much. Then later on, if I was with someone special, I'd have more chance of doing everything right. What I mean is, if Miss Emily was correct and sex was this really big deal between people, then I didn't want to be doing it for the first time when it was really important how well it went.

So I had my eye on Harry C. I chose him for a number of reasons. First, I knew he'd definitely done it before, with Sharon D. Next, I didn't fancy him that much, but I certainly didn't find him sick-making. Also, he was quiet and decent, so unlikely to go round gossiping afterwards if it was a complete disaster. And he'd hinted a few times he'd like to have sex with me. Okay, a lot of the boys were making flirty noises in those days, but it was clear by then what was a real proposition and what was the usual boys' stuff.

So I'd chosen Harry, and I only delayed those couple of months because I wanted to make sure I'd be all right physically. Miss Emily had told us it could be painful and a big failure if you didn't get wet enough and this was my one real worry. It wasn't being ripped apart down there, which we often joked about, and was the secret fear of quite a few girls. I kept thinking, as long as I got wet quick enough, there'd be no problem, and I did it a lot on my own just to make sure.

I realise this may sound like I was getting obsessive, but I remember I also spent a lot of time re-reading passages from books where people had sex, going over the lines again and again, trying to tease out clues. The trouble was, the books we had at Hailsham weren't at all helpful. We had a lot of nineteenth-century stuff by Thomas Hardy and people like that, which was more or less useless. Some modern books, by people like Edna O'Brien and Margaret Drabble, had some sex in them, but it wasn't ever very clear what was happening because the authors always assumed you'd already had a lot of sex before and there was no need to go into details. So I was having a frustrating time with the books, and the videos weren't much better. We'd got a video player in the billiards room a couple of years earlier, and by that spring had built up quite a good collection of movies. A lot of them had sex in them, but most scenes would end just as the sex was starting up, or else you'd only see their faces and their backs. And when there *was* a useful scene, it was difficult to see it more than fleetingly because there were usually twenty others in the room watching with you. We'd evolved this system where we called for particular favourite scenes to be played again – like, for instance, the moment the American jumps over the barbed wire on his bike in *The Great Escape*. There'd be a chant of: 'Rewind! Rewind!' until someone got the remote and we'd see the portion again, sometimes three, four times. But I could hardly, by myself, start shouting for rewinds just to see sex scenes again.

So I kept delaying week by week, while I went on preparing,

until the summer came and I decided I was as ready as I'd ever be. By then, I was even feeling reasonably confident about it, and began dropping hints to Harry. Everything was going fine and according to plan, when Ruth and Tommy split up and it all got confused.

CHAPTER NINE

What happened was that a few days after they split, I was in the Art Room with some other girls, working on a still life. I remember it being stifling that day, even though we had the fan rattling behind us. We were using charcoal, and because someone had commandeered all the easels, we were having to work with our boards propped up on our laps. I was sitting beside Cynthia E., and we'd just been chatting and complaining about the heat. Then somehow we'd got onto the subject of boys, and she'd said, not looking up from her work:

'And Tommy. I knew it wouldn't last with Ruth. Well, I suppose you're the natural successor.'

She'd said it in a throwaway manner. But Cynthia was a perceptive person, and the fact that she wasn't part of our group just gave her remark more weight. What I mean is, I couldn't help thinking she represented what anyone with any distance on the subject would think. After all, I'd been Tommy's friend for years until all this couples stuff had come up. It was perfectly possible that to someone on the outside, I'd look like Ruth's 'natural successor'. I just let it go, though, and Cynthia, who wasn't trying to make any big point, said nothing else about it.

Then maybe a day or two later, I was coming out of the pavilion with Hannah when she suddenly nudged me and nodded towards a group of boys over on the North Playing Field.

'Look,' she said quietly. 'Tommy. Sitting by himself.'

I shrugged, as though to say: 'So what?' And that's all there was to it. But afterwards I found myself thinking a lot about it. Maybe all Hannah had meant to do was point out how Tommy, since splitting with Ruth, looked a bit of a spare part. But I couldn't quite buy this; I knew Hannah too well. The way she'd nudged me and lowered her voice had made it all too obvious she too was expressing some assumption, probably doing the rounds, about me being the 'natural successor'.

All this did, as I say, put me in a bit of a confusion, because until then I'd been all set on my Harry plan. In fact, looking back now, I'm sure I *would* have had sex with Harry if it hadn't been for this 'natural successor' business. I'd had it all sorted, and my preparations had gone well. And I still think Harry was a good choice for that stage in my life. I think he would have been considerate and gentle, and have understood what I was wanting from him.

I saw Harry fleetingly a couple of years ago at the recovery centre in Wiltshire. He was being brought in after a donation. I wasn't in the best of moods because my own donor had just completed the night before. No one was blaming me for that – it had been a particularly untidy operation – but I wasn't feeling great all the same. I'd been up most of the night, sorting all the arrangements, and I was in the front reception getting ready to leave when I saw Harry coming in. He was in a wheelchair – because he was so weak, I found out later, not because he couldn't actually walk – and I'm not sure he recognised me when I went up and said hello. I suppose there's no reason I should have any special place in his memory. We'd never had much to do with each other apart from that one time. To him, if he remembered me at all, I'd just be this daft girl who came up to him once, asked if he wanted sex, then backed off. He must have been pretty mature for his age, because he didn't get annoyed or go round telling people I was a tease, or any of that. So when I saw him being brought in that day, I felt grateful to him and wished I was his carer. I looked about, but whoever *was* his carer wasn't even around. The orderlies were impatient to get him to his room, so I didn't talk with him long. I just said hello, that I hoped he'd feel better soon, and he smiled tiredly. When I mentioned Hailsham he did a thumbs-up, but I could tell he didn't recognise me. Maybe later, when he wasn't so tired, or when the medication wasn't so strong, he'd have tried to place me and remembered.

Anyway, I was talking about back then: about how after Ruth and Tommy split, all my plans got confused. Looking at it now, I feel a bit sorry for Harry. After all the hints I'd been dropping the previous week, there I was, suddenly whispering stuff to put him off. I suppose I must have assumed he was raring to go, that I had my work cut out just to hold him off. Because whenever I saw him, I'd always get something in quick, then rush off before he could say anything back. It was only much later, when I thought about it, it occurred to me he might not have had sex on his mind at all. For all I know, he might have been happy to forget the whole thing, except that every time he saw me, along a corridor or in the grounds, I'd come up and whisper some excuse why I didn't want sex with him just then. It must have looked pretty daft from his side, and if he hadn't been such a decent type, I'd have been a laughing stock in no time. Well, anyway, this era of putting Harry off lasted maybe a couple of weeks, and then came Ruth's request.

That summer, right up until the warm weather faded, we developed this odd way of listening to music together in the fields. Walkmans had started appearing at Hailsham since the previous year's Sales and by that summer there were at least six of them in circulation. The craze was for several people to sit on the grass around a single Walkman, passing the headset around. Okay, it sounds a stupid way to listen to music, but it created a really good feeling. You listened for maybe twenty seconds, took off the headset, passed it on. After a while, provided you kept the same tape going over and over, it was surprising how close it was to having heard all of it by yourself. As I say, the craze really took off that summer, and during the lunch breaks you'd see all these clusters of students lying about the grass around the Walkmans. The guardians weren't too keen, saying we'd spread ear infections, but they let us carry on. I can't remember that last summer without thinking about those afternoons around the Walkmans. Someone would wander up and ask: 'What's the sound?' and if they liked the answer, they'd sit down on the grass and wait their turn. There was almost always a good atmosphere around these sessions and I don't remember anyone being refused a share of the headset.

Anyway, that's what I was up to with a few other girls when Ruth came up to ask if we could have a talk. I could tell it was something important, so I left my other friends and the two of us walked off, all the way to our dorm hut. When we got to our room, I sat down on Ruth's bed, close to the window – the sun had warmed the blanket – and she sat on mine over by the back wall. There was a bluebottle buzzing around, and for a minute we had a laugh playing 'bluebottle tennis', throwing our hands about to make the demented creature go from one to the other of us. Then it found its way out of the window, and Ruth said:

'I want me and Tommy to get back together again. Kathy, will you help?' Then she asked: 'What's the matter?'

'Nothing. I was just a bit surprised, after what's happened. Of course I'll help.'

'I haven't told anybody else about wanting to get back with Tommy. Not even Hannah. You're the only one I trust.'

'What do you want me to do?'

'Just talk to him. You've always had this way with him. He'll listen to you. And he'll know you're not bullshitting about me.'

For a moment we sat there swinging our feet under our beds.

'It's really good you're telling me this,' I said eventually. 'I probably am the best person. Talking to Tommy and all that.'

'What I want is for us to make a fresh start. We're about evens now, we've both done daft things just to hurt each other, but it's enough now. Martha bloody H., I ask you! Maybe he did it just to give me a good laugh. Well you can tell him he succeeded, and the scores are all even again. It's time we grew up and started afresh. I know you can reason with him, Kathy. You'll deal with it the best way possible. Then if he's still not prepared to be sensible, I'll know there's no point carrying on with him.'

I shrugged. 'As you say, Tommy and I, we've always been able to talk.'

'Yeah, and he really respects you. I know because he's often talked about it. How you've got guts and how you always do what you say you're going to do. He told me once if he was in a corner, he'd rather have you backing him than any of the boys.' She did a quick laugh. 'Now you've got to admit, that's a *real* compliment. So you see, it's got to be you to our rescue. Tommy and I were made for each other and he'll listen to you. You'll do it for us, won't you, Kathy?'

I didn't say anything for a moment. Then I asked: 'Ruth, are you serious about Tommy? I mean, if I do persuade him, and you get back together, you won't hurt him again?'

Ruth gave an impatient sigh. 'Of course I'm serious. We're adults now. Soon we'll be leaving Hailsham. It's not a game any more.'

'Okay. I'll talk to him. Like you say, we'll be leaving here soon. We can't afford to waste time.'

After that, I remember us sitting on those beds, talking for some time. Ruth wanted to go over everything again and again: how stupid he was being, why they were really suited to each other, how differently they'd do things next time round, how they'd keep much more private, how they'd have sex in better places at better times. We talked about it all and she wanted my advice on everything. Then at one point, I was looking out of the window towards the hills in the distance, when I was startled to feel Ruth, suddenly beside me, squeeze my shoulders.

'Kathy, I knew we could depend on you,' she said. 'Tommy's right. You're just the person to have when you're in a corner.'

What with one thing and another, I didn't get a chance to talk to Tommy for the next few days. Then one lunch-time I spotted him on the edge of the South Playing Field practising with his football. He'd been having a kickabout earlier with two other boys, but now he was alone, juggling the ball about in the air. I went over and sat down on the grass behind him, putting my back against a fence post. This couldn't have been long after that time I'd shown him Patricia C.'s calendar and he'd marched off, because I remember we weren't sure how we stood with each other. He went on with his ball-juggling, scowling with concentration – knee, foot, head, foot – while I sat there picking away at clovers and gazing at the woods in the distance that we'd once been so frightened of. In the end I decided to break the deadlock and said:

'Tommy, let's talk now. There's something I want to talk to you about.'

As soon as I said this, he let the ball roll away and came to sit down beside me. It was typical of Tommy that once he knew I was willing to talk, there was suddenly no trace left of any sulkiness; just a kind of grateful eagerness that reminded me of the way we were back in the Juniors when a guardian who'd been telling us off went back to being normal. He was panting a bit, and though I knew this was from the football, it added to his overall impression of eagerness. In other words, before we'd said anything, he'd already got my back up. Then when I said to him: 'Tommy, I can tell. You haven't been too happy lately,' he said: 'What do you mean? I'm perfectly happy. I really am.' And he did a big beam, followed by this hearty laugh. That was what did it. Years later, when I saw a shadow of it every now and then, I'd just smile. But back then, it really used to get to me. If Tommy happened to say to you: 'I'm really upset about it,' he'd have to put on a long, downcast face, then and there, to back up his words. I don't mean he did this ironically. He actually thought he'd be more convincing. So now, to prove he was happy, here he was, trying to sparkle with bonhomie. As I say, there would come a time when I'd think this was sweet; but that summer all I could see was that it advertised what a child he still was, and how easily you could take advantage of him. I didn't know much then about the world that awaited us beyond Hailsham, but I'd guessed we'd need all our wits about us, and when Tommy did anything like this, I felt something close to panic. Until that afternoon I'd always let it go – it always seemed too difficult to explain – but this time I burst out, saying:

'Tommy, you look so *stupid*, laughing like that! If you want to pretend you're happy, you don't do it that way! Just take it from me, you don't do it that way! You definitely don't! Look, you've got to grow up. And you've got to get yourself back on track. Everything's been falling apart for you just lately, and we both know why.'

Tommy was looking puzzled. When he was sure I'd finished, he said: 'You're right. Things have been falling apart for me. But I don't see what you mean, Kath. What do you mean, we both know? I don't see how you could know. I haven't told anyone.'

'Obviously I don't have all the details. But we all know about you splitting with Ruth.'

Tommy still looked puzzled. Finally he did another little laugh, but this time it was a real one. 'I see what you mean,' he mumbled, then paused a moment to think something over. 'To be honest, Kath,' he said eventually, 'that's not really what's bothering me. It's really something else altogether. I just keep thinking about it all the time. About Miss Lucy.'

And that was how I came to hear about it, about what had happened between Tommy and Miss Lucy at the start of that summer. Later, when I'd had time to think it over, I worked out it must have happened no more than a few days after the morning I'd seen Miss Lucy up in Room 22 scrawling over her paperwork. And like I said, I felt like kicking myself I hadn't found out from him earlier.

It had been in the afternoon near the 'dead hour' – when the lessons were finished but there was still some time to go until supper. Tommy had seen Miss Lucy coming out of the main house, her arms loaded with flipcharts and box files, and because it looked like she'd drop something any moment, he'd run over and offered to help.

'Well, she gave me a few things to carry and said we were headed back to her study with it all. Even between the two of us there was too much and I dropped a couple of things on the way. Then when we were coming up to the Orangery, she suddenly stopped, and I thought she'd dropped something else. But she was looking at me, like *this*, straight in the face, all serious. Then she says we've got to have a talk, a good talk. I say fine, and so we go into the Orangery, into her study, put all the stuff down. And she tells me to sit down, and I end up exactly where I was the last time, you know, that time years ago. And I can tell she's remembering that time as well, because she starts talking about it like it was only the day before. No explanations, nothing, she just starts off saying something like: "Tommy, I made a mistake, when I said what I did to you. And I should have put you right about it long before now." Then she's saying I should forget everything she told me before. That she'd done me a big disservice telling me not to worry about being creative. That the other guardians had been right all along, and there was no excuse for my art being so rubbish . . .'

'Hold on, Tommy. Did she actually say your art was "rubbish"?'

'If it wasn't "rubbish" it was something like it. Negligible. That might have been it. Or incompetent. She might as well have said rubbish. She said she was sorry she'd told me what she had the last time because if she hadn't, I might have sorted it all by now.'

'What were you saying through all this?'

'I didn't know *what* to say. In the end, she actually asked. She said: "Tommy, what are you thinking?" So I said I wasn't sure but that she shouldn't worry either way because I was all right now. And she said, no, I wasn't all right. My art was rubbish, and that was partly her fault for telling me what she had. And I said to her, but what does it matter? I'm all right now, no one laughs at me about that any more. But she keeps shaking her head saying: "It does matter. I shouldn't have said what I did." So it occurs to me she's talking about later, you know, about after we leave here. So I say: "But I'll be all right, Miss. I'm really fit, I know how to look after myself. When it's time for donations, I'll be able to do it really well." When I said this, she starts shaking her head, shaking it really hard so I'm worried she'll get dizzy. Then she says: "Listen, Tommy, your art, it *is* important. And not just because it's evidence. But for your own sake. You'll get a lot from it, just for yourself."'

'Hold on. What did she mean, "evidence"?'

'I don't know. But she definitely said that. She said our art was important, and "not just because it's evidence". God knows what she meant. I did actually ask her, when she said that. I said I didn't understand what she was telling me, and was it something to do with Madame and her gallery? And she did a big sigh and said: "Madame's gallery, yes, that's important. Much more important than I once thought. I see that now." Then she said: "Look, there are all kinds of things you don't understand, Tommy, and I can't tell you about them. Things about Hailsham, about your place in the wider world, all kinds of things. But perhaps one day, you'll try and find out. They won't make it easy for you, but if you want to, really want to, you might find out." She started shaking her head again after that, though not as bad as before, and she says: "But why should you be any different? The students who leave here, they never find out much. Why should you be any different?" I didn't know what she was talking about, so I just said again: "I'll be all right, Miss." She was quiet for a time, then she suddenly stood up and kind of bent over me and hugged me. Not in a sexy way. More like they used to do when we were little. I just kept as still as possible. Then she stood back and said again she was sorry for what she'd told me before. And that it wasn't too late, I should start straight away, making up the lost time. I don't think I said anything, and she looked at me and I thought she'd hug me again. But instead she said: "Just do it for my sake, Tommy." I told her I'd do my best, because by then I just wanted out of there. I was probably bright scarlet, what with her hugging me and everything. I mean, it's not the same, is it, now we've got bigger.'

Until this point I'd been so engrossed in Tommy's story, I'd forgotten my reason for having this talk with him. But this reference to our getting 'bigger' reminded me of my original mission.

'Look, Tommy,' I said, 'we'll have to talk this over carefully soon. It's really interesting and I can see how it must have made you miserable. But either way, you're going to have to pull yourself together a bit more. We're going to be leaving here this summer. You've got to get yourself sorted again, and there's one thing you can straighten out right now. Ruth told me she's prepared to call it quits and have you get back with her again. I think that's a good chance for you. Don't mess it up.'

He was quiet for a few seconds, then said: 'I don't know, Kath. There are all these other things to think about.'

'Tommy, just listen. You're really lucky. Of all the people here, you've got Ruth fancying you. After we leave, if you're with her, you won't have to worry. She's the best, you'll be fine so long as you're with her. She's saying she wants a fresh start. So don't blow it.'

I waited but Tommy gave no response, and again I felt something like panic coming over me. I leaned forward and said: 'Look, you fool, you're not going to get many more chances. Don't you realise, we won't be here together like this much longer?'

To my surprise Tommy's response, when it came, was calm and considered – the side of Tommy that was to emerge more and more in the years ahead.

'I do realise that, Kath. That's exactly why I can't rush back into it with Ruth. We've got to think about the next move really carefully.' Then he sighed and looked right at me. 'Like you say, Kath. We're going to be leaving here soon. It's not like a game any more. We've got to think carefully.'

I was suddenly lost for what to say and just sat there tugging away at the clovers. I could feel his eyes on me, but I didn't look up. We might have gone on that way for a while longer, except we were interrupted. I think the boys he'd been playing football with earlier came back, or maybe it was some students strolling by who came and sat down with us. Anyway, our little heart-to-heart was at an end and I came away feeling I hadn't done what I'd set out to do – that I'd somehow let Ruth down.

I never got to assess what kind of impact my talk with Tommy had had, because it was the very next day the news broke. It was midway through the morning and we'd been in yet another Culture Briefing. These were classes where we had to role play various people we'd find out there – waiters in cafés, policemen and so on. The sessions always got us excited and worried all at the same time, so we were pretty keyed up anyway. Then at the end of the lesson, as we were filing out, Charlotte F. came rushing into the room and the news about Miss Lucy leaving Hailsham spread through us in an instant. Mr Chris, who'd been taking the class and who must have known all along, shuffled off guiltily before we could ask him anything. At first we weren't sure if Charlotte was just reporting a rumour, but the more she told us, the clearer it became this was for real. Earlier in the morning, one of the other Senior classes had gone into Room 12 expecting Music Appreciation with Miss Lucy. But Miss Emily had been there instead and she'd told them Miss Lucy couldn't come just at that moment, so she would take the class. For the next twenty minutes or so everything had gone quite normally. Then suddenly – right in mid-sentence, apparently – Miss Emily had broken off from talking about Beethoven and announced that Miss Lucy had left Hailsham and wouldn't be returning. That class had finished several minutes early – Miss Emily had rushed off with a preoccupied frown – and the word had started to go round as soon as the students had come out.

I immediately set off to look for Tommy, because I desperately wanted him to hear it first from me. But when I stepped into the courtyard, I saw I was too late. There was Tommy, over on the far side, on the edge of a circle of boys, nodding to what was being said. The other boys were animated, maybe excited even, but Tommy's eyes looked empty. That very evening, Tommy and Ruth got back together again, and I remember Ruth finding me a few days later to thank me for 'sorting it all out so well'. I told her I probably hadn't helped much, but she was having none of that. I was most definitely in her good books. And that was more or less the way things stayed throughout our last days at Hailsham.

PART TWO

CHAPTER TEN

Sometimes I'll be driving on a long weaving road across marsh-land, or maybe past rows of furrowed fields, the sky big and grey and never changing mile after mile, and I find I'm thinking about my essay, the one I was supposed to be writing back then, when we were at the Cottages. The guardians had talked to us about our essays on and off throughout that last summer, trying to help each of us choose a topic that would absorb us properly for any-thing up to two years. But somehow – maybe we could see some-thing in the guardians' manner – no one really believed the essays were that important, and among ourselves we hardly dis-cussed the matter. I remember when I went in to tell Miss Emily my chosen topic was Victorian novels, I hadn't really thought about it much and I could see she knew it. But she just gave me one of her searching stares and said nothing more.

Once we got to the Cottages, though, the essays took on a new importance. In our first days there, and for some of us a lot longer, it was like we were each clinging to our essay, this last task from Hailsham, like it was a farewell gift from the guardians. Over time, they would fade from our minds, but for a while those essays helped keep us afloat in our new surroundings.

When I think about my essay today, what I do is go over it in some detail: I may think of a completely new approach I could have taken, or about different writers and books I could have focused on. I might be having coffee in a service station, staring at the motorway through the big windows, and my essay will pop into my head for no reason. Then I quite enjoy sitting there, going through it all again. Just lately, I've even toyed with the idea of going back and working on it, once I'm not a carer any more and I've got the time. But in the end, I suppose I'm not really serious about it. It's just a bit of nostalgia to pass the time. I think about the essay the same way I might a rounders match at Hailsham I did particularly well in, or else an argument from long ago where I can now think of all the clever things I should have said. It's at that sort of level – daydream stuff. But as I say, that's not how it was when we first got to the Cottages.

Eight of us who left Hailsham that summer ended up at the Cottages. Others went to the White Mansion in the Welsh hills, or to Poplar Farm in Dorset. We didn't know then that all these places had only the most tenuous links with Hailsham. We arrived at the Cottages expecting a version of Hailsham for older students, and I suppose that was the way we continued to see them for some time. We certainly didn't think much about our lives beyond the Cottages, or about who ran them, or how they fitted into the larger world. None of us thought like that in those days.

The Cottages were the remains of a farm that had gone out of business years before. There was an old farmhouse, and around it, barns, outhouses, stables all converted for us to live in. There were other buildings, usually the outlying ones, that were virtually falling down, which we couldn't use for much, but for which we felt in some vague way responsible – mainly on account of Keffers. He was this grumpy old guy who turned up two or three times a week in his muddy van to look the place over. He didn't like to talk to us much, and the way he went round sighing and shaking his head disgustedly implied we weren't doing nearly enough to keep the place up. But it was never clear what more he wanted us to do. He'd shown us a list of chores when we'd first arrived, and the students who were already there – 'the veterans', as Hannah called them – had long since worked out a rota which we kept to conscientiously. There really wasn't much else we could do other than report leaking gutters and mop up after floods.

The old farmhouse – the heart of the Cottages – had a number of fireplaces where we could burn the split logs stacked in the outer barns. Otherwise we had to make do with big boxy heaters. The problem with these was they worked on gas canisters, and unless it was really cold, Keffers wouldn't bring many in. We kept asking him to leave a big supply with us, but he'd shake his head gloomily, like we were bound to use them up frivolously or else cause an explosion. So I remember a lot of the time, outside the summer months, being chilly. You went around with two, even three jumpers on, and your jeans felt cold and stiff. We sometimes kept our Wellingtons on the whole day, leaving trails of mud and damp through the rooms. Keffers, observing this, would again shake his head, but when we asked him what else we were supposed to do, the floors being in the state they were, he'd make no reply.

I'm making it sound pretty bad, but none of us minded the discomforts one bit – it was all part of the excitement of being at the Cottages. If we were honest, though, particularly near the beginning, most of us would have admitted missing the guardians. A few of us, for a time, even tried to think of Keffers as a sort of guardian, but he was having none of it. You went up to greet him when he arrived in his van and he'd stare at you like you were mad. But this was one thing we'd been told over and over: that after Hailsham there'd be no more guardians, so we'd have to look after each other. And by and large, I'd say Hailsham prepared us well on that score.

Most of the students I was close to at Hailsham ended up at the Cottages that summer. Cynthia E. – the girl who'd said about me being Ruth's 'natural successor' that time in the Art Room – I wouldn't have minded her, but she went to Dorset with the rest of her crowd. And Harry, the boy I'd nearly had sex with, I heard he went to Wales. But all our gang had stayed together. And if we ever missed the others, we could tell ourselves there was nothing stopping us going to visit them. For all our map lessons with Miss Emily, we had no real idea at that point about distances and how easy or hard it was to visit a particular place. We'd talk about getting lifts from the veterans when they were going on their trips, or else how in time we'd learn to drive ourselves and then we'd be able to see them whenever we pleased.

Of course, in practice, especially during the first months, we rarely stepped beyond the confines of the Cottages. We didn't even walk about the surrounding countryside or wander into the nearby village. I don't think we were afraid exactly. We all knew no one would stop us if we wandered off, provided we were back by the day and the time we entered into Keffers's ledgerbook. That summer we arrived, we were constantly seeing veterans packing their bags and rucksacks and going off for two or three days at a time with what seemed to us scary nonchalance. We'd watched them with astonishment, wondering if by the following summer we'd be doing the same. Of course, we were, but in those early days, it didn't seem possible. You have to remember that until that point we'd never been beyond the grounds of Hailsham, and we were just bewildered. If you'd told me then that within a year, I'd not only develop a habit of taking long solitary walks, but that I'd start learning to drive a car, I'd have thought you were mad.

Even Ruth looked daunted that sunny day the minibus dropped us in front of the farmhouse, circled round the little pond and disappeared up the slope. We could see hills in the distance that reminded us of the ones in the distance at Hailsham, but they seemed to us oddly crooked, like when you draw a picture of a friend and it's almost right but not quite, and the face on the sheet gives you the creeps. But at least it was the summer, not the way the Cottages would get a few months on, with all the puddles frozen over and the rough ground frosted bone hard. The place looked beautiful and cosy, with overgrown grass everywhere – a novelty to us. We stood together in a huddle, the eight of us, and watched Keffers go in and out of the farmhouse, expecting him to address us at any moment. But he didn't, and all we could catch was the odd irritated mutter about the students who already lived there. Once, as he went to get something from his van, he gave us a moody glance, then returned to the farmhouse and closed the door behind him.

Before too long, though, the veterans, who'd been having a bit of fun watching us being pathetic – we were to do much the same the following summer – came out and took us in hand. In fact, looking back, I see they really went out of their way helping us settle in. Even so, those first weeks were strange and we were glad we had each other. We'd always move about together and seemed to spend large parts of the day awkwardly standing outside the farmhouse, not knowing what else to do.

It's funny now recalling the way it was at the beginning, because when I think of those two years at the Cottages, that scared, bewildered start doesn't seem to go with any of the rest of it. If someone mentions the Cottages today, I think of easy-going days drifting in and out of each other's rooms, the languid way the afternoon would fold into evening then into night. I think of my pile of old paperbacks, their pages gone wobbly, like they'd once belonged to the sea. I think about how I read them, lying on my front in the grass on warm afternoons, my hair – which I was growing long then – always falling across my vision. I think about the mornings waking up in my room at the top of the Black Barn to the voices of students outside in the field, arguing about poetry or philosophy; or the long winters, the breakfasts in steamed-up kitchens, meandering discussions around the table about Kafka or Picasso. It was always stuff like that at breakfast; never who you'd had sex with the night before, or why Larry and Helen weren't talking to each other any more.

But then again, when I think about it, there's a sense in which that picture of us on that first day, huddled together in front of the farmhouse, isn't so incongruous after all. Because maybe, in a way, we didn't leave it behind nearly as much as we might once have thought. Because somewhere underneath, a part of us stayed like that: fearful of the world around us, and – no matter how much we despised ourselves for it – unable quite to let each other go.

The veterans, who of course knew nothing about the history of Tommy and Ruth's relationship, treated them as a long-established couple, and this seemed to please Ruth no end. For the first weeks after we arrived, she made a big deal of it, always putting her arm around Tommy, sometimes snogging him in the corner of a room while other people were still about. Well, this kind of thing might have been fine at Hailsham, but looked immature at the Cottages. The veteran couples never did anything showy in public, going about in a sensible sort of way, like a mother and father might do in a normal family.

There was, incidentally, something I noticed about these veteran couples at the Cottages – something Ruth, for all her close study of them, failed to spot – and this was how so many of their mannerisms were copied from the television. It first came to me watching this couple, Susie and Greg – probably the oldest students at the Cottages and generally thought to be 'in charge' of the place. There was this particular thing Susie did whenever Greg set off on one of his speeches about Proust or whoever: she'd smile at the rest of us, roll her eyes, and mouth very emphatically, but only just audibly: 'Gawd help us.' Television at Hailsham had been pretty restricted, and at the Cottages too – though there was nothing to stop us watching all day – no one was very keen on it. But there was an old set in the farmhouse and another in the Black Barn, and I'd watch every now and then. That's how I realised that this 'Gawd help us' stuff came from an American series, one of those with an audience laughing along at everything anyone said or did. There was a character – a large woman who lived next door to the main characters – who did exactly what Susie did, so when her husband went off on a big spiel, the audience would be waiting for her to roll her eyes and say 'Gawd help us' so they could burst out with this huge laugh. Once I'd spotted this, I began to notice all kinds of other things the veteran couples had taken from TV programmes: the way they gestured to each other, sat together on sofas, even the way they argued and stormed out of rooms.

Anyway, my point is, it wasn't long before Ruth realised the way she'd been carrying on with Tommy was all wrong for the Cottages, and she set about changing how they did things in front of people. And there was in particular this one gesture Ruth picked up from the veterans. Back at Hailsham, if a couple were parting, even for a few minutes, it had been an excuse for big embraces and snogging. At the Cottages, though, when a couple were saying goodbye to each other, there'd be hardly any words, never mind embraces or kisses. Instead, you slapped your partner's arm near the elbow, lightly with the back of your knuckles, the way you might do to attract someone's attention. Usually the girl did it to the boy, just as they were moving apart. This custom had faded out by the winter, but when we arrived, it was what was going on and Ruth was soon doing it to Tommy. Mind you, at first, Tommy didn't have a clue what was going on, and would turn abruptly to Ruth and go: 'What?', so that she'd have to glare furiously at him, like they were in a play and he'd forgotten his lines. I suppose she eventually had a word with him, because after a week or so they were managing to do it right, more or less exactly like the veteran couples.

I'd not actually seen the slap on the elbow on the television, but I was pretty sure that's where the idea had come from, and just as sure Ruth hadn't realised it. That was why, that afternoon I was reading *Daniel Deronda* on the grass and Ruth was being irritating, I decided it was time someone pointed it out to her.

It was nearly autumn and starting to get chilly. The veterans were spending more time indoors and generally going back to whatever routines they'd had before the summer. But those of us who'd arrived from Hailsham kept sitting outside on the uncut grass – wanting to keep going for as long as possible the only routine we'd got used to. Even so, by that particular afternoon, there were maybe only three or four apart from me reading in the field, and since I'd gone out of my way to find a quiet corner to myself, I'm pretty sure what happened between me and Ruth wasn't overheard.

I was lying on a piece of old tarpaulin reading, as I say, *Daniel Deronda*, when Ruth came wandering over and sat down beside me. She studied the cover of my book and nodded to herself. Then after about a minute, just as I knew she would, she began to outline to me the plot of *Daniel Deronda*. Until that point, I'd been in a perfectly okay mood, and had been pleased to see Ruth, but now I was irritated. She'd done this to me a couple of times before, and I'd seen her doing it to others. For one thing, there was the manner she put on: a kind of nonchalant but sincere one as though she expected people to be really grateful for her assistance. Okay, even at the time, I was vaguely aware what was behind it. In those early months, we'd somehow developed this idea that how well you were settling in at the Cottages – how well you were *coping* – was somehow reflected by how many books you'd read. It sounds odd, but there you are, it was just something that developed between us, the ones who'd arrived from Hailsham. The whole notion was kept deliberately hazy – in fact, it was pretty reminiscent of the way we'd dealt with sex at Hailsham. You could go around implying you'd read all kinds of things, nodding knowingly when someone mentioned, say, *War and Peace*, and the understanding was that no one would scrutinise your claim too rationally. You have to remember, since we'd been in each other's company constantly since arriving at the Cottages, it wasn't possible for any of us to have read *War and Peace* without the rest noticing. But just like with the sex at Hailsham, there was an unspoken agreement to allow for a mysterious dimension where we went off and did all this reading.

It was, as I say, a little game we all indulged in to some extent. Even so, it was Ruth who took it further than anyone else. She was the one always pretending to have finished anything anyone happened to be reading; and she was the only one with this notion that the way to demonstrate your superior reading was to go around telling people the plots of novels they were in the middle of. That's why, when she started on *Daniel Deronda*, even though I'd not been enjoying it much, I closed the book, sat up and said to her, completely out of the blue:

'Ruth, I've been meaning to ask you. Why do you always hit Tommy on the arm like that when you're saying goodbye? You know what I mean.'

Of course she claimed not to, so I patiently explained what I was talking about. Ruth heard me out then shrugged.

'I didn't realise I was doing it. I must have just picked it up.'

A few months before I might have let it go at that – or probably wouldn't have brought it up in the first place. But that afternoon I just pressed on, explaining to her how it was something from a television series. 'It's not something worth copying,' I told her. 'It's not what people really do out there, in normal life, if that's what you were thinking.'

Ruth, I could see, was now angry but unsure how to fight back. She looked away and did another shrug. 'So what?' she said. 'It's no big deal. A lot of us do it.'

'What you mean is Chrissie and Rodney do it.'

As soon as I said this I realised I'd made a mistake; that until I'd mentioned these two, I'd had Ruth in a corner, but now she was out. It was like when you make a move in chess and just as you take your finger off the piece, you see the mistake you've made, and there's this panic because you don't know yet the scale of disaster you've left yourself open to. Sure enough, I saw a gleam come into Ruth's eyes and when she spoke again it was in an entirely new voice.

'So that's it, that's what's upsetting poor little Kathy. Ruth isn't paying enough attention to her. Ruth's got big new friends and baby sister isn't getting played with so often . . .'

'Stop all that. Anyway that's not how it works in real families. You don't know anything about it.'

'Oh Kathy, the great expert on real families. So sorry. But that's what this is, isn't it? You've still got this idea. Us Hailsham lot, we have to stay together, a tight little bunch, must never make any new friends.'

'I've never said that. I'm just talking about Chrissie and Rodney. It looks daft, the way you copy everything they do.'

'But I'm right, aren't I?' Ruth went on. 'You're upset because I've managed to move on, make new friends. Some of the veterans hardly remember your name, and who can blame them? You never talk to anyone unless they're Hailsham. But you can't expect me to hold your hand the whole time. We've been here nearly two months now.'

I didn't take the bait, but said instead: 'Never mind me, never mind Hailsham. But you keep leaving Tommy in the lurch. I've watched you, you've done it a few times just this week. You leave him stranded, looking like a spare part. That's not fair. You and Tommy are supposed to be a couple. That means you look out for him.'

'Quite right, Kathy, we're a couple, like you say. And if you must intrude, I'll tell you. We've talked about this, and we've agreed. If he sometimes doesn't feel like doing things with Chrissie and Rodney, that's his choice. I'm not going to make him do anything he's not yet ready for. But we've agreed, he shouldn't hold me back. Nice of you to be concerned though.' Then she added, in a quite different voice: 'Come to think of it, I suppose you haven't been *that* slow making friends with at least *some* of the veterans.'

She watched me carefully, then did a laugh, as though to say: 'We're still friends, aren't we?' But I didn't find anything to laugh about in this last remark of hers. I just picked up my book and walked off without another word.

CHAPTER ELEVEN

I should explain why I got so bothered by Ruth saying what she did. Those early months at the Cottages had been a strange time in our friendship. We were quarrelling over all kinds of little things, but at the same time we were confiding in each other more than ever. In particular, we used to have these talks, the two of us, usually up in my room at the top of the Black Barn just before going to bed. You could say they were a sort of hangover from those talks in our dorm after lights out. Anyway, the thing was, however much we might have fallen out during the day, come bed-time, Ruth and I would still find ourselves sitting side by side on my mattress, sipping our hot drinks, exchanging our deepest feelings about our new life like nothing had ever come between us. And what made these heart-to-hearts possible – you might even say what made the whole friendship possible during that time – was this understanding we had that anything we told each other during these moments would be treated with careful respect: that we'd honour confidences, and that no matter how much we rowed, we wouldn't use against each other anything we'd talked about during those sessions. Okay, this had never been spelt out exactly, but it was definitely, as I say, an understanding, and until the afternoon of the *Daniel Deronda* business, neither of us had come anywhere near breaching it. That was why, when Ruth said what she did about my not being slow making friends with certain veterans, I wasn't just cross. To me, it was a betrayal. Because there wasn't any doubt what she'd meant by it; she was referring to something I'd confided in her one night about me and sex.

As you'd expect, sex was different at the Cottages from how it had been at Hailsham. It was a lot more straightforward – more 'grown up'. You didn't go around gossiping and giggling about who'd been doing it with whom. If you knew two students had had sex, you didn't immediately start speculating about whether they'd become a proper couple. And if a new couple did emerge one day, you didn't go around talking about it like it was a big event. You just accepted it quietly, and from then on, when you referred to one, you also referred to the other, as in 'Chrissie and Rodney' or 'Ruth and Tommy'. When someone wanted sex with you, that too was much more straightforward. A boy would come up and ask if you wanted to spend the night in his room 'for a change', something like that, it was no big deal. Sometimes it was because he was interested in becoming a couple with you; other times it was just for a one-nighter.

The atmosphere, like I say, was much more grown up. But when I look back, the sex at the Cottages seems a bit functional. Maybe it was precisely because all the gossip and secrecy had gone. Or maybe it was because of the cold.

When I remember sex at the Cottages, I think about doing it in freezing rooms in the pitch dark, usually under a ton of blankets. And the blankets often weren't even blankets, but a really odd assortment – old curtains, even bits of carpet. Sometimes it got so cold you just had to pile anything you could over you, and if you were having sex at the bottom of it, it felt like a mountain of bedding was pounding at you, so that half the time you weren't sure if you were doing it with the boy or all that stuff.

Anyway, the point is, I'd had a few one-nighters shortly after getting to the Cottages. I hadn't planned it that way. My plan had been to take my time, maybe become part of a couple with someone I chose carefully. I'd never been in a couple before, and especially after watching Ruth and Tommy for a while, I was quite curious to give it a try for myself. As I say, that had been my plan, and when the one-nighters kept happening, it unsettled me a bit. That was why I'd decided to confide in Ruth that night.

It was in many ways a typical evening session for us. We'd brought up our mugs of tea, and we were sitting in my room, side by side on the mattress, our heads slightly stooped because of the rafters. We talked about the different boys at the Cottages, and whether any of them might be right for me. And Ruth had been at her best: encouraging, funny, tactful, wise. That's why I decided to tell her about the one-nighters. I told her how they'd happened without my really wanting them to; and how, even though we couldn't have babies from doing it, the sex had done funny things to my feelings, just as Miss Emily had warned. Then I said to her:

'Ruth, I wanted to ask you. Do you ever get so you just really have to do it? With anybody almost?'

Ruth shrugged, then said: 'I'm in a couple. So if I want to do it, I just do it with Tommy.'

'I suppose so. Maybe it's just me anyway. There might be something not quite right with me, down there. Because sometimes I just really, really need to do it.'

'That's strange, Kathy.' She fixed me with a concerned look, which made me feel all the more worried.

'So you don't ever get like that.'

She shrugged again. 'Not so as I'd do it with just anybody. What you're saying does sound a bit weird, Kathy. But maybe it'll calm down after a while.'

'Sometimes it won't be there for ages. Then it suddenly comes on. It was like that, the first time it happened. He started snogging me and I just wanted him to get off. Then suddenly it just came on, out of nowhere. I just really had to do it.'

Ruth shook her head. 'It does sound a bit weird. But it'll probably go away. It's probably just to do with the different food we're eating here.'

She hadn't been a huge help, but she'd been sympathetic and I'd felt a little better about it all afterwards. That's why it was such a jolt to have Ruth suddenly bring it up the way she did in the middle of the argument we were having that afternoon in the field. Okay, there was probably no one to overhear us, but even so, there was something not at all right about what she'd done. In those first months at the Cottages, our friendship had stayed intact because, on my side at least, I'd had this notion there were two quite separate Ruths. There was one Ruth who was always trying to impress the veterans, who wouldn't hesitate to ignore me, Tommy, any of the others, if she thought we'd cramp her style. This was the Ruth I wasn't pleased with, the one I could see every day putting on airs and pretending – the Ruth who did the slap-on-the-elbow gesture. But the Ruth who sat beside me in my little attic room at the day's close, legs outstretched over the edge of my mattress, her steaming mug held in both her hands, that was the Ruth from Hailsham, and whatever had been happening during the day, I could just pick up with her where we'd left off the last time we'd sat together like that. And until that afternoon in the field, there'd been a definite understanding these two Ruths wouldn't merge; that the one I confided in before bed was one I could absolutely trust. That's why when she said that, about my 'not being slow making friends with at least some of the veterans', I got so upset. That's why I just picked up my book and walked off.

But when I think about it now, I can see things more from Ruth's viewpoint. I can see, for instance, how she might have felt *I* had been the one to first violate an understanding, and that her little dig had just been a retaliation. This never occurred to me at the time, but I see now it's a possibility, and an explanation for what happened. After all, immediately before she made that remark, I'd been talking about the arm-slapping business. Now it's a bit hard to explain this, but some sort of understanding had definitely developed between the two of us about the way Ruth behaved in front of the veterans. Okay, she often bluffed and implied all sorts of things I knew weren't true. Sometimes, as I said, she did things to impress the veterans at our expense. But it seems to me Ruth believed, at some level, she was doing all this *on behalf of us all*. And my role, as her closest friend, was to give her silent support, as if I was in the front row of the audience when she was performing on stage. She was struggling to become someone else, and maybe felt the pressure more than the rest of us because, as I say, she'd somehow taken on the responsibility for all of us. In that case, then, the way I'd talked about her slap on the elbow thing could be seen as a betrayal, and she might well then have felt justified retaliating as she had. As I say, this expla-

nation only occurred to me recently. At the time I didn't look at
the larger picture or at my own part in it. I suppose, in general, I
never appreciated in those days the sheer effort Ruth was making
to move on, to grow up and leave Hailsham behind. Thinking
about this now, I'm reminded of something she told me once,
when I was caring for her in the recovery centre at Dover. We'd
been sitting in her room, watching the sunset, as we so often did,
enjoying the mineral water and biscuits I'd brought, and I'd been
telling her how I still had most of my old Hailsham collection box
safely stowed inside my pine chest in my bedsit. Then – I wasn't
trying to lead onto anything, or make any kind of point – I just
happened to say to her:

'You never had a collection after Hailsham, did you?'

Ruth, who was sitting up in bed, was quiet for a long time, the
sunset falling over the tiled wall behind her. Then she said:

'Remember the guardians, before we left, how they kept
reminding us we could take our collections with us. So I'd taken
everything out of my box and put it into this holdall bag. My
plan was I'd find a really good wooden box for it all once I got to
the Cottages. But when we got there, I could see none of the veterans had collections. It was only us, it wasn't normal. We must
all have realised it, I wasn't the only one, but we didn't really
talk about it, did we? So I didn't go looking for a new box. My
things all stayed in the holdall bag for months, then in the end I
threw them away.'

I stared at her. 'You put your collection out with the rubbish?'

Ruth shook her head, and for the next few moments seemed to
be going through in her mind all the different items in her collection. Finally she said:

'I put them all in a bin bag, but I couldn't stand the idea of
putting them out with the rubbish. So I asked old Keffers, once
when he was about to drive off, if he'd take the bin bag to a shop.
I knew about charity shops, I'd found it all out. Keffers rummaged in the bag a bit, he didn't know what any of it was – why
should he? – and he did this laugh and said no shop he knew
would want stuff like that. And I said, but it's good stuff, really

good stuff. And he could see I was getting a bit emotional, and he changed his tune then. He said something like: "All right, missy, I'll take it along to the Oxfam people." Then he made a real effort and said: "Now I've had a closer look, you're right, it *is* pretty good stuff!" He wasn't very convincing though. I suppose he just took it away and put it in some bin somewhere. But at least I didn't have to know that.' Then she smiled and said: 'You were different. I remember. You were never embarrassed about your collection and you kept it. I wish now I'd done that too.'

What I'm saying is that we were all of us struggling to adjust to our new life, and I suppose we all did things back then we later regretted. I was really upset by Ruth's remark at the time, but it's pointless now trying to judge her or anyone else for the way they behaved during those early days at the Cottages.

As the autumn came on, and I got more familiar with our surroundings, I began noticing things I'd missed earlier. There was, for instance, the odd attitude to students who'd recently left. The veterans were never slow coming out with funny anecdotes about characters they'd met on trips to the White Mansion or to Poplar Farm; but they hardly ever mentioned students who, right up until just before we'd arrived, must have been their intimate friends.

Another thing I noticed – and I could see it tied in – was the big hush that would descend around certain veterans when they went off on 'courses' – which even we knew had to do with becoming carers. They could be gone for four or five days, but were hardly mentioned in that time; and when they came back, no one really asked them anything. I suppose they might have talked to their closest friends in private. But there was definitely an understanding that you didn't mention these trips out in the open. I can remember one morning watching, through the misted-up windows of our kitchen, two veterans leaving for a course, and wondering if by the next spring or summer, they'd have gone altogether, and we'd be taking care not to mention them.

But it's perhaps stretching it to claim students who'd left were an actual taboo. If they had to be mentioned, they got mentioned. Most commonly, you'd hear them referred to indirectly, in connection with an object or a chore. For example, if repairs were needed to a downpipe, there'd be a lot of discussion about 'the way Mike used to do it'. And there was a tree stump outside the Black Barn everyone called 'Dave's stump' because for over three years, until a few weeks before our arrival, he'd sat on it to read and write, sometimes even when it was raining or cold. Then, maybe most memorably, there was Steve. None of us ever discovered anything much about the sort of person Steve had been – except that he'd liked porn magazines.

Every now and again, you'd come across a porn mag at the Cottages, thrown behind a sofa or amidst a pile of old newspapers. They were what you'd call 'soft' porn, though we didn't know about such distinctions then. We'd never come across anything like that before and didn't know what to think. The veterans usually laughed when one showed up and flicked through it quickly in a blasé way before throwing it aside, so we did the same. When Ruth and I were remembering all this a few years ago, she claimed there were dozens of these magazines circulating around the Cottages. 'No one admitted to liking them,' she said. 'But you remember how it was. If one turned up in a room, everyone pretended to find it dead boring. Then you came back half an hour later and it would always be gone.'

Anyway, my point is that whenever one of these magazines turned up, people would claim it was a left-over from 'Steve's collection'. Steve, in other words, was responsible for every porn mag that ever showed up. As I say, we never found out much else about Steve. We did, though, see the funny side of it even then, so that when someone pointed and said: 'Oh look, one of Steve's magazines,' they did it with a bit of irony.

These magazines, incidentally, used to drive old Keffers mad. There was a rumour that he was religious and dead against not just porn, but sex in general. Sometimes he'd work himself into a complete state – you could see his face under his grey whiskers blotchy with fury – and he'd go thudding around the place, barging into people's rooms without knocking, determined to round up every one of 'Steve's magazines'. We did our best to find him amusing on these occasions, but there was something truly scary about him in these moods. For one thing, the grumbling he usually kept up suddenly stopped and this silence alone gave him an alarming aura.

I remember one particular time when Keffers had collected up six or seven of 'Steve's mags' and stormed out with them to his van. Laura and I were watching him from up in my room, and I'd been laughing at something Laura had just said. Then I saw Keffers opening his van door, and maybe because he needed both hands to move some stuff about, he put the mags down on top of some bricks stacked outside the boiler hut – some veterans had tried to build a barbecue there a few months earlier. Keffers's figure, bent forwards, his head and shoulders hidden in the van, went on rummaging about for ages, and something told me that, for all his fury of a moment ago, he'd now forgotten about the magazines. Sure enough, a few minutes later, I saw him straighten, climb in behind the wheel, slam the door and drive off.

When I pointed out to Laura that Keffers had left the magazines behind, she said: 'Well, they won't stay put for long. He'll just have to collect them all up again, next time he decides on a purge.'

But when I found myself strolling past the boiler hut about half an hour later, I saw the magazines hadn't been touched. I thought for a moment about taking them up to my room, but then I could see if they were ever found there, I'd get no end of teasing; and how there was no way people would understand my reasons for doing such a thing. That was why I picked up the magazines and went inside the boiler hut with them.

The boiler hut was really just another barn, built onto the end of the farmhouse, filled with old mowers and pitch-forks – stuff Keffers reckoned wouldn't catch alight too easily if one day the boiler decided to blow up. Keffers also kept a workbench in there, and so I put the magazines down on it, pushed aside some old rags and heaved myself up to sit on the tabletop. The light wasn't too good, but there was a grimy window somewhere behind me, and when I opened the first magazine I found I could see well enough.

There were lots of pictures of girls holding their legs open or sticking their bottoms out. I'll admit, there have been times when I've looked at pictures like that and felt excited, though I've never fancied doing it with a girl. But that's not what I was after that afternoon. I moved through the pages quickly, not wanting to be distracted by any buzz of sex coming off those pages. In fact, I hardly saw the contorted bodies, because I was focusing on the faces. Even in the little adverts for videos or whatever tucked away to the side, I checked each model's face before moving on.

It wasn't until I was nearing the end of the pile that I became certain there was somebody standing outside the barn, just beside the doorway. I'd left the door open because that's how it was normally, and because I wanted the light; and twice already I'd found myself glancing up, thinking I'd heard some small noise. But there'd been no one there, and I'd just gone on with what I was doing. Now I was certain, though, and lowering my magazine I made a heavy sighing sound that would be clearly audible.

I waited for giggling, or maybe for two or three students to come bursting into the barn, eager to make the best of having caught me with a pile of porn mags. But nothing happened. So I called out, in what I tried to make a weary tone:

'Delighted you could join me. Why be so shy?'

There was a little chuckle, then Tommy appeared at the threshold. 'Hi, Kath,' he said sheepishly.

'Come on in, Tommy. Join in the fun.'

He came towards me cautiously, then stopped a few steps away. Then he looked over to the boiler, and said: 'I didn't know you liked that sort of stuff.'

'Girls are allowed too, aren't we?'

I kept going through the pages, and for the next few seconds he stayed silent. Then I heard him say:

'I wasn't trying to spy on you. But I saw you from my room. I saw you come out here and pick up that pile Keffers left.'

'You're very welcome to them when I've finished.'

He laughed awkwardly. 'It's just sex stuff. I expect I've seen them all already.' He did another laugh, but then when I glanced up, I saw he was watching me with a serious expression. Then he asked:

'Are you looking for something, Kath?'

'What do you mean? I'm just looking at dirty pictures.'

'Just for kicks?'

'I suppose you could say that.' I put down one mag and started on the next one.

Then I heard Tommy's steps coming nearer until he was right up to me. When I looked up again, his hands were hovering fretfully in the air, like I was doing a complicated manual task and he was itching to help.

'Kath, you don't . . . Well, if it's for kicks, you don't do it like that. You've got to look at the pictures much more carefully. It doesn't really work if you go that fast.'

'How do you know what works for girls? Or maybe you've looked these over with Ruth. Sorry, not thinking.'

'Kath, what are you looking for?'

I ignored him. I was nearly at the end of the pile and I was now keen to finish. Then he said:

'I saw you doing this once before.'

This time I did stop and look at him. 'What's going on here, Tommy? Has Keffers recruited you for his porn patrol?'

'I wasn't trying to spy on you. But I did see you, that time last week, after we'd all been up in Charley's room. There was one of these mags there, and you thought we'd all left and gone. But I came back to get my jumper, and Claire's doors were open so I could see straight through to Charley's room. That's how I saw you in there, going through the magazine.'

'Well, so what? We all have to get our kicks some way.'

'You weren't doing it for kicks. I could tell, just like I can now. It's your face, Kath. That time in Charley's room, you had a strange face. Like you were sad, maybe. And a bit scared.'

I jumped off the workbench, gathered up the mags and dumped them in his arms. 'Here. Give these to Ruth. See if they do anything for her.'

I walked past him and out of the barn. I knew he'd be disappointed I hadn't told him anything, but at that point I hadn't thought things through properly myself and wasn't ready to tell anyone. But I hadn't minded him coming into the boiler hut after me. I hadn't minded at all. I'd felt comforted, protected almost. I did tell him eventually, but that wasn't until a few months later, when we went on our Norfolk trip.

CHAPTER TWELVE

I want to talk about the Norfolk trip, and all the things that happened that day, but I'll first have to go back a bit, to give you the background and explain why it was we went.

Our first winter was just about over by then and we were all feeling much more settled. For all our little hiccups, Ruth and I had kept up our habit of rounding off the day in my room, talking over our hot drinks, and it was during one of those sessions, when we were larking around about something, that she suddenly said:

'I suppose you've heard what Chrissie and Rodney have been saying.'

When I said I hadn't, she did a laugh and continued: 'They're probably just having me on. Their idea of a joke. Forget I mentioned it.'

But I could see she wanted me to drag it out of her, so I kept pressing until in the end she said in a lowered voice:

'You remember last week, when Chrissie and Rodney were away? They'd been up to this town called Cromer, up on the north Norfolk coast.'

'What were they doing there?'

'Oh, I think they've got a friend there, someone who used to live here. That's not the point. The point is, they claim they saw this . . . person. Working there in this open-plan office. And, well, you know. They reckon this person's a *possible*. For me.'

Though most of us had first come across the idea of 'possibles' back at Hailsham, we'd sensed we weren't supposed to discuss it, and so we hadn't – though for sure, it had both intrigued and disturbed us. And even at the Cottages, it wasn't a topic you could bring up casually. There was definitely more awkwardness around any talk of possibles than there was around, say, sex. At the same time, you could tell people were fascinated – obsessed, in some cases – and so it kept coming up, usually in solemn arguments, a world away from our ones about, say, James Joyce.

The basic idea behind the possibles theory was simple, and didn't provoke much dispute. It went something like this. Since each of us was copied at some point from a normal person, there must be, for each of us, somewhere out there, a model getting on with his or her life. This meant, at least in theory, you'd be able to find the person you were modelled from. That's why, when you were out there yourself – in the towns, shopping centres, transport cafés – you kept an eye out for 'possibles' – the people who might have been the models for you and your friends.

Beyond these basics, though, there wasn't much consensus. For a start, no one could agree what we were looking for when we looked for possibles. Some students thought you should be looking for a person twenty to thirty years older than yourself – the sort of age a normal parent would be. But others claimed this was sentimental. Why would there be a 'natural' generation between us and our models? They could have used babies, old people, what difference would it have made? Others argued back that they'd use for models people at the peak of their health, and that's why they were likely to be 'normal parent' age. But around here, we'd all sense we were near territory we didn't want to enter, and the arguments would fizzle out.

Then there were those questions about why we wanted to track down our models at all. One big idea behind finding your model was that when you did, you'd glimpse your future. Now I don't mean anyone really thought that if your model turned out to be, say, a guy working at a railway station, that's what you'd end up doing too. We all realised it wasn't that simple. Nevertheless, we all of us, to varying degrees, believed that when you saw the person you were copied from, you'd get *some* insight into who you were deep down, and maybe too, you'd see something of what your life held in store.

There were some who thought it stupid to be concerned about

possibles at all. Our models were an irrelevance, a technical necessity for bringing us into the world, nothing more than that. It was up to each of us to make of our lives what we could. This was the camp Ruth always claimed to side with, and I probably did too. All the same, whenever we heard reports of a possible – whoever it was for – we couldn't help getting curious.

The way I remember it, sightings of possibles tended to come in batches. Weeks could go by with no one mentioning the subject, then one reported sighting would trigger off a whole spate of others. Most of them were obviously not worth pursuing: someone seen in a car going by, stuff like that. But every now and then, a sighting seemed to have substance to it – like the one Ruth told me about that night.

According to Ruth, Chrissie and Rodney had been busy exploring this seaside town they'd gone to and had split up for a while. When they'd met up again, Rodney was all excited and had told Chrissie how he'd been wandering the side-streets off the High Street, and had gone past an office with a large glass front. Inside had been a lot of people, some of them at their desks, some walking about and chatting. And that's where he'd spotted Ruth's possible.

'Chrissie came and told me as soon as they got back. She made Rodney describe everything, and he did his best, but it was impossible to tell anything. Now they keep talking about driving me up there, but I don't know. I don't know if I ought to do anything about it.'

I can't remember exactly what I said to her that night, but I was at that point pretty sceptical. In fact, to be honest, my guess was that Chrissie and Rodney had made the whole thing up. I don't really want to suggest Chrissie and Rodney were bad people – that would be unfair. In many ways, I actually liked them. But the fact was, the way they regarded us newcomers, and Ruth in particular, was far from straightforward.

Chrissie was a tall girl who was quite beautiful when she stood up to her full height, but she didn't seem to realise this and spent her time crouching to be the same as the rest of us. That's why she often looked more like the Wicked Witch than a movie star – an impression reinforced by her irritating way of jabbing you with a finger the second before she said something to you. She always wore long skirts rather than jeans, and little glasses pressed too far into her face. She'd been one of the veterans who'd really welcomed us when we'd first arrived in the summer, and I'd at first been really taken by her and looked to her for guidance. But as the weeks had passed, I'd begun to have reservations. There was something odd about the way she was always mentioning the fact that we'd come from Hailsham, like that could explain almost anything to do with us. And she was always asking us questions about Hailsham – about little details, much like my donors do now – and although she tried to make out these were very casual, I could see there was a whole other dimension to her interest. Another thing that got to me was the way she always seemed to want to separate us: taking one of us aside when a few of us were doing something together, or else inviting two of us to join in something while leaving another two stranded – that sort of thing.

You'd hardly ever see Chrissie without her boyfriend, Rodney. He went around with his hair tied back in a ponytail, like a rock musician from the seventies, and talked a lot about things like reincarnation. I actually got to quite like him, but he was pretty much under Chrissie's influence. In any discussion, you knew he'd back up Chrissie's angle, and if Chrissie ever said anything mildly amusing, he'd be chortling and shaking his head like he couldn't believe how funny it was.

Okay, I'm maybe being a bit hard on these two. When I was remembering them with Tommy not so long ago, he thought they were pretty decent people. But I'm telling you all this now to explain why I was so sceptical about their reported sighting of Ruth's possible. As I say, my first instinct was not to believe it, and to suppose Chrissie was up to something.

The other thing that made me doubtful about all this had to do with the actual description given by Chrissie and Rodney: their picture of a woman working in a nice glass-fronted office. To me, at the time, this seemed just too close a match to what we then knew to be Ruth's 'dream future'.

I suppose it was mainly us newcomers who talked about 'dream futures' that winter, though a number of veterans did too. Some older ones – especially those who'd started their training – would sigh quietly and leave the room when this sort of talk began, but for a long time we didn't even notice this happening. I'm not sure what was going on in our heads during those discussions. We probably knew they couldn't be serious, but then again, I'm sure we didn't regard them as fantasy either. Maybe once Hailsham was behind us, it was possible, just for that half year or so, before all the talk of becoming carers, before the driving lessons, all those other things, it was possible to forget for whole stretches of time who we really were; to forget what the guardians had told us; to forget Miss Lucy's outburst that rainy afternoon at the pavilion, as well as all those theories we'd developed amongst ourselves over the years. It couldn't last, of course, but like I say, just for those few months, we somehow managed to live in this cosy state of suspension in which we could ponder our lives without the usual boundaries. Looking back now, it feels like we spent ages in that steamed-up kitchen after breakfast, or huddled around half-dead fires in the small hours, lost in conversation about our plans for the future.

Mind you, none of us pushed it *too* far. I don't remember anyone saying they were going to be a movie star or anything like that. The talk was more likely to be about becoming a postman or working on a farm. Quite a few students wanted to be drivers of one sort or other, and often, when the conversation went this way, some veterans would begin comparing particular scenic routes they'd travelled, favourite roadside cafés, difficult roundabouts, that sort of thing. Today, of course, I'd be able to talk the lot of them under the table on those topics. Back then, though, I used to just listen, not saying a thing, drinking in their talk. Sometimes, if it was late, I'd close my eyes and nestle against the arm of a sofa – or of a boy, if it was during one of those brief phases I was officially 'with' someone – and drift in and out of sleep, letting images of the roads move through my head.

Anyway, to get back to my point, when this sort of talk was going on, it was often Ruth who took it further than anybody – especially when there were veterans around. She'd been talking about offices right from the start of the winter, but when it really took on life, when it became her 'dream future', was after that morning she and I walked into the village.

It was during a bitterly cold spell, and our boxy gas heaters had been giving us trouble. We'd spend ages trying to get them to light, clicking away with no result, and we'd had to give up on more and more – and along with them, the rooms they were supposed to heat. Keffers refused to deal with it, claiming it was our responsibility, but in the end, when things were getting really cold, he'd handed us an envelope with money and a note of some igniter fuel we had to buy. So Ruth and I had volunteered to walk to the village to get it, and that's why we were going down the lane that frosty morning. We'd reached a spot where the hedges were high on both sides, and the ground was covered in frozen cowpats, when Ruth suddenly stopped a few steps behind me.

It took me a moment to realise, so that by the time I turned back to her she was breathing over her fingers and looking down, engrossed by something beside her feet. I thought maybe it was some poor creature dead in the frost, but when I came up, I saw it was a colour magazine – not one of 'Steve's magazines', but one of those bright cheerful things that come free with newspapers. It had fallen open at this glossy double page advert, and though the paper had gone soggy and there was mud at one corner, you could see it well enough. It showed this beautifully modern open-plan office with three or four people who worked in it having some kind of joke with each other. The place looked sparkling and so did the people. Ruth was staring at this picture and, when she noticed me beside her, said: 'Now *that* would be a *proper* place to work.'

Then she got self-conscious – maybe even cross that I'd caught her like that – and set off again much faster than before.

But a few evenings later, when several of us were sitting around a fire in the farmhouse, Ruth began telling us about the sort of office she'd ideally work in, and I immediately recognised it. She went into all the details – the plants, the gleaming equipment, the chairs with their swivels and castors – and it was so vivid everyone let her talk uninterrupted for ages. I was watching her closely, but it never seemed to occur to her I might make the connection – maybe she'd even forgotten herself where the image had come from. She even talked at one point about how the people in her office would all be 'dynamic, go-ahead types', and I remembered clearly those same words written in big letters across the top of the advert: 'Are you the dynamic, go-ahead type?' – something like that. Of course, I didn't say anything. In fact, listening to her, I even started wondering if maybe it was all feasible: if one day we might all of us move into a place like that and carry on our lives together.

Chrissie and Rodney were there that night, of course, hanging onto every word. And then for days afterwards, Chrissie kept trying to get Ruth to talk some more about it. I'd pass them sitting together in the corner of a room and Chrissie would be asking 'Are you sure you wouldn't put each other off, working all together in a place like that?' just to get Ruth going on it again.

The point about Chrissie – and this applied to a lot of the veterans – was that for all her slightly patronising manner towards us when we'd first arrived, she was awestruck about our being from Hailsham. It took me a long time to realise this. Take the business about Ruth's office: Chrissie would never herself have talked about working in *any* office, never mind one like that. But because Ruth was from Hailsham, somehow the whole notion came within the realms of the possible. That's how Chrissie saw it, and I suppose Ruth did say a few things every now and then to encourage the idea that, sure enough, in some mysterious way, a separate set of rules applied to us Hailsham students. I never heard Ruth actually lie to veterans; it was more to do with not denying certain things, implying others. There were occasions when I could have brought the whole thing down over her head. But I

Ruth was sometimes embarrassed, catching my eye in the middle of some story or other, she seemed confident I wouldn't give her away. And of course, I didn't.

So that was the background to Chrissie and Rodney's claim to have seen Ruth's 'possible', and you can maybe see now why I was wary about it. I wasn't keen on Ruth going with them to Norfolk, though I couldn't really say why. And once it became clear she was completely set on going, I told her I'd come too. At first, she didn't seem too delighted, and there was even a hint that she wouldn't let Tommy come with her either. In the end, though, we all went, the five of us: Chrissie, Rodney, Ruth, Tommy and me.

CHAPTER THIRTEEN

Rodney, who had a driver's licence, had made an arrangement to borrow a car for the day from the farm-workers at Metchley a couple of miles down the road. He'd regularly got cars this way in the past, but this particular time, the arrangement broke down the day before we were due to set off. Though things got sorted out fairly easily – Rodney walked over to the farm and got a promise on another car – the interesting thing was the way Ruth responded during those few hours when it looked like the trip might have to be called off.

Until then, she'd been making out the whole thing was a bit of a joke, that if anything she was going along with it to please Chrissie. And she'd talked a lot about how we weren't exploring our freedom nearly enough since leaving Hailsham; how anyway she'd always wanted to go to Norfolk to 'find all our lost things'. In other words, she'd gone out of her way to let us know she wasn't very serious about the prospect of finding her 'possible'.

That day before we went, I remember Ruth and I had been out for a stroll, and we came into the farmhouse kitchen where Fiona and a few veterans were making a huge stew. And it was Fiona herself, not looking up from what she was doing, who told us how the farm boy had come in earlier with the message. Ruth was standing just in front of me, so I couldn't see her face, but her whole posture froze up. Then without a word, she turned and pushed past me out of the cottage. I got a glimpse of her face then, and that's when I realised how upset she was. Fiona started to say something like: 'Oh, I didn't know . . .' But I said quickly: 'That's not what Ruth's upset about. It's about something else, something that happened earlier on.' It wasn't very good, but it was the best I could do on the spur of the moment.

In the end, as I said, the vehicle crisis got resolved, and early the next morning, in the pitch dark, the five of us got inside a bashed but perfectly decent Rover car. The way we sat was with Chrissie up front next to Rodney, and the three of us in the back. That was what had felt natural, and we'd got in like that without thinking about it. But after only a few minutes, once Rodney had brought us out of the dark winding lanes onto the proper roads, Ruth, who was in the middle, leaned forward, put her hands on the front seats, and began talking to the two veterans. She did this in a way that meant Tommy and I, on either side of her, couldn't hear anything they were saying, and because she was between us, couldn't talk to or even see each other. Sometimes, on the rare occasions she did lean back, I tried to get something going between the three of us, but Ruth wouldn't pick up on it, and before long, she'd be crouched forwards again, her face stuck between the two front seats.

After about an hour, with day starting to break, we stopped to stretch our legs and let Rodney go for a pee. We'd pulled over beside a big empty field, so we jumped over the ditch and spent a few minutes rubbing our hands together and watching our breaths rise. At one point, I noticed Ruth had drifted away from the rest of us and was gazing across the field at the sunrise. So I went over to her and made the suggestion that, since she only wanted to talk to the veterans, she swap seats with me. That way she could go on talking at least with Chrissie, and Tommy and I could have some sort of conversation to while away the journey. I'd hardly finished before Ruth said in a whisper:

'Why do you have to be difficult? Now of all times! I don't get it. Why do you want to make trouble?' Then she yanked me round so both our backs were to the others and they wouldn't see if we started to argue. It was the way she did this, rather than her words, that suddenly made me see things her way; I could see that Ruth was making a big effort to present not just herself, but all of us, in the right way to Chrissie and Rodney; and here I was, threatening to undermine her and start an embarrassing scene. I saw all this, and so I touched her on the shoulder and went off back to the others. And when we returned to the car, I made sure the three of us sat exactly as before. But now, as we drove on, Ruth stayed more or less silent, sitting right back in her seat, and even when Chrissie or Rodney shouted things to us from the front, responded only in sulky monosyllables.

Things cheered up considerably, though, once we arrived in our seaside town. We got there around lunch-time and left the Rover in a car park beside a mini-golf course full of fluttering flags. It had turned into a crisp, sunny day, and my memory of it is that for the first hour we all felt so exhilarated to be out and about we didn't give much thought to what had brought us there. At one point Rodney actually let out a few whoops, waving his arms around as he led the way up a road climbing steadily past rows of houses and the occasional shop, and you could sense just from the huge sky, that you were walking towards the sea.

Actually, when we did reach the sea, we found we were standing on a road carved into a cliff edge. It seemed at first there was a sheer drop down to the sands, but once you leant over the rail, you could see zigzagging footpaths leading you down the cliff-face to the seafront.

We were starving by now and went into a little café perched on the cliff just where one of the footpaths began. When we went in, the only people inside were the two chubby women in aprons who worked there. They were smoking cigarettes at one of the tables, but they quickly got up and disappeared into the kitchen, so then we had the place to ourselves.

We took the table right at the back – which meant the one stuck out closest to the cliff edge – and when we sat down it felt like we were virtually suspended over the sea. I didn't have anything to compare it with at the time, but I realise now the café was tiny, with just three or four little tables. They'd left a window open – probably to stop the place filling up with frying smells – so that every now and then a gust would pass through the room making all the signs advertising their good deals flutter about. There was one cardboard notice pinned over the counter that had been done in coloured felt-tips, and at the top of it was the word 'look' with a staring eye drawn inside each 'o'. I see the same thing so often these days I don't even register it, but back then I hadn't seen it before. So I was looking at it admiringly, then caught Ruth's eye, and realised she too was looking at it amazed, and we both burst out laughing. That was a cosy little moment, when it felt like we'd left behind the bad feeling that had grown between us in the car. As it turned out, though, it was just about the last moment like that between me and Ruth for the rest of that outing.

We hadn't mentioned the 'possible' at all since arriving in the town, and I'd assumed when we sat down we'd finally discuss the matter properly. But once we'd started on our sandwiches, Rodney began talking about their old friend, Martin, who'd left the Cottages the year before and was now living somewhere in the town. Chrissie eagerly took up the subject and soon both veterans were coming out with anecdotes about all the hilarious things Martin had got up to. We couldn't follow much of it, but Chrissie and Rodney were really enjoying themselves. They kept exchanging glances and laughing, and although they pretended it was for our benefit, it was clear they were remembering for each other. Thinking about it now, it occurs to me the near-taboo at the Cottages surrounding people who'd left might well have stopped them talking about their friend even to each other, and it was only once we'd come away they'd felt able to indulge themselves in this way.

Whenever they laughed, I laughed too just to be polite. Tommy seemed to be understanding things even less than me and was letting out hesitant little half-laughs that lagged some way behind. Ruth, though, was laughing and laughing, and kept nodding to everything being said about Martin just like she too was remembering them. Then once, when Chrissie made a really obscure reference – she'd said something like: 'Oh, yes, the time he put out his jeans!' – Ruth gave a big laugh and signalled in our direction, as though to say to Chrissie: 'Go on, explain it to them so they can enjoy it too.' I let this all go, but when Chrissie and Rodney started discussing whether we should go round to Martin's flat, I finally said, maybe a bit coldly:

'What exactly is he doing here? Why's he got a flat?'

There was a silence, then I heard Ruth let out an exasperated sigh. Chrissie leaned over the table towards me and said quietly, like she was explaining to a child: 'He's being a carer. What else do you think he'd be doing here? He's a proper carer now.'

There was a bit of shifting, and I said: 'That's what I mean. We can't just go and visit him.'

Chrissie sighed. 'Okay. We're not *supposed* to visit carers. Absolutely strictly speaking. Certainly not encouraged.'

Rodney chuckled and added: 'Definitely not encouraged. Naughty naughty to go and visit him.'

'Very naughty,' Chrissie said and made a tutting noise.

Then Ruth joined in, saying: 'Kathy *hates* to be naughty. So we'd better not go and visit him.'

Tommy was looking at Ruth, clearly puzzled about whose side she'd taken, and I wasn't sure either. It occurred to me she didn't want the expedition side-tracked and was reluctantly siding with me, so I smiled at her, but she didn't return my look. Then Tommy asked suddenly:

'Whereabouts was it you saw Ruth's possible, Rodney?'

'Oh . . .' Rodney didn't seem nearly so interested in the possible now we were in the town, and I could see anxiety cross Ruth's face. Finally Rodney said: 'It was a turning off the High Street, somewhere up the other end. Of course, it might be her day off.' Then when no one said anything, he added: 'They do have days off, you know. They're not always at their work.'

For a moment, as he said this, the fear passed through me that we'd misjudged things badly; that for all we knew, veterans often used talk of possibles just as a pretext to go on trips, and didn't really expect to take it any further. Ruth might well have been thinking along the same lines, because she was now looking definitely worried, but in the end she did a little laugh, like Rodney had made a joke.

Then Chrissie said in a new voice: 'You know, Ruth, we might be coming here in a few years' time to visit *you*. Working in a nice office. I don't see how anyone could stop us visiting you then.'

'That's right,' Ruth said quickly. 'You can all come and see me.'

'I suppose,' Rodney said, 'there aren't any rules about visiting people if they're working in an office.' He laughed suddenly. 'We don't know. It hasn't really happened with us before.'

'It'll be all right,' Ruth said. 'They let you do it. You can all come and visit me. Except Tommy, that is.'

Tommy looked shocked. 'Why can't I come?'

'Because you'll already be with me, stupid,' Ruth said. 'I'm keeping you.'

We all laughed, Tommy again a little behind the rest of us.

'I heard about this girl up in Wales,' Chrissie said. 'She was Hailsham, maybe a few years before you lot. Apparently she's working in this clothes shop right now. A really smart one.'

There were murmurs of approval and for a while we all looked dreamily out at the clouds.

'That's Hailsham for you,' Rodney said eventually, and shook his head as though in amazement.

'And then there was that other person' – Chrissie had turned to Ruth – 'that boy you were telling us about the other day. The one a couple of years above you who's a park keeper now.'

Ruth was nodding thoughtfully. It occurred to me that I should shoot Tommy a warning glance, but by the time I'd turned to him, he'd already started to speak.

'Who was that?' he asked in a bewildered voice.

'You know who it is, Tommy,' I said quickly. It was too risky to kick him, or even to make my voice wink-wink: Chrissie would have picked it up in a flash. So I said it dead straight, with a bit of weariness, like we were all fed up with Tommy forgetting all the time. But this just meant Tommy still didn't twig.

'Someone *we* knew?'

'Tommy, let's not go through this again,' I said. 'You'll have to have your brains tested.'

At last the penny seemed to drop, and Tommy shut up.

Chrissie said: 'I know how lucky I am, getting to be at the Cottages. But you Hailsham lot, you're *really* lucky. You know . . .' She lowered her voice and leaned forward again. 'There's something I've been wanting to talk to you lot about. It's just that back there, at the Cottages, it's impossible. Everyone always listening in.'

She looked around the table, then fixed her gaze on Ruth. Rodney suddenly tensed and he too leaned forward. And something told me we were coming to what was, for Chrissie and Rodney, the central purpose of this whole expedition.

'When Rodney and I, we were up in Wales,' she said. 'The same time we heard about this girl in the clothes shop. We heard something else, something about Hailsham students. What they were saying was that some Hailsham students in the past, in special circumstances, had managed to get a deferral. That this was something you could do if you were a Hailsham student. You could ask for your donations to be put back by three, even four years. It wasn't easy, but just sometimes they'd let you do it. So long as you could convince them. So long as you *qualified*.'

Chrissie paused and looked at each of us, maybe for dramatic effect, maybe to check us for signs of recognition. Tommy and I probably had puzzled looks, but Ruth had on one of her faces where you couldn't tell what was going on.

'What they said,' Chrissie continued, 'was that if you were a boy and a girl, and you were in love with each other, really, properly in love, and if you could show it, then the people who run Hailsham, they sorted it out for you. They sorted it out so you could have a few years together before you began your donations.'

There was now a strange atmosphere around the table, a kind of tingle going round.

'When we were in Wales,' Chrissie went on, 'the students at the White Mansion. They'd heard of this Hailsham couple, the guy had only a few weeks left before he became a carer. And they went to see someone and got everything put back three years. They were allowed to go on living there together, up at the White Mansion, three years straight, didn't have to go on with their training or anything. Three years just to themselves, because they could prove they were properly in love.'

It was at this point I noticed Ruth nodding with a lot of authority. Chrissie and Rodney noticed too and for a few seconds they watched her like they were hypnotised. And I had a kind of vision of Chrissie and Rodney, back at the Cottages, in the months leading up to this moment, probing and prodding this subject between them. I could see them bringing it up, at first very tentatively, shrugging, putting it to one side, bringing it up again, never able quite to leave it alone. I could see them toying with the idea of talking to us about it, see them refining how they'd do it, what exactly they'd say. I looked again at Chrissie and Rodney in front of me, gazing at Ruth, and tried to read their faces. Chrissie looked both afraid and hopeful. Rodney looked on edge, like he didn't trust himself not to blurt out something he wasn't supposed to.

This wasn't the first time I'd come across the rumour about deferrals. Over the past several weeks, I'd caught more and more snatches of it at the Cottages. It was always veterans talking among themselves, and when any of us showed up, they'd look awkward and go quiet. But I'd heard enough to get the gist of it; and I knew it had specifically to do with us Hailsham students. Even so, it was only that day, in that seafront café, that it really came home to me how important this whole notion had become for some veterans.

'I suppose,' Chrissie went on, her voice wobbling slightly, 'you lot would know about it. The rules, all that sort of thing.'

She and Rodney looked at each of us in turn, then their gazes settled back on Ruth.

Ruth sighed and said: 'Well, they told us a few things, obviously. But' – she gave a shrug – 'it's not something we know much about. We never talked about it really. Anyway, we should get going soon.'

'Who is it you go to?' Rodney suddenly asked. 'Who did they say you had to go to if you wanted, you know, to *apply*?'

Ruth shrugged again. 'Well, I told you. It wasn't something we talked about much.' Almost instinctively she looked to me and Tommy for support, which was probably a mistake, because Tommy said:

'To be honest, I don't know what you're all talking about. What rules are these?'

Ruth stared daggers at him, and I said quickly: 'You know, Tommy. All that talk that used to go round at Hailsham.'

Tommy shook his head. 'I don't remember it,' he said flatly. And this time I could see – and Ruth could too – that he wasn't being slow. 'I don't remember anything like that at Hailsham.'

Ruth turned away from him. 'What you've got to realise,' she said to Chrissie, 'is that even though Tommy was at Hailsham, he isn't like a real Hailsham student. He was left out of everything and people were always laughing at him. So there's no point in asking him about anything like this. Now, I want to go and find this person Rodney saw.'

A look had appeared in Tommy's eyes that made me catch my breath. It was one I hadn't seen for a long time and that belonged to the Tommy who'd had to be barricaded inside a classroom while he kicked over desks. Then the look faded, he turned to the sky outside and let out a heavy breath.

The veterans hadn't noticed anything because Ruth, at the same moment, had risen to her feet and was fiddling with her coat. Then there was a bit of confusion as the rest of us all moved back our chairs from the little table all at once. I'd been put in charge of the spending money, so I went up to pay. The others filed out behind me, and while I was waiting for the change, I watched them through one of the big misty windows, shuffling about in the sunshine, not talking, looking down at the sea.

CHAPTER FOURTEEN

When I got outside, it was obvious the excitement from when we'd first arrived had evaporated completely. We walked in silence, Rodney leading the way, through little backstreets hardly penetrated by the sun, the pavements so narrow we often had to shuffle along in single file. It was a relief to come out onto the High Street where the noise made our rotten mood less obvious. As we crossed at a pelican to the sunnier side, I could see Rodney and Chrissie conferring about something and I wondered how much of the bad atmosphere had to do with their believing we were holding back on some big Hailsham secret, and how much was just to do with Ruth's having a go at Tommy.

Then once we'd crossed the High Street, Chrissie announced she and Rodney wanted to go shopping for birthday cards. Ruth was stunned by this, but Chrissie just went on:

'We like buying them in big batches. It's always cheaper in the long run. And you've always got one handy when it's someone's birthday.' She pointed to the entrance of a Woolworth's shop. 'You can get pretty good cards in there really cheap.'

Rodney was nodding, and I thought there was something a little bit mocking around the edges of his smile. 'Of course,' he said, 'you end up with a lot of cards the same, but you can put your own illustrations on them. You know, personalise them.'

Both veterans were now standing in the middle of the pavement, letting people with pushchairs move round them, waiting for us to put up a challenge. I could tell Ruth was furious, but without Rodney's co-operation there wasn't much that could be done anyway.

So we went into the Woolworth's, and immediately I felt much more cheerful. Even now, I like places like that: a large store with lots of aisles displaying bright plastic toys, greeting cards, loads of cosmetics, maybe even a photo booth. Today, if I'm in a town and find myself with some time to kill, I'll stroll into somewhere just like that, where you can hang around and enjoy yourself, not buying a thing, and the assistants don't mind at all.

Anyway, we went in and before long we'd wandered apart to look at different aisles. Rodney had stayed near the entrance beside a big rack of cards, and further inside, I spotted Tommy under a big pop-group poster, rummaging through the music cassettes. After about ten minutes, when I was somewhere near the back of the store, I thought I heard Ruth's voice and wandered towards it. I'd already turned into the aisle – one with fluffy animals and big boxed jigsaws – before I realised Ruth and Chrissie were standing together at the end of it, having some sort of tête-à-tête. I wasn't sure what to do: I didn't want to interrupt, but it was time we were leaving and I didn't want to turn and walk off again. So I just stopped where I was, pretended to examine a jigsaw and waited for them to notice me.

That was when I realised they were back on the subject of this rumour. Chrissie was saying, in a lowered voice, something like:

'But all that time you were there, I'm amazed you didn't think more about how you'd do it. About who you'd go to, all of that.'

'You don't understand,' Ruth was saying. 'If you were from Hailsham, then you'd see. It's never been such a big deal for us. I suppose we've always known if we ever wanted to look into it, all we'd have to do is get word back to Hailsham . . .'

Ruth saw me and broke off. When I lowered the jigsaw and turned to them, they were both looking at me angrily. At the same time, it was like I'd caught them doing something they shouldn't, and they moved apart self-consciously.

'It's time we were off,' I said, pretending to have heard nothing.

But Ruth wasn't fooled. As they came past, she gave me a really dirty look.

So by the time we set off again, following Rodney in search of the office where he'd seen Ruth's possible the month before, the atmosphere between us was worse than ever. Things weren't helped either by Rodney repeatedly taking us down the wrong streets. At least four times, he led us confidently down a turning off the High Street, only for the shops and offices to run out, and we'd have to turn and come back. Before long, Rodney was looking defensive and on the verge of giving up. But then we found it.

Again, we'd turned and were heading back towards the High Street, when Rodney had stopped suddenly. Then he'd indicated silently an office on the other side of the street.

There it was, sure enough. It wasn't exactly like the magazine advert we'd found on the ground that day, but then it wasn't so far off either. There was a big glass front at street-level, so anyone going by could see right into it: a large open-plan room with maybe a dozen desks arranged in irregular L-patterns. There were the potted palms, the shiny machines and swooping desk lamps. People were moving about between desks, or leaning on a partition, chatting and sharing jokes, while others had pulled their swivel chairs close to each other and were enjoying a coffee and sandwich.

'Look,' Tommy said. 'It's their lunch break, but they don't go out. Don't blame them either.'

We kept on staring, and it looked like a smart, cosy, self-contained world. I glanced at Ruth and noticed her eyes moving anxiously around the faces behind the glass.

'Okay, Rod,' Chrissie said. 'So which one's the possible?'

She said this almost sarcastically, like she was sure the whole thing would turn out to be a big mistake on his part. But Rodney said quietly, with a tremor of excitement:

'There. Over in that corner. In the blue outfit. Her, talking now to the big red woman.'

It wasn't obvious, but the longer we kept looking, the more it seemed he had something. The woman was around fifty, and had kept her figure pretty well. Her hair was darker than Ruth's – though it could have been dyed – and she had it tied back in a simple pony-tail the way Ruth usually did. She was laughing at something her friend in the red outfit was saying, and her face,

145

especially when she was finishing her laugh with a shake of her head, had more than a hint of Ruth about it.

We all kept on watching her, not saying a word. Then we became aware that in another part of the office, a couple of the other women had noticed us. One raised a hand and gave us an uncertain wave. This broke the spell and we took to our heels in giggly panic.

We stopped again further down the street, talking excitedly all at once. Except for Ruth, that is, who remained silent in the middle of it. It was hard to read her face at that moment: she certainly wasn't disappointed, but then she wasn't elated either. She had on a half-smile, the sort a mother might have in an ordinary family, weighing things up while the children jumped and screamed around her asking her to say, yes, they could do whatever. So there we were, all coming out with our views, and I was glad I could say honestly, along with the others, that the woman we'd seen was by no means out of the question. The truth was, we were all relieved: without quite realising it, we'd been bracing ourselves for a let-down. But now we could go back to the Cottages, Ruth could take encouragement from what she'd seen, and the rest of us could back her up. And the office life the woman appeared to be leading was about as close as you could hope to the one Ruth had often described for herself. Regardless of what had been going on between us that day, deep down, none of us wanted Ruth to return home despondent, and at that moment we thought we were safe. And so we would have been, I'm pretty sure, had we put an end to the matter at that point.

But then Ruth said: 'Let's sit over there, over on that wall. Just for a few minutes. Once they've forgotten about us, we can go and have another look.'

We agreed to this, but as we walked towards the low wall around the small car park Ruth had indicated, Chrissie said, perhaps a little too eagerly:

'But even if we don't get to see her again, we're all agreed she's a possible. And it's a lovely office. It really is.'

146

'Let's just wait a few minutes,' Ruth said. 'Then we'll go back.'

I didn't sit on the wall myself because it was damp and crumbling, and because I thought someone might appear any minute and shout at us for sitting there. But Ruth did sit on it, knees on either side like she was astride a horse. And today I have these vivid images of the ten, fifteen minutes we waited there. No one's talking about the possible any more. We're pretending instead that we're just killing a bit of time, maybe at a scenic spot during a carefree day-trip. Rodney's doing a little dance to demonstrate what a good feeling there is. He gets up on the wall, balances along it then deliberately falls off. Tommy's making jokes about some passers-by, and though they're not very funny, we're all laughing. Just Ruth, in the middle, astride the wall, remains silent. She keeps the smile on her face, but hardly moves. There's a breeze messing up her hair, and the bright winter sun's making her crinkle up her eyes, so you're not sure if she's smiling at our antics, or just grimacing in the light. These are the pictures I've kept of those moments we waited by that car park. I suppose we were waiting for Ruth to decide when it was time to go back for a second look. Well, she never got to make that decision because of what happened next.

Tommy, who had been mucking about on the wall with Rodney, suddenly jumped down and went still. Then he said: 'That's her. That's the same one.'

We all stopped what we were doing and watched the figure coming from the direction of the office. She was now wearing a cream-coloured overcoat, and struggling to fasten her briefcase as she walked. The buckle was giving her trouble, so she kept slowing down and starting again. We went on watching her in a kind of trance as she went past on the other side. Then as she was turning into the High Street, Ruth leapt up and said: 'Let's see where she goes.'

We came out of our trance and were off after her. In fact, Chrissie had to remind us to slow down or someone would think we were a gang of muggers going after the woman. We followed along the High Street at a reasonable distance, giggling, dodging past people, separating and coming together again. It must have been around two o'clock by then, and the pavement was busy with shoppers. At times we nearly lost sight of her, but we kept up, loitering in front of window displays when she went into a shop, squeezing past pushchairs and old people when she came out again.

Then the woman turned off the High Street into the little lanes near the seafront. Chrissie was worried she'd notice us away from the crowds, but Ruth just kept going, and we followed behind her.

Eventually we came into a narrow side-street that had the occasional shop, but was mainly just ordinary houses. We had to walk again in single file, and once when a van came the other way, we had to press ourselves into the houses to let it pass. Before long there was only the woman and us in the entire street, and if she'd glanced back, there was no way she wouldn't have noticed us. But she just kept walking, a dozen or so steps ahead, then went in through a door – into 'The Portway Studios'.

I've been back to the Portway Studios a number of times since then. It changed owners a few years ago and now sells all kinds of arty things: pots, plates, clay animals. Back then, it was two big white rooms just with paintings – beautifully displayed with plenty of spaces between them. The wooden sign hanging over the door is still the same one though. Anyway, we decided to go in after Rodney pointed out how suspicious we looked in that quiet little street. Inside the shop, we could at least pretend we were looking at the pictures.

We came in to find the woman we'd been following talking to a much older woman with silver hair, who seemed to be in charge of the place. They were sitting on either side of a small desk near the door, and apart from them, the gallery was empty. Neither woman paid much attention as we filed past, spread out and tried to look fascinated by the pictures.

Actually, preoccupied though I was with Ruth's possible, I did begin to enjoy the paintings and the sheer peacefulness of the place. It felt like we'd come a hundred miles from the High Street.

The walls and ceilings were peppermint, and here and there, you'd see a bit of fishing net, or a rotted piece from a boat stuck up high near the cornicing. The paintings too – mostly oils in deep blues and greens – had sea themes. Maybe it was the tiredness suddenly catching up with us – after all, we'd been travelling since before dawn – but I wasn't the only one who went off into a bit of a dream in there. We'd all wandered into different corners, and were staring at one picture after another, only occasionally making the odd hushed remark like: 'Come and look at this!' All the time, we could hear Ruth's possible and the silver-haired lady talking on and on. They weren't especially loud, but in that place, their voices seemed to fill the entire space. They were discussing some man they both knew, how he didn't have a clue with his children. And as we kept listening to them, stealing the odd glance in their direction, bit by bit, something started to change. It did for me, and I could tell it was happening for the others. If we'd left it at seeing the woman through the glass of her office, even if we'd followed her through the town then lost her, we could still have gone back to the Cottages excited and triumphant. But now, in that gallery, the woman was too close, much closer than we'd ever really wanted. And the more we heard her and looked at her, the less she seemed like Ruth. It was a feeling that grew among us almost tangibly, and I could tell that Ruth, absorbed in a picture on the other side of the room, was feeling it as much as anyone. That was probably why we went on shuffling around that gallery for so long; we were delaying the moment when we'd have to confer.

Then suddenly the woman had left, and we all kept standing about, avoiding each other's eyes. But none of us had thought to follow the woman, and as the seconds kept ticking on, it became like we were agreeing, without speaking, about how we now saw the situation.

Eventually the silver-haired lady came out from behind her desk and said to Tommy, who was the nearest to her: 'That's a *particularly* lovely work. That one's a favourite of mine.'

Tommy turned to her and let out a laugh. Then as I was hurrying over to help him out, the lady asked: 'Are you art students?'

'Not exactly,' I said before Tommy could respond. 'We're just, well, keen.'

The silver-haired lady beamed, then started to tell us how the artist whose work we were looking at was related to her, and all about the artist's career thus far. This had the effect, at least, of breaking the trance-like state we'd been in, and we gathered round her to listen, the way we might have done at Hailsham when a guardian started to speak. This really got the silver-haired lady going, and we kept nodding and exclaiming while she talked about where the paintings had been done, the times of day the artist liked to work, how some had been done without sketches. Then there came a kind of natural end to her lecture, and we all gave a sigh, thanked her and went out.

The street outside being so narrow, we couldn't talk properly for a while longer, and I think we were all grateful for that. As we walked away from the gallery in single file, I could see Rodney, up at the front, theatrically stretching out his arms, like he was exhilarated the way he'd been when we'd first arrived in the town. But it wasn't convincing, and once we came out onto a wider street, we all shuffled to a halt.

We were once again near a cliff edge. And like before, if you peered over the rail, you could see the paths zigzagging down to the seafront, except this time you could see the promenade at the bottom with rows of boarded-up stalls.

We spent a few moments just looking out, letting the wind hit us. Rodney was still trying to be cheerful, like he'd decided not to let any of this business spoil a good outing. He was pointing out to Chrissie something in the sea, way off on the horizon. But Chrissie turned away from him and said:

'Well, I think we're agreed, aren't we? That *isn't* Ruth.' She gave a small laugh and laid a hand on Ruth's shoulder. 'I'm sorry. We're all sorry. But we can't blame Rodney really. It wasn't that wild a try. You've got to admit, when we saw her through those windows, it did look . . .' She trailed off, then touched Ruth on the shoulder again.

Ruth said nothing, but gave a little shrug, almost as if to shrug off the touch. She was squinting into the distance, at the sky rather than the water. I could tell she was upset, but someone who didn't know her well might well have supposed she was being thoughtful.

'Sorry, Ruth,' Rodney said, and he too gave Ruth a pat on the shoulder. But he had a smile on his face like he didn't expect for one moment to be blamed for anything. It was the way someone apologised when they'd tried to do you a favour, but it hadn't worked out.

Watching Chrissie and Rodney at that moment, I remember thinking, yes, they were okay. They were kind in their way and were trying to cheer Ruth up. At the same time, though, I remember feeling – even though they were the ones doing the talking, and Tommy and I were silent – a sort of resentment towards them on Ruth's behalf. Because however sympathetic they were, I could see that deep down they were relieved. They were relieved things had turned out the way they had; that they were in a position to comfort Ruth, instead of being left behind in the wake of a dizzying boost to her hopes. They were relieved they wouldn't have to face, more starkly than ever, the notion which fascinated and nagged and scared them: this notion of theirs that there were all kinds of possibilities open to us Hailsham students that weren't open to them. I remember thinking then how different they actually were, Chrissie and Rodney, from the three of us.

Then Tommy said: 'I don't see what difference it makes. It was just a bit of fun we were having.'

'A bit of fun for you maybe, Tommy,' Ruth said coldly, still gazing straight ahead of her. 'You wouldn't think so if it was *your* possible we'd been looking for.'

'I think I would,' Tommy said. 'I don't see how it matters. Even if you found your possible, the actual model they got you from. Even then, I don't see what difference it makes to anything.'

'Thank you for your profound contribution, Tommy,' said Ruth.

'But I think Tommy's right,' I said. 'It's daft to assume you'll

151

have the same sort of life as your model. I agree with Tommy. It's just a bit of fun. We shouldn't get so serious about it.'

I too reached out and touched Ruth on the shoulder. I wanted her to feel the contrast to when Chrissie and Rodney had touched her, and I deliberately chose exactly the same spot. I expected some response, some signal that she accepted understanding from me and Tommy in a way she didn't from the veterans. But she gave me nothing, not even the shrug she'd given Chrissie.

Somewhere behind me I could hear Rodney pacing about, making noises to suggest he was getting chilly in the strong wind. 'How about going to visit Martin now?' he said. 'His flat's just over there, behind those houses.'

Ruth suddenly sighed and turned to us. 'To be honest,' she said, 'I knew all along it was stupid.'

'Yeah,' said Tommy, eagerly. 'Just a bit of fun.'

Ruth gave him an irritated look. 'Tommy, please shut up with all this "bit of fun" stuff. No one's listening.' Then turning to Chrissie and Rodney she went on: 'I didn't want to say when you first told me about this. But look, it was never on. They don't ever, *ever*, use people like that woman. Think about it. Why would she want to? We all know it, so why don't we all face it. We're not modelled from that sort . . .'

'Ruth,' I cut in firmly. 'Ruth, don't.'

But she just carried on: 'We all know it. We're modelled from *trash*. Junkies, prostitutes, winos, tramps. Convicts, maybe, just so long as they aren't psychos. That's what we come from. We all know it, so why don't we say it? A woman like that? Come on. Yeah, right, Tommy. A bit of fun. Let's have a bit of fun pretending. That other woman in there, her friend, the old one in the gallery. *Art* students, that's what she thought we were. Do you think she'd have talked to us like that if she'd known what we really were? What do you think she'd have said if we'd asked her? "Excuse me, but do you think your friend was ever a clone model?" She'd have thrown us out. We know it, so we might as well just say it. If you want to look for possibles, if you want to do it properly, then you look in the gutter. You look in rubbish bins.

Look down the toilet, that's where you'll find where we all came from.'

'Ruth' – Rodney's voice was steady and had a warning in it – 'let's forget about it and go and see Martin. He's off this afternoon. You'll like him, he's a real laugh.'

Chrissie put an arm around Ruth. 'Come on, Ruth. Let's do what Rodney says.'

Ruth got to her feet and Rodney started to walk.

'Well, you lot can go,' I said quietly. 'I'm not going.'

Ruth turned and looked at me carefully. 'Well, what do you know? Who's the upset one now?'

'I'm not upset. But sometimes you speak garbage, Ruth.'

'Oh, look who's upset now. Poor Kathy. She never likes straight talking.'

'It's nothing to do with that. I don't want to visit a carer. We're not supposed to and I don't even know this guy.'

Ruth shrugged and exchanged glances with Chrissie. 'Well,' she said, 'there's no reason we've got to go round together the whole time. If little Miss here doesn't want to join us, she doesn't have to. Let her go off by herself.' Then she leaned over to Chrissie and said in a stage whisper: 'That's always the best way when Kathy's in a mood. Leave her alone and she'll walk it off.'

'Be back at the car by four o'clock,' Rodney said to me. 'Otherwise you'll have to hitch-hike.' Then he did a laugh. 'Come on, Kathy, don't get in a sulk. Come with us.'

'No. You go on. I don't feel like it.'

Rodney shrugged and started to move off again. Ruth and Chrissie followed, but Tommy didn't move. Only when Ruth stared at him did he say:

'I'll stay with Kath. If we're splitting, then I'll stay with Kath.'

Ruth glared at him in fury, then turned and strode off. Chrissie and Rodney looked at Tommy awkwardly, then they too began walking again.

CHAPTER FIFTEEN

Tommy and I leaned on the rail and stared at the view until the others had gone out of sight.

'It's just talk,' he said eventually. Then after a pause: 'It's just what people say when they're feeling sorry for themselves. It's just talk. The guardians never told us anything like that.'

I started to walk – the opposite way to the others – and let Tommy fall in step beside me.

'It's not worth getting upset about,' Tommy went on. 'Ruth's always doing things like that now. It's just her letting off steam. Anyway, like we were telling her, even if it's true, even a little bit true, I don't see how it makes any difference. Our models, what they were like, that's nothing to do with us, Kath. It's just not worth getting upset about.'

'Okay,' I said, and deliberately bumped my shoulder into his. 'Okay, okay.'

I had the impression we were walking towards the town cen- tre, though I couldn't be sure. I was trying to think of a way to change the subject, when Tommy said first:

'You know when we were in that Woolworth's place earlier? When you were down at the back with the others? I was trying to find something. Something for you.'

'A present?' I looked at him in surprise. 'I'm not sure Ruth would approve of that. Not unless you got her a bigger one.'

'A sort of present. But I couldn't find it. I wasn't going to tell you, but now, well, I've got another chance to find it. Except you might have to help me. I'm not very good at shopping.'

'Tommy, what are you talking about? You want to get me a present, but you want me to help you choose it . . .'

'No, I know what it is. It's just that . . .' He laughed and shrugged. 'Oh, I might as well tell you. In that shop we were in,

they had this shelf with loads of records and tapes. So I was looking for the one you lost that time. Do you remember, Kath?
Except I couldn't remember what it was any more.'

'My tape? I didn't realise you ever knew about it, Tommy.'

'Oh yeah. Ruth was getting people to look for it and saying you
were really upset about losing it. So I tried to find it. I never told
you at the time, but I did try really hard. I thought there'd be
places I could look where you couldn't. In boys' dorms, stuff like
that. I remember looking for ages, but I couldn't find it.'

I glanced at him and felt my rotten mood evaporating. 'I never
knew that, Tommy. That was really sweet of you.'

'Well, it didn't help much. But I really wanted to find it for you.
And when it looked in the end like it wasn't going to turn up, I
just said to myself, one day I'll go to Norfolk and I'll find it there
for her.'

'The lost corner of England,' I said, and looked around me.
'And here we are!'

Tommy too looked around him, and we came to a halt. We
were in another side-street, not as narrow as the one with the
gallery. For a moment we both kept glancing around theatrically,
then giggled.

'So it wasn't such a daft idea,' Tommy said. 'That Woolworth's
shop earlier, it had all these tapes, so I thought they were bound
to have yours. But I don't think they did.'

'You don't *think* they did? Oh, Tommy, you mean you didn't
even look properly!'

'I did, Kath. It's just that, well, it's really annoying but I couldn't
remember what it was called. All that time at Hailsham, I was
opening boys' collection chests and everything, and now I can't
remember. It was Julie Bridges or something . . .'

'Judy Bridgewater. *Songs After Dark.*'

Tommy shook his head solemnly. 'They definitely didn't have
that.'

I laughed and punched his arm. He looked puzzled so I said:
'Tommy, they wouldn't have something like that in Woolworth's. They have the latest hits. Judy Bridgewater, she's some-

one from ages ago. It just happened to turn up, at one of our Sales. It's not going to be in Woolworth's now, you idiot!'

'Well, like I said, I don't know about things like that. But they had so many tapes . . .'

'They had *some*, Tommy. Oh, never mind. It was a sweet idea. I'm really touched. It was a great idea. This is Norfolk, after all.'

We started walking again and Tommy said hesitantly: 'Well, that's why I had to tell you. I wanted to surprise you, but it's useless. I don't know where to look, even if I do know the name of the record. Now I've told you, you can help me. We can look for it together.'

'Tommy, what are you talking about?' I was trying to sound reproachful, but I couldn't help laughing.

'Well, we've got over an hour. This is a real chance.'

'Tommy, you idiot. You really believe it, don't you? All this lost-corner stuff.'

'I don't necessarily believe it. But we might as well look now we're here. I mean, you'd like to find it again, wouldn't you? What have we got to lose?'

'All right. You're a complete idiot, but all right.'

He opened his arms out helplessly. 'Well, Kath, where do we go? Like I say, I'm no good at shopping.'

'We have to look in second-hand places,' I said, after a moment's thought. 'Places full of old clothes, old books. They'll sometimes have a box full of records and tapes.'

'Okay. But where are these shops?'

When I think of that moment now, standing with Tommy in the little side-street about to begin our search, I feel a warmth welling up through me. Everything suddenly felt perfect: an hour set aside, stretching ahead of us, and there wasn't a better way to spend it. I had to really hold myself back from giggling stupidly, or jumping up and down on the pavement like a little kid. Not long ago, when I was caring for Tommy, and I brought up our Norfolk trip, he told me he'd felt exactly the same. That moment when we decided to go searching for my lost tape, it was like sud-

156

denly every cloud had blown away, and we had nothing but fun and laughter before us.

At the start, we kept going into the wrong sort of places: second-hand bookshops, or shops full of old vacuum cleaners, but no music at all. After a while Tommy decided I didn't know any better than he did and announced he would lead the way. As it happened, by sheer luck really, he discovered straight away a street with four shops of just the kind we were after, standing virtually in a row. Their front windows were full of dresses, handbags, children's annuals, and when you went inside, a sweet stale smell. There were piles of creased paperbacks, dusty boxes full of postcards or trinkets. One shop specialised in hippie stuff, while another had war medals and photos of soldiers in the desert. But they all had somewhere a big cardboard box or two with LPs and cassette tapes. We rummaged around those shops, and in all honesty, after the first few minutes, I think Judy Bridgewater had more or less slipped from our minds. We were just enjoying looking through all those things together; drifting apart then finding ourselves side by side again, maybe competing for the same box of bric-a-brac in a dusty corner lit up by a shaft of sun.

Then of course I found it. I'd been flicking through a row of cassette cases, my mind on other things, when suddenly there it was, under my fingers, looking just the way it had all those years ago: Judy, her cigarette, the coquettish look for the barman, the blurred palms in the background.

I didn't exclaim, the way I'd been doing when I'd come across other items that had mildly excited me. I stood there quite still, looking at the plastic case, unsure whether or not I was delighted. For a second, it even felt like a mistake. The tape had been the perfect excuse for all this fun, and now it had turned up, we'd have to stop. Maybe that was why, to my own surprise, I kept silent at first; why I thought about pretending never to have seen it. And now it was there in front of me, there was something vaguely embarrassing about the tape, like it was something I should have grown out of. I actually went as far as flicking the cassette on and letting its neighbour fall on it. But there was the spine, looking up at me, and in the end I called Tommy over.

'Is that it?' He seemed genuinely sceptical, perhaps because I wasn't making more fuss. I pulled it out and held it in both hands. Then suddenly I felt a huge pleasure – and something else, something more complicated that threatened to make me burst into tears. But I got a hold of the emotion, and just gave Tommy's arm a tug.

'Yes, this is it,' I said, and for the first time smiled excitedly. 'Can you believe it? We've really found it!'

'Do you think it could be the same one? I mean, the *actual* one. The one you lost?'

As I turned it in my fingers, I found I could remember all the design details on the back, the titles of the tracks, everything.

'For all I know, it might be,' I said. 'But I have to tell you, Tommy, there might be thousands of these knocking about.'

Then it was my turn to notice Tommy wasn't as triumphant as he might be.

'Tommy, you don't seem very pleased for me,' I said, though in an obviously jokey voice.

'I *am* pleased for you, Kath. It's just that, well, I wish I'd found it.' Then he did a small laugh and went on: 'Back then, when you lost it, I used to think about it, in my head, what it would be like, if I found it and brought it to you. What you'd say, your face, all of that.'

His voice was softer than usual and he kept his eyes on the plastic case in my hand. And I suddenly became very conscious of the fact that we were the only people in the shop, except for the old guy behind the counter at the front engrossed in his paperwork. We were right at the back of the shop, on a raised platform where it was darker and more secluded, like the old guy didn't want to think about the stuff in our area and had mentally curtained it off. For several seconds, Tommy stayed in a sort of trance, for all I know playing over in his mind one of these old fantasies of giving me back my lost tape. Then suddenly he snatched the case out of my hand.

'Well at least I can *buy* it for you,' he said with a grin, and before I could stop him, he'd started down the floor towards the front.

I went on browsing around the back of the shop while the old guy searched around for the tape to go with the case. I was still feeling a pang of regret that we'd found it so quickly, and it was only later, when we were back at the Cottages and I was alone in my room, that I really appreciated having the tape – and that song – back again. Even then, it was mainly a nostalgia thing, and today, if I happen to get the tape out and look at it, it brings back memories of that afternoon in Norfolk every bit as much as it does our Hailsham days.

As we came out of the shop, I was keen to regain the carefree, almost silly mood we'd been in before. But when I made a few little jokes, Tommy was lost in his thoughts and didn't respond.

We began going up a steeply climbing path, and we could see – maybe a hundred yards further up – a kind of viewing area right on the cliff edge with benches facing out to sea. It would have made a nice spot in the summer for an ordinary family to sit and eat a picnic. Now, despite the chilly wind, we found ourselves walking up towards it, but when there was still some way left to go, Tommy slowed to a dawdle and said to me:

'Chrissie and Rodney, they're really obsessed with this idea. You know, the one about people having their donations deferred if they're really in love. They're convinced we know all about it, but no one said anything like that at Hailsham. At least, I never heard anything like that, did you, Kath? No, it's just something going around recently among the veterans. And people like Ruth, they've been stoking it up.'

I looked at him carefully, but it was hard to tell if he'd just spoken with mischievous affection or else a kind of disgust. I could see anyway there was something else on his mind, nothing to do with Ruth, so I didn't say anything and waited. Eventually he came to a complete halt and started to poke around with his foot a squashed paper cup on the ground.

'Actually, Kath,' he said, 'I've been thinking about it for a while. I'm sure we're right, there was no talk like that when we were at Hailsham. But there were a lot of things that didn't make sense back then. And I've been thinking, if it's true, this rumour, then it could explain quite a lot. Stuff we used to puzzle over.'

'What do you mean? What sort of stuff?'

'The Gallery, for instance.' Tommy had lowered his voice and I stepped in closer, just as though we were still at Hailsham, talking in the dinner queue or beside the pond. 'We never got to the bottom of it, what the Gallery was for. Why Madame took away all the best work. But now I think I know. Kath, you remember that time everyone was arguing about tokens? Whether they should get them or not to make up for stuff they'd had taken away by Madame? And Roy J. went in to see Miss Emily about it? Well, there was something Miss Emily said then, something she let drop, and that's what's been making me think.'

Two women were passing by with dogs on leads, and although it was completely stupid, we both stopped talking until they'd gone further up the slope and out of earshot. Then I said:

'What thing, Tommy? What thing Miss Emily let drop?'

'When Roy J. asked her why Madame took our stuff away. Do you remember what she's supposed to have said?'

'I remember her saying it was a privilege, and we should be proud . . .'

'But that wasn't all.' Tommy's voice was now down to a whisper. 'What she told Roy, what she let slip, which she probably didn't mean to let slip, do you remember, Kath? She told Roy that things like pictures, poetry, all that kind of stuff, she said they *revealed what you were like inside*. She said *they revealed your soul.*'

When he said this, I suddenly remembered a drawing Laura had done once of her intestines and laughed. But something was coming back to me.

'That's right,' I said. 'I remember. So what are you getting at?'

'What I think,' said Tommy slowly, 'is this. Suppose it's true, what the veterans are saying. Suppose some special arrangement *has* been made for Hailsham students. Suppose two people say they're truly in love, and they want extra time to be together.

Then you see, Kath, there has to be a way to judge if they're really telling the truth. That they aren't just saying they're in love, just to defer their donations. You see how difficult it could be to decide? Or a couple might really believe they're in love, but it's just a sex thing. Or just a crush. You see what I mean, Kath? It'll be really hard to judge, and it's probably impossible to get it right every time. But the point is, whoever decides, Madame or whoever it is, *they need something to go on.*'

I nodded slowly. 'So that's why they took away our art . . .'

'It could be. Madame's got a gallery somewhere filled with stuff by students from when they were tiny. Suppose two people come up and say they're in love. She can find the art they've done over years and years. She can see if they go. If they match. Don't forget, Kath, what she's got reveals our souls. She could decide for herself what's a good match and what's just a stupid crush.'

I started to walk slowly again, hardly looking in front of me. Tommy fell in step, waiting for my response.

'I'm not sure,' I said in the end. 'What you're saying could certainly explain Miss Emily, what she said to Roy. And I suppose it explains too why the guardians always thought it was so important for us, to be able to paint and all of that.'

'Exactly. And that's why . . .' Tommy sighed and went on with some effort. 'That's why Miss Lucy had to admit she'd been wrong, telling me it didn't really matter. She'd said that because she was sorry for me at the time. But she knew deep down it *did* matter. The thing about being from Hailsham was that you had this special chance. And if you didn't get stuff into Madame's gallery, then you were as good as throwing that chance away.'

It was after he said this that it suddenly dawned on me, with a real chill, where this was leading. I stopped and turned to him, but before I could speak, Tommy let out a laugh.

'If I've got this right, then, well, it looks like I might have blown my chance.'

'Tommy, did you *ever* get anything into the Gallery? When you were much younger maybe?'

He was already shaking his head. 'You know how useless I

was. And then there was that stuff with Miss Lucy. I know she meant well. She was sorry for me and she wanted to help me. I'm sure she did. But if my theory's right, well . . .'

'It's only a theory, Tommy,' I said. 'You know what your theories are like.'

I'd wanted to lighten things a bit, but I couldn't get the tone right, and it must have been obvious I was still thinking hard about what he'd just said. 'Maybe they've got all sorts of ways to judge,' I said after a moment. 'Maybe the art's just one out of all kinds of different ways.'

Tommy shook his head again. 'Like what? Madame never got to know us. She wouldn't remember us individually. Besides, it's probably not just Madame that decides. There's probably people higher up than her, people who never set foot in Hailsham. I've thought about this a lot, Kath. It all fits. That's why the Gallery was so important, and why the guardians wanted us to work so hard on our art and our poetry. Kath, what are you thinking?'

Sure enough, I'd drifted off a bit. Actually, I was thinking about that afternoon I'd been alone in our dorm, playing the tape we'd just found; how I'd been swaying around, clutching a pillow to my breast, and how Madame had been watching me from the doorway, tears in her eyes. Even this episode, for which I'd never yet found a convincing explanation, seemed to fit Tommy's theory. In my head, I'd been imagining I was holding a baby, but of course, there'd have been no way for Madame to know that. She'd have supposed I was holding a lover in my arms. If Tommy's theory was right, if Madame was connected to us for the sole purpose of deferring our donations when, later on, we fell in love, then it made sense – for all her usual coldness towards us – she'd be really moved stumbling on a scene like that. All this flashed through my mind, and I was on the point of blurting it all out to Tommy. But I held back because I wanted now to play down his theory.

'I was just thinking over what you said, that's all,' I said. 'We should start going back now. It might take us a while to find the car park.'

162

We began to retrace our steps down the slope, but we knew we still had time and didn't hurry.

'Tommy,' I asked, after we'd been walking for a while. 'Have you said any of this to Ruth?'

He shook his head and went on walking. Eventually he said: 'The thing is, Ruth believes it all, everything the veterans are saying. Okay, she likes to pretend she knows much more than she does. But she does believe it. And sooner or later, she's going to want to take it further.'

'You mean, she'll want to . . .'

'Yeah. She'll want to apply. But she hasn't thought it through yet. Not the way we just did.'

'You've never told her your theory about the Gallery?'

He shook his head again, but said nothing.

'If you tell her your theory,' I said, 'and she buys it . . . Well, she's going to be furious.'

Tommy seemed thoughtful, but still didn't say anything. It wasn't until we were back down in the narrow side-streets that he spoke again, and then his voice was suddenly sheepish.

'Actually, Kath,' he said, 'I *have* been doing some stuff. Just in case. I haven't told anyone, not even Ruth. It's just a start.'

That was when I first heard about his imaginary animals. When he started to describe what he'd been doing – I didn't actually see anything until a few weeks later – I found it hard to show much enthusiasm. In fact, I have to admit, I was reminded of the original elephant-in-the-grass picture that had started off all Tommy's problems at Hailsham. The inspiration, he explained, had come from an old children's book with the back cover missing which he'd found behind one of the sofas at the Cottages. He'd then persuaded Keffers to give him one of the little black notebooks he scribbled his figures in, and since then, Tommy had finished at least a dozen of his fantastic creatures.

'The thing is, I'm doing them really small. Tiny. I'd never thought of that at Hailsham. I think maybe that's where I went wrong. If you make them tiny, and you have to because the pages are only about this big, then everything changes. It's like they come to life by themselves. Then you have to draw in all these different details for them. You have to think about how they'd protect themselves, how they'd reach things. Honest, Kath, it's nothing like anything I ever did at Hailsham.'

He started describing his favourites, but I couldn't really concentrate; the more excited he got telling me about his animals, the more uneasy I was growing. 'Tommy,' I wanted to say to him, 'you're going to make yourself a laughing stock all over again. Imaginary animals? What's up with you?' But I didn't. I just looked at him cautiously and kept saying: 'That sounds really good, Tommy.'

Then he said at one point: 'Like I said, Kath, Ruth doesn't know about the animals.' And when he said this, he seemed to remember everything else, and why we'd been talking about his animals in the first place, and the energy faded from his face. Then we were walking in silence again, and as we came out onto the High Street, I said:

'Well, even if there's something to your theory, Tommy, there's a lot more we'll have to find out. For one thing, how's a couple supposed to apply? What are they supposed to do? There aren't exactly forms lying about.'

'I've been wondering about all of that too.' His voice was quiet and solemn again. 'As far as I can see, there's only one obvious way forward. And that's to find Madame.'

I gave this a think, then said: 'That might not be so easy. We don't really know a thing about her. We don't even know her name. And you remember how she was? She didn't like us even coming near her. Even if we did ever track her down, I don't see her helping much.'

Tommy sighed. 'I know,' he said. 'Well, I suppose we've got time. None of us are in any particular hurry.'

By the time we got back to the car park, the afternoon had clouded over and was growing pretty chilly. There was no sign of the others yet, so Tommy and I leaned against our car and looked towards the mini-golf course. No one was playing and the flags

164

were fluttering away in the wind. I didn't want to talk any more about Madame, the Gallery or any of the rest of it, so I got the Judy Bridgewater tape out from its little bag and gave it a good look-over.

'Thanks for buying this for me,' I said.

Tommy smiled. 'If I'd got to that tape box and you were on the LPs, I'd have found it first. It was bad luck for poor old Tommy.'

'It doesn't make any difference. We only found it because you said to look for it. I'd forgotten about all this lost-corner stuff. After Ruth going on like that, I was in such a mood. Judy Bridgewater. My old friend. It's like she's never been away. I wonder who stole it back then?'

For a moment, we turned towards the street, looking for the others.

'You know,' Tommy said, 'when Ruth said what she did earlier on, and I saw how upset you looked . . .'

'Leave it, Tommy. I'm all right about it now. And I'm not going to bring it up with her when she comes back.'

'No, that's not what I was getting at.' He took his weight off the car, turned and pressed a foot against the front tyre as though to test it. 'What I meant was, I realised then, when Ruth came out with all that, I realised why you keep looking through those porn mags. Okay, I haven't *realised*. It's just a theory. Another of my theories. But when Ruth said what she did earlier on, it kind of clicked.'

I knew he was looking at me, but I kept my eyes straight ahead and made no response.

'But I still don't really get it, Kath,' he said eventually. 'Even if what Ruth says is right, and I don't think it is, why are you looking through old porn mags for your possibles? Why would your model have to be one of those girls?'

I shrugged, still not looking at him. 'I don't claim it makes sense. It's just something I do.' There were tears filling my eyes now and I tried to hide them from Tommy. But my voice wobbled as I said: 'If it annoys you so much, I won't do it any more.'

I don't know if Tommy saw the tears. In any case, I'd got them under control by the time he came close to me and gave my shoulders a squeeze. This was something he'd done before from time to time, it wasn't anything special or new. But somehow I did feel better and gave a little laugh. He let go of me then, but we stayed almost touching, side by side again, our backs to the car.

'Okay, there's no sense in it,' I said. 'But we all do it, don't we? We all wonder about our model. After all, that's why we came out here today. We all do it.'

'Kath, you know, don't you, I haven't told anyone. About that time in the boiler hut. Not Ruth, not anyone. But I just don't get it. I don't get what it's about.'

'All right, Tommy. I'll tell you. It may not make any more sense after you've heard it, but you can hear it anyway. It's just that sometimes, every now and again, I get these really strong feelings when I want to have sex. Sometimes it just comes over me and for an hour or two it's scary. For all I know, I could end up doing it with old Keffers, it's that bad. That's why . . . that's the only reason I did it with Hughie. And with Oliver. It didn't mean anything deep down. I don't even like them much. I don't know what it is, and afterwards, when it's passed over, it's just scary. That's why I started thinking, well, it has to come from somewhere. It must be to do with the way I am.' I stopped, but when Tommy didn't say anything, I went on: 'So I thought if I find her picture, in one of those magazines, it'll at least explain it. I wouldn't want to go and find her or anything. It would just, you know, kind of explain why I am the way I am.'

'I get it too sometimes,' said Tommy. 'When I really feel like doing it. I reckon everyone does, if they're honest. I don't think there's anything different about you, Kath. In fact, I get like that quite a lot . . .' He broke off and laughed, but I didn't laugh with him.

'What I'm talking about's different,' I said. 'I've watched other people. They get in the mood for it, but that doesn't make them do things. They never do things like I've done, going with people like that Hughie . . .'

I might have started crying again, because I felt Tommy's arm going back around my shoulders. Upset as I was, I remained conscious of where we were, and I made a kind of check in my mind that if Ruth and the others came up the street, even if they saw us at that moment, there'd be no room for misunderstanding. We were still side by side, leaning against the car, and they'd see I was upset about something and Tommy was just comforting me. Then I heard him say:

'I don't think it's necessarily a bad thing. Once you find someone, Kath, someone you really want to be with, then it could be really good. Remember what the guardians used to tell us? If it's with the right person, it makes you feel really good.'

I made a movement with my shoulder to get Tommy's arm off me, then took a deep breath. 'Let's forget it. Anyway, I've got much better at controlling these moods when they come on. So let's just forget it.'

'All the same, Kath, it's stupid looking through those magazines.'

'It's stupid, okay. Tommy, let's leave it. I'm all right now.'

I don't remember what else we talked about until the others showed up. We didn't discuss any more of those serious things, and if the others sensed something still in the air, they didn't remark on it. They were in good spirits, and Ruth in particular seemed determined to make up for the bad scene earlier on. She came up and touched my cheek, making some joke or other, and once we got in the car, she made sure the jovial mood kept going. She and Chrissie had found everything about Martin comical and were relishing the chance to laugh openly about him now they'd left his flat. Rodney looked disapproving, and I realised Ruth and Chrissie were making a song and dance of it mainly to tease him. It all seemed good-natured enough. But what I noticed was that whereas before Ruth would have taken the opportunity to keep me and Tommy in the dark about all the jokes and references, throughout the journey back, she kept turning to me and explaining carefully everything they were talking about. In fact it got a bit tiring after a while because it was like everything being said in the car was for our – or at least my – special benefit. But I was pleased Ruth was making such a fuss. I understood – as did Tommy – that she'd recognised she'd behaved badly before, and this was her way of admitting it. We were sitting with her in the middle, just as we'd done on the journey out, but now she spent all her time talking to me, turning occasionally to her other side to give Tommy a little squeeze or the odd kiss. It was a good atmosphere, and no one brought up Ruth's possible or anything like that. And I didn't mention the Judy Bridgewater tape Tommy had bought me. I knew Ruth would find out about it sooner or later, but I didn't want her to find out just yet. On that journey home, with the darkness setting in over those long empty roads, it felt like the three of us were close again and I didn't want anything to come along and break that mood.

CHAPTER SIXTEEN

The odd thing about our Norfolk trip was that once we got back, we hardly talked about it. So much so that for a while all kinds of rumours went around about what we'd been up to. Even then, we kept pretty quiet, until eventually people lost interest.

I'm still not sure why this happened. Perhaps we felt it was up to Ruth, that it was her call how much got told, and we were waiting to take our cue from her. And Ruth, for one reason or another – maybe she was embarrassed how things had turned out with her possible, maybe she was enjoying the mystery – had remained completely closed on the subject. Even among ourselves, we avoided talking about the trip.

This air of secrecy made it easier for me to keep from telling Ruth about Tommy buying me the Judy Bridgewater tape. I didn't go as far as actually hiding the thing. It was always there in my collection, in one of my little piles next to the skirting board. But I always made sure not to leave it out or on top of a pile. There were times when I wanted badly to tell her, when I wanted us to reminisce about Hailsham with the tape playing in the background. But the further away we got from the Norfolk trip, and I still hadn't told her, the more it came to feel like a guilty secret. Of course, she did spot the tape in the end, much later, and it was probably a much worse time for her to find it, but that's the way your luck sometimes goes.

As spring came on, there seemed to be more and more veterans leaving to start their training, and though they left without fuss in the usual way, the increased numbers made them impossible to ignore. I'm not sure what our feelings were, witnessing these departures. I suppose to some extent we envied the people leaving. It did feel like they were headed for a bigger, more exciting world. But of course, without a doubt, their going made us increasingly uneasy.

Then, I think it was around April, Alice F. became the first of our Hailsham bunch to leave, and not long after that Gordon C. did too. They'd both asked to start their training, and went off with cheerful smiles, but after that, for our lot anyway, the atmosphere at the Cottages changed forever.

Many veterans, too, seemed affected by the flurry of departures, and maybe as a direct result, there was a fresh spate of rumours of the sort Chrissie and Rodney had spoken about in Norfolk. Talk went around of students, somewhere else in the country, getting deferrals because they'd shown they were in love – and now, just sometimes, the talk was of students with no connections to Hailsham. Here again, the five of us who'd been to Norfolk backed away from these topics: even Chrissie and Rodney, who'd once been at the centre of just this sort of talk, now looked awkwardly away when these rumours got going.

The 'Norfolk effect' even got to me and Tommy. I'd been assuming, once we were back, we'd be taking little opportunities, whenever we were alone, to exchange more thoughts on his theory about the Gallery. But for some reason – and it wasn't any more him than me – this never really happened. The one exception, I suppose, was that time in the goosehouse, the morning when he showed me his imaginary animals.

The barn we called the goosehouse was on the outer fringes of the Cottages, and because the roof leaked badly and the door was permanently off its hinges, it wasn't used for anything much other than as a place for couples to sneak off to in the warmer months. By then I'd taken to going for long solitary walks, and I think I was setting out on one of these, and had just gone past the goosehouse, when I heard Tommy calling me. I turned to see him in his bare feet, perched awkwardly on a bit of dry ground surrounded by huge puddles, one hand on the side of the barn to keep his balance.

'What happened to your Wellies, Tommy?' I asked. Aside from his bare feet, he was dressed in his usual thick jumper and jeans.

'I was, you know, *drawing* . . .' He laughed, and held up a little black notebook similar to the ones Keffers always went around with. It was by then over two months since the Norfolk trip, but I realised as soon as I saw the notebook what this was about. But I waited for him to say:

'If you like, Kath, I'll show you.'

He led the way into the goosehouse, hopping over the jaggy ground. I'd expected it to be dark inside, but the sunlight was pouring through the skylights. Pushed against one wall were various bits of furniture heaved out over the past year or so – broken tables, old fridges, that kind of thing. Tommy appeared to have dragged into the middle of the floor a two-seater settee with stuffing poking out of its black plastic, and I guessed he'd been sitting in it doing his drawing when I'd gone past. Just nearby, his Wellingtons were lying fallen on their sides, his football socks peeking out of the tops.

Tommy jumped back onto the settee, nursing his big toe. 'Sorry my feet poo a bit. I took everything off without realising. I think I've cut myself now. Kath, do you want to see these? Ruth looked at them last week, so I've been meaning to show you ever since. No one's seen them apart from Ruth. Have a look, Kath.'

That was when I first saw his animals. When he'd told me about them in Norfolk, I'd seen in my mind scaled-down versions of the sort of pictures we'd done when we were small. So I was taken aback at how densely detailed each one was. In fact, it took a moment to see they were animals at all. The first impression was like one you'd get if you took the back off a radio set: tiny canals, weaving tendons, miniature screws and wheels were all drawn with obsessive precision, and only when you held the page away could you see it was some kind of armadillo, say, or a bird.

'It's my second book,' Tommy said. 'There's no way anyone's seeing the first one! It took me a while to get going.'

He was lying back on the settee now, tugging a sock over his foot and trying to sound casual, but I knew he was anxious for my reaction. Even so, for some time, I didn't come up with wholehearted praise. Maybe it was partly my worry that any art-work was liable to get him into trouble all over again. But also, what I was looking at was so different from anything the guardians had taught us to do at Hailsham, I didn't know how to judge it. I did say something like:

'God, Tommy, these must take so much concentration. I'm sur-prised you can see well enough in here to do all this tiny stuff.' And then, as I flicked through the pages, perhaps because I was still struggling to find the right thing to say, I came out with: 'I wonder what Madame would say if she saw these.'

I'd said it in a jokey tone, and Tommy responded with a little snigger, but then there was something hanging in the air that hadn't been there before. I went on turning the pages of the note-book – it was about a quarter full – not looking up at him, wish-ing I'd never brought up Madame. Finally I heard him say:

'I suppose I'll have to get a lot better before *she* gets to see any of it.'

I wasn't sure if this was a cue for me to say how good the draw-ings were, but by this time, I was becoming genuinely drawn to these fantastical creatures in front of me. For all their busy, metal-lic features, there was something sweet, even vulnerable about each of them. I remembered him telling me, in Norfolk, that he worried, even as he created them, how they'd protect themselves or be able to reach and fetch things, and looking at them now, I could feel the same sort of concerns. Even so, for some reason I couldn't fathom, something continued to stop me coming out with praise. Then Tommy said:

'Anyway, it's not only because of all that I'm doing the ani-mals. I just like doing them. I was wondering, Kath, if I should go on keeping it secret. I was thinking, maybe there's no harm in people knowing I do these. Hannah still does her watercolours, a lot of the veterans do stuff. I don't mean I'm going to go round *showing* everyone exactly. But I was thinking, well, there's no rea-son why I should keep it all secret any more.'

At last I was able to look up at him and say with some convic-tion: 'Tommy, there's no reason, no reason at all. These are good.

Really, really good. In fact, if that's why you're hiding in here now, it's really daft.'

He didn't say anything in response, but a kind of smirk appeared over his face, like he was enjoying a joke with himself, and I knew how happy I'd made him. I don't think we spoke much more to each other after that. I think before long he got his Wellingtons on, and we both left the goosehouse. As I say, that was about the only time Tommy and I touched directly on his theory that spring.

Then the summer came, and the one year point from when we'd first arrived. A batch of new students turned up in a minibus, much as we'd done, but none of them were from Hailsham. This was in some ways a relief: I think we'd all been getting anxious about how a fresh lot of Hailsham students might complicate things. But for me at least, this non-appearance of Hailsham students just added to a feeling that Hailsham was now far away in the past, and that the ties binding our old crowd were fraying. It wasn't just that people like Hannah were always talking about following Alice's example and starting their training; others, like Laura, had found boyfriends who weren't Hailsham and you could almost forget they'd ever had much to do with us.

And then there was the way Ruth kept pretending to forget things about Hailsham. Okay, these were mostly trivial things, but I got more and more irritated with her. There was the time, for instance, we were sitting around the kitchen table after a long breakfast, Ruth, me and a few veterans. One of the veterans had been talking about how eating cheese late at night always disturbed your sleep, and I'd turned to Ruth to say something like: 'You remember how Miss Geraldine always used to tell us that?' It was just a casual aside, and all it needed was for Ruth to smile or nod. But she made a point of staring back at me blankly, like she didn't have the faintest what I was talking about. Only when I said to the veterans, by way of explanation: 'One of our guardians,' did Ruth give a frowning nod, as though she'd just that moment remembered.

I let her get away with it that time. But there was another occasion when I didn't, that evening we were sitting out in the ruined bus shelter. I got angry then because it was one thing to play this game in front of veterans; quite another when it was just the two of us, in the middle of a serious talk. I'd referred, just in passing, to the fact that at Hailsham, the short-cut down to the pond through the rhubarb patch was out of bounds. When she put on her puzzled look, I abandoned whatever point I'd been trying to make and said: 'Ruth, there's no way you've forgotten. So don't give me that.'

Perhaps if I hadn't pulled her up so sharply – perhaps if I'd just made a joke of it and carried on – she'd have seen how absurd it was and laughed. But because I'd snapped at her, Ruth glared back and said:

'What does it matter anyway? What's the rhubarb patch got to do with any of this? Just get on with what you were saying.'

It was getting late, the summer evening was fading, and the old bus shelter felt musty and damp after a recent thunderstorm. So I didn't have the head to go into why it mattered so much. And though I did just drop it and carry on with the discussion we'd been having, the atmosphere had gone chilly, and could hardly have helped us get through the difficult matter in hand.

But to explain what we were talking about that evening, I'll have to go back a little bit. In fact, I'll have to go back several weeks, to the earlier part of the summer. I'd been having a relationship with one of the veterans, a boy called Lenny, which, to be honest, had been mainly about the sex. But then he'd suddenly opted to start his training and left. This unsettled me a little, and Ruth had been great about it, watching over me without seeming to make a fuss, always ready to cheer me up if I seemed gloomy. She also kept doing little favours for me, like making me sandwiches, or taking on parts of my cleaning rota.

Then about a fortnight after Lenny had gone, the two of us were sitting in my attic room some time after midnight chatting over mugs of tea, and Ruth got me really laughing about Lenny. He hadn't been such a bad guy, but once I'd started telling Ruth some of the more intimate things about him, it did seem like everything to do with him was hilarious, and we just kept laughing and laughing. Then at one point Ruth was running a finger up and down the cassettes stacked in little piles along my skirting board. She was doing this in an absent-minded sort of way while she kept laughing, but afterwards, I went through a spell of suspecting it hadn't been by chance at all; that she'd noticed it there maybe days before, perhaps even examined it to make sure, then had waited for the best time to 'find' it. Years later, I gently hinted this to Ruth, and she didn't seem to know what I was talking about, so maybe I was wrong. Anyway, there we were, laughing and laughing each time I came out with another detail about poor Lenny, and then suddenly it was like a plug had been pulled out. There was Ruth, lying on her side across my rug, peering at the spines of the cassettes in the low light, and then the Judy Bridgewater tape was in her hands. After what seemed an eternity, she said:

'So how long have you had this again?'

I told her, as neutrally as I could, about how Tommy and I had come across it that day while she'd been gone with the others. She went on examining it, then said:

'So Tommy found it for you.'

'No. I found it. I saw it first.'

'Neither of you told me.' She shrugged. 'At least, if you did, I never heard.'

'The Norfolk thing was true,' I said. 'You know, about it being the lost corner of England.'

It did flash through my mind Ruth would pretend not to remember this reference, but she nodded thoughtfully.

'I should have remembered at the time,' she said. 'I might have found my red scarf then.'

We both laughed and the uneasiness seemed to pass. But there was something about the way Ruth put the tape back without discussing it any further that made me think it wasn't finished with yet.

I don't know if the way the conversation went after that was something controlled by Ruth in the light of her discovery, or if we were headed that way anyway, and that it was only afterwards Ruth realised she could do with it what she did. We went back to discussing Lenny, in particular a lot of stuff about how he had sex, and we were laughing away again. At that point, I think I was just relieved she'd finally found the tape and not made a huge scene about it, and so maybe I wasn't being as careful as I might have been. Because before long, we'd drifted from laughing about Lenny to laughing about Tommy. At first it had all felt good-natured enough, like we were just being affectionate towards him. But then we were laughing about his animals.

As I say, I've never been sure whether or not Ruth deliberately moved things round to this. To be fair, I can't even say for certain she was the one who first mentioned the animals. And once we started, I was laughing just as much as she was – about how one of them looked like it was wearing underpants, how another had to have been inspired by a squashed hedgehog. I suppose I should have said in there somewhere that the animals were good, that he'd done really well to have got where he had with them. But I didn't. That was partly because of the tape; and maybe, if I have to be honest, because I was pleased by the notion that Ruth wasn't taking the animals seriously, and everything that implied. I think when we eventually broke up for the night, we felt as close as we'd ever done. She touched my cheek on her way out, saying: 'It's really good the way you always keep your spirits up, Kathy.'

So I wasn't prepared at all for what happened at the churchyard several days later. Ruth had discovered that summer a lovely old church about half a mile from the Cottages, which had behind it rambling grounds with very old gravestones leaning in the grass. Everything was overgrown, but it was really peaceful and Ruth had taken to doing a lot of her reading there, near the back railings, on a bench under a big willow. I hadn't at first been too keen on this development, remembering how the previous summer we'd all sat around together in the grass right outside the Cottages. All the same, if I was headed that way on one of my walks, and I knew Ruth was likely to be there, I'd find myself

176

going through the low wooden gate and along the overgrown path past the gravestones. On that afternoon, it was warm and still, and I'd come down the path in a dreamy mood, reading off names on the stones, when I saw not only Ruth, but Tommy on the bench under the willow.

Ruth was actually sitting on the bench, while Tommy was standing with one foot up on its rusty armrest, doing a kind of stretching exercise as they talked. It didn't look like they were having any big conversation and I didn't hesitate to go up to them. Maybe I should have picked up something in the way they greeted me, but I'm sure there wasn't anything obvious. I had some gossip I was dying to tell them – something about one of the newcomers – and so for a while it was just me blabbing on while they nodded and asked the odd question. It was some time before it occurred to me something wasn't right, and even then, when I paused and asked: 'Did I interrupt something here?' it was in a jokey sort of way.

But then Ruth said: 'Tommy's been telling me about his big theory. He says he's already told you. Ages ago. But now, very kindly, he's allowing me to share in it too.'

Tommy gave a sigh and was about to say something, but Ruth said in a mock whisper: 'Tommy's big Gallery theory!'

Then they were both looking at me, like I was now in charge of everything and it was up to me what happened next.

'It's not a bad theory,' I said. 'It might be right, I don't know. What do you think, Ruth?'

'I had to really dig it out of Sweet Boy here. Not very keen at all on letting me in on it, were you, sweety gums? It was only when I kept pressing him to tell me what was behind all this *art*.'

'I'm not doing it just for that,' Tommy said sulkily. His foot was still up on the armrest and he kept on with his stretching. 'All I said was, if it *was* right, about the Gallery, then I could always try and put in the animals . . .'

'Tommy, sweety, don't make a fool of yourself in front of our friend. Do it to me, that's all right. But not in front of our dear Kathy.'

'I don't see why it's such a joke,' Tommy said. 'It's as good a theory as anyone else's.'

'It's not the *theory* people will find funny, sweety gums. They might well buy the theory, right enough. But the idea that you'll swing it by showing Madame your little animals . . .' Ruth smiled and shook her head.

Tommy said nothing and continued with his stretching. I wanted to come to his defence and was trying to think of just the right thing that would make him feel better without making Ruth even more angry. But that was when Ruth said what she did. It felt bad enough at the time, but I had no idea in the churchyard that day how far-reaching the repercussions would be. What she said was:

'It's not just me, sweety. Kathy here finds your animals a complete hoot.'

My first instinct was to deny it, then just to laugh. But there was a real authority about the way Ruth had spoken, and the three of us knew each other well enough to know there had to be something behind her words. So in the end I stayed silent, while my mind searched back frantically, and with a cold horror, settled on that night up in my room with our mugs of tea. Then Ruth said:

'As long as people think you're doing those little creatures as a kind of joke, fine. But don't give out you're serious about it. Please.'

Tommy had stopped his stretching and was looking questioningly at me. Suddenly he was really child-like again, with no front whatsoever, and I could see too something dark and troubling gathering behind his eyes.

'Look, Tommy, you've got to understand,' Ruth went on. 'If Kathy and I have a good laugh about you, it doesn't really matter. Because that's just us. But please, let's not bring everyone else in on it.'

I've thought about those moments over and over. I should have found something to say. I could have just denied it, though Tommy probably wouldn't have believed me. And to try to explain the thing truthfully would have been too complicated. But I could have done something. I could have challenged Ruth, told her she was twisting things, that even if I might have laughed, it wasn't in the way she was implying. I could even have gone up to Tommy and hugged him, right there in front of Ruth. That's something that came to me years later, and probably wasn't a real option at the time, given the person I was, and the way the three of us were with each other. But that might have done it, where words would only have got us in deeper.

But I didn't say or do anything. It was partly, I suppose, that I was so floored by the fact that Ruth would come out with such a trick. I remember a huge tiredness coming over me, a kind of lethargy in the face of the tangled mess before me. It was like being given a maths problem when your brain's exhausted, and you know there's some far-off solution, but you can't work up the energy even to give it a go. Something in me just gave up. A voice went: 'All right, let him think the absolute worst. Let him think it, let him think it.' And I suppose I looked at him with resignation, with a face that said: 'Yes, it's true, what else did you expect?' And I can recall now, as fresh as anything, Tommy's own face, the anger receding for the moment, being replaced by an expression almost of wonder, like I was a rare butterfly he'd come across on a fence-post.

It wasn't that I thought I'd burst into tears or lose my temper or anything like that. But I decided just to turn and go. Even later that day, I realised this was a bad mistake. All I can say is that at the time what I feared more than anything was that one or the other of them would stalk off first, and I'd be left with the remaining one. I don't know why, but it didn't seem an option for more than one of us to storm off, and I wanted to make sure that one was me. So I turned and marched back the way I'd come, past the gravestones towards the low wooden gate, and for several minutes, I felt as though I'd triumphed; that now they'd been left in each other's company, they were suffering a fate they thoroughly deserved.

CHAPTER SEVENTEEN

As I've said, it wasn't until a long time afterwards – long after I'd left the Cottages – that I realised just how significant our little encounter in the churchyard had been. I was upset at the time, yes. But I didn't believe it to be anything so different from other tiffs we'd had. It never occurred to me that our lives, until then so closely interwoven, could unravel and separate over a thing like that.

But the fact was, I suppose, there were powerful tides tugging us apart by then, and it only needed something like that to finish the task. If we'd understood that back then – who knows? – maybe we'd have kept a tighter hold of one another.

For one thing, more and more students were going off to be carers, and among our old Hailsham crowd, there was a growing feeling this was the natural course to follow. We still had our essays to finish, but it was well known we didn't really have to finish them if we chose to start our training. In our early days at the Cottages, the idea of not finishing our essays would have been unthinkable. But the more distant Hailsham grew, the less important the essays seemed. I had this idea at the time – and I was probably right – that if our sense of the essays being important was allowed to seep away, then so too would whatever bound us together as Hailsham students. That's why I tried for a while to keep going our enthusiasm for all the reading and note-taking. But with no reason to suppose we'd ever see our guardians again, and with so many students moving on, it soon began to feel like a lost cause.

Anyway, in the days after that talk in the churchyard, I did what I could to put it behind us. I behaved towards both Tommy and Ruth as though nothing special had occurred, and they did much the same. But there was always something there now, and it wasn't just between me and them. Though they still made a show of being a couple – they still did the punching-on-the-arm thing when they parted – I knew them well enough to see they'd grown quite distant from each other.

Of course I felt bad about it all, especially about Tommy's animals. But it wasn't as simple any more as going to him and saying sorry and explaining how things really were. A few years earlier, even six months earlier, it might have worked out that way. Tommy and I would have talked it over and sorted it out. But somehow, by that second summer, things were different. Maybe it was because of this relationship with Lenny, I don't know. Anyway, talking to Tommy wasn't so easy any more. On the surface, at least, it was much like before, but we never mentioned the animals or what had happened in the churchyard.

So that was what had been happening just before I had that conversation with Ruth in the old bus shelter, when I got so annoyed with her for pretending to forget about the rhubarb patch at Hailsham. Like I said, I'd probably not have got nearly so cross if it hadn't come up in the middle of such a serious conversation. Okay, we'd got through a lot of the meat of it by then, but even so, even if we were just easing off and chatting by that point, that was still all part of our trying to sort things with each other, and there was no room for any pretend stuff like that.

What had happened was this. Although something had come between me and Tommy, it hadn't quite got like that with Ruth – or at least that's what I'd thought – and I'd decided it was time I talked with her about what had happened in the churchyard. We'd just had one of those summer days of rain and thunderstorms, and we'd been cooped up indoors despite the humidity. So when it appeared to clear for the evening, with a nice pink sunset, I suggested to Ruth we get a bit of air. There was a steep footpath I'd discovered leading up along the edge of the valley and just where it came out onto the road was an old bus shelter. The buses had stopped coming ages ago, the bus stop sign had been taken away, and on the wall at the back of the shelter, there was left only the frame of what must have once been a glassed-in notice displaying all the bus times. But the shelter itself – which was like a lovingly constructed wooden hut with one side open to the fields going down the valleyside – was still standing, and even had its bench intact. So that's where Ruth and I were sitting to get our breath back, looking at the cobwebs up on the rafters and the summer evening outside. Then I said something like:

'You know, Ruth, we should try and sort it out, what happened the other day.'

I'd made my voice conciliatory, and Ruth responded. She said immediately how daft it was, the three of us having rows over the most stupid things. She brought up other times we'd rowed and we laughed a bit about them. But I didn't really want Ruth just to bury the thing like that, so I said, still in the least challenging voice I could:

'Ruth, you know, I think sometimes, when you're in a couple, you don't see things as clearly as maybe someone can from the outside. Just sometimes.'

She nodded. 'That's probably right.'

'I don't want to interfere. But sometimes, just lately, I think Tommy's been quite upset. You know. About certain things you've said or done.'

I was worried Ruth would get angry, but she nodded and sighed. 'I think you're right,' she said in the end. 'I've been think-ing about it a lot too.'

'Then maybe I shouldn't have brought it up. I should have known you'd see what was happening. It's not my business really.'

'But it is, Kathy. You're really one of us, and so it's always your business. You're right, it hasn't been good. I know what you mean. That stuff the other day, about his animals. That wasn't good. I told him I was sorry about that.'

'I'm glad you talked it over. I didn't know if you had.'

Ruth had been picking at some moulding flakes of wood on the bench beside her, and for a moment she seemed completely absorbed in this task. Then she said:

'Look, Kathy, it's good we're talking now about Tommy. I've

been wanting to tell you something, but I've never quite known how to say it, or when, really. Kathy, promise you won't be too cross with me.'

I looked at her and said: 'As long as it's not about those T-shirts again.'

'No, seriously. Promise you won't get too cross. Because I've got to tell you this. I wouldn't forgive myself if I kept quiet much longer.'

'Okay, what is it?'

'Kathy, I've been thinking this for some time. You're no fool, and you can see that maybe me and Tommy, we might not be a couple for ever. That's no tragedy. We were right for each other once. Whether we always will be, that's anyone's guess. And now there's all this talk, about couples getting deferrals if they can prove, you know, that they're really right. Okay, look, what I wanted to say, Kathy, is this. It'd be completely natural if you'd thought about, you know, what would happen if me and Tommy decided we shouldn't be together any more. We're not about to split, don't get me wrong. But I'd think it was completely normal if you at least wondered about it. Well, Kathy, what you have to realise is that Tommy doesn't see you like that. He really, really likes you, he thinks you're really great. But I know he doesn't see you like, you know, a proper girlfriend. Besides . . .' Ruth paused, then sighed. 'Besides, you know how Tommy is. He can be fussy.'

I stared at her. 'What do you mean?'

'You must know what I mean. Tommy doesn't like girls who've been with . . . well, you know, with this person and that. It's just a thing he has. I'm sorry, Kathy, but it wouldn't be right not to have told you.'

I thought about it, then said: 'It's always good to know these things.'

I felt Ruth touch my arm. 'I knew you'd take it the right way. What you've got to understand, though, is that he thinks the world of you. He really does.'

I wanted to change the subject, but for the moment my mind

183

was a blank. I suppose Ruth must have picked up on this, because she stretched out her arms and did a kind of yawn, saying:

'If I ever learn to drive a car, I'd take us all on a trip to some wild place. Dartmoor, say. The three of us, maybe Laura and Hannah too. I'd love to see all the bogs and stuff.'

We spent the next several minutes talking about what we'd do on a trip like that if we ever went on one. I asked where we'd stay, and Ruth said we could borrow a big tent. I pointed out the wind could get really fierce in places like that and our tent could easily blow away in the night. None of this was that serious. But it was around here I remembered the time back at Hailsham, when we'd still been Juniors and we were having a picnic by the pond with Miss Geraldine. James B. had been sent to the main house to fetch the cake we'd all baked earlier, but as he was carrying it back, a strong gust of wind had taken off the whole top layer of sponge, tossing it into the rhubarb leaves. Ruth said she could only vaguely remember the incident, and I'd said, trying to clinch it for her memory:

'The thing was, he got into trouble because that proved he'd been coming down through the rhubarb patch.'

And that was when Ruth looked at me and said: 'Why? What was wrong with that?'

It was just the way she said it, suddenly so false even an onlooker, if there'd been one, would have seen through it. I sighed with irritation and said:

'Ruth, don't give me that. There's no way you've forgotten. You know that route was out of bounds.'

Maybe it was a bit sharp, the way I said it. Anyway, Ruth didn't back down. She continued pretending to remember nothing, and I got all the more irritated. And that was when she said:

'What does it matter anyway? What's the rhubarb patch got to do with anything? Just get on with what you were saying.'

After that I think we went back to talking in a more or less friendly way, and then before long we were making our way down the footpath in the half-light back to the Cottages. But the atmosphere never quite righted itself, and when we said our goodnights in front of the Black Barn, we parted without our usual little touches on the arms and shoulders.

It wasn't long after that I made my decision, and once I'd made it, I never wavered. I just got up one morning and told Keffers I wanted to start my training to become a carer. It was surprisingly easy. He was walking across the yard, his Wellingtons covered in mud, grumbling to himself and holding a piece of piping. I went up and told him, and he just looked at me like I'd bothered him about more firewood. Then he mumbled something about coming to see him later that afternoon to go through the forms. It was that easy.

It took a little while after that, of course, but the whole thing had been set in motion, and I was suddenly looking at everything – the Cottages, everybody there – in a different light. I was now one of the ones leaving, and soon enough, everyone knew it. Maybe Ruth thought we'd be spending hours talking about my future; maybe she thought she'd have a big influence on whether or not I changed my mind. But I kept a certain distance from her, just as I did from Tommy. We didn't really talk properly again at the Cottages, and before I knew it, I was saying my goodbyes.

Part Three

CHAPTER EIGHTEEN

For the most part being a carer's suited me fine. You could even say it's brought the best out of me. But some people just aren't cut out for it, and for them the whole thing becomes a real struggle. They might start off positively enough, but then comes all that time spent so close to the pain and the worry. And sooner or later a donor doesn't make it, even though, say, it's only the second donation and no one anticipated complications. When a donor completes like that, out of the blue, it doesn't make much difference what the nurses say to you afterwards, and neither does that letter saying how they're sure you did all you could and to keep up the good work. For a while at least, you're demoralised. Some of us learn pretty quick how to deal with it. But others – like Laura, say – they never do.

Then there's the solitude. You grow up surrounded by crowds of people, that's all you've ever known, and suddenly you're a carer. You spend hour after hour, on your own, driving across the country, centre to centre, hospital to hospital, sleeping in overnights, no one to talk to about your worries, no one to have a laugh with. Just now and again you run into a student you know – a carer or donor you recognise from the old days – but there's never much time. You're always in a rush, or else you're too exhausted to have a proper conversation. Soon enough, the long hours, the travelling, the broken sleep have all crept into your being and become part of you, so everyone can see it, in your posture, your gaze, the way you move and talk.

I don't claim I've been immune to all of this, but I've learnt to live with it. Some carers, though, their whole attitude lets them down. A lot of them, you can tell, are just going through the motions, waiting for the day they're told they can stop and become donors. It really gets me, too, the way so many of them 'shrink' the moment they step inside a hospital. They don't know what to say to the whitecoats, they can't make themselves speak up on behalf of their donor. No wonder they end up feeling frustrated and blaming themselves when things go wrong. I try not to make a nuisance of myself, but I've figured out how to get my voice heard when I have to. And when things go badly, of course I'm upset, but at least I can feel I've done all I could and keep things in perspective.

Even the solitude, I've actually grown to quite like. That's not to say I'm not looking forward to a bit more companionship come the end of the year when I'm finished with all of this. But I do like the feeling of getting into my little car, knowing for the next couple of hours I'll have only the roads, the big grey sky and my daydreams for company. And if I'm in a town somewhere with several minutes to kill, I'll enjoy myself wandering about looking in the shop windows. Here in my bedsit, I've got these four desk-lamps, each a different colour, but all the same design – they have these ribbed necks you can bend whichever way you want. So I might go looking for a shop with another lamp like that in its window – not to buy, but just to compare with my ones at home.

Sometimes I get so immersed in my own company, if I unexpectedly run into someone I know, it's a bit of a shock and takes me a while to adjust. That's the way it was the morning I was walking across the windswept car park of the service station and spotted Laura, sitting behind the wheel of one of the parked cars, looking vacantly towards the motorway. I was still some way away, and just for a second, even though we hadn't met since the Cottages seven years before, I was tempted to ignore her and keep walking. An odd reaction, I know, considering she'd been one of my closest friends. As I say, it may have been partly because I didn't like being bumped out of my daydreams. But also, I suppose, when I saw Laura slumped in her car like that, I saw immediately she'd become one of these carers I've just been describing, and a part of me just didn't want to find out much more about it.

But of course I did go to her. There was a chilly wind blowing against me as I walked over to her hatchback, parked away from the other vehicles. Laura was wearing a shapeless blue anorak, and her hair – a lot shorter than before – was sticking to her forehead. When I tapped on her window, she didn't start, or even look surprised to see me after all that time. It was almost like she'd been sitting there waiting, if not for me precisely, then for someone more or less like me from the old days. And now I'd shown up, her first thought seemed to be: 'At last!' Because I could see her shoulders move in a kind of sigh, then without further ado, she reached over to open the door for me.

We talked for about twenty minutes: I didn't leave until the last possible moment. A lot of it was about her, how exhausted she'd been, how difficult one of her donors was, how much she loathed this nurse or that doctor. I waited to see a flash of the old Laura, with the mischievous grin and inevitable wisecrack, but none of that came. She talked faster than she used to, and although she seemed pleased to see me, I sometimes got the impression it wouldn't have mattered much if it wasn't me, but someone else, so long as she got to talk.

Maybe we both felt there was something dangerous about bringing up the old days, because for ages we avoided any mention of them. In the end, though, we found ourselves talking about Ruth, who Laura had run into at a clinic a few years earlier, when Ruth was still a carer. I began quizzing her about how Ruth had been, but she was so unforthcoming, in the end I said to her:

'Look, you must have talked about *something*.'

Laura let out a long sigh. 'You know how it gets,' she said. 'We were both in a hurry.' Then she added: 'Anyway, we hadn't parted the best of friends, back at the Cottages. So maybe we weren't so delighted to see one another.'

'I didn't realise you'd fallen out with her too,' I said.

She shrugged. 'It wasn't any big deal. You remember the way she was back then. If anything, after you left, she got worse. You know, always telling everyone what to do. So I was keeping out

191

of her way, that was all. We never had a big fight or anything. So you haven't seen her since then?'

'No. Funny, but I've never even glimpsed her.'

'Yeah, it's funny. You'd think we'd all run into each other much more. I've seen Hannah a few times. And Michael H. too.' Then she said: 'I heard this rumour, that Ruth had a really bad first donation. Just a rumour, but I heard it more than once.'

'I heard that too,' I said.

'Poor Ruth.'

We were quiet for a moment. Then Laura asked: 'Is it right, Kathy? That they let you choose your donors now?'

She'd not asked in the accusing way people do sometimes, so I nodded and said: 'Not every time. But I did well with a few donors, so yeah, I get to have a say every now and then.'

'If you can choose,' Laura said, 'why don't you become Ruth's carer?'

I shrugged. 'I've thought about it. But I'm not sure it's such a great idea.'

Laura looked puzzled. 'But you and Ruth, you were so close.'

'Yeah, I suppose so. But like with you, Laura. She and I weren't such great friends by the end.'

'Oh, but that was back then. She's had a bad time. And I've heard she's had trouble with her carers too. They've had to change them around a lot for her.'

'Not surprising really,' I said. 'Can you imagine? Being Ruth's carer?'

Laura laughed, and for a second a look came into her eyes that made me think she was finally going to come out with a crack. But then the light died, and she just went on sitting there looking tired.

We talked a little more about Laura's problems – in particular about a certain nursing sister who seemed to have it in for her. Then it was time for me to go, and I reached for the door and was telling her we'd have to talk more the next time we met. But we were both of us by then acutely aware of something we'd not yet mentioned, and I think we both sensed there'd be something wrong about us parting like that. In fact, I'm pretty sure now, at that moment, our minds were running along exactly the same lines. Then she said:

'It's weird. Thinking it's all gone now.'

I turned in my seat to face her again. 'Yeah, it's really strange,' I said. 'I can't really believe it's not there any more.'

'It's so weird,' Laura said. 'I suppose it shouldn't make any difference to me now. But somehow it does.'

'I know what you mean.'

It was that exchange, when we finally mentioned the closing of Hailsham, that suddenly brought us close again, and we hugged, quite spontaneously, not so much to comfort one another, but as a way of affirming Hailsham, the fact that it was still there in both our memories. Then I had to hurry off to my own car.

I'd first started hearing rumours about Hailsham closing a year or so before that meeting with Laura in the car park. I'd be talking to a donor or a carer and they'd bring it up in passing, like they expected me to know all about it. 'You were at Hailsham, weren't you? So is it really true?' That sort of thing. Then one day I was coming out of a clinic in Suffolk and ran into Roger C., who'd been in the year below, and he told me with complete certainty it was about to happen. Hailsham was going to close any day and there were plans to sell the house and grounds to a hotel chain. I remember my first response when he told me this. I said: 'But what'll happen to all the students?' Roger obviously thought I'd meant the ones still there, the little ones dependent on their guardians, and he put on a troubled face and began speculating how they'd have to be transferred to other houses around the country, even though some of these would be a far cry from Hailsham. But of course, that wasn't what I'd meant. I'd meant *us*, all the students who'd grown up with me and were now spread across the country, carers and donors, all separated now but still somehow linked by the place we'd come from.

That same night, trying to get to sleep in an overnight, I kept thinking about something that had happened to me a few days earlier. I'd been in a seaside town in North Wales. It had been raining hard all morning, but after lunch, it had stopped and the sun had come out a bit. I was walking back to where I'd left my car, along one of those long straight seafront roads. There was hardly anyone else about, so I could see an unbroken line of wet paving stones stretching on in front of me. Then after a while a van pulled up, maybe thirty yards ahead of me, and a man got out dressed as a clown. He opened the back of the van and took out a bunch of helium balloons, about a dozen of them, and for a moment, he was holding the balloons in one hand, while he bent down and rummaged about in his vehicle with the other. As I came closer, I could see the balloons had faces and shaped ears, and they looked like a little tribe, bobbing in the air above their owner, waiting for him.

Then the clown straightened, closed up his van and started walking, in the same direction I was walking, several paces ahead of me, a small suitcase in one hand, the balloons in the other. The seafront continued long and straight, and I was walking behind him for what seemed like ages. Sometimes I felt awkward about it, and I even thought the clown might turn and say something. But since that was the way I had to go, there wasn't much else I could do. So we just kept walking, the clown and me, on and on along the deserted pavement still wet from the morning, and all the time the balloons were bumping and grinning down at me. Every so often, I could see the man's fist, where all the balloon strings converged, and I could see he had them securely twisted together and in a tight grip. Even so, I kept worrying that one of the strings would come unravelled and a single balloon would sail off up into that cloudy sky.

Lying awake that night after what Roger had told me, I kept seeing those balloons again. I thought about Hailsham closing, and how it was like someone coming along with a pair of shears and snipping the balloon strings just where they entwined above the man's fist. Once that happened, there'd be no real sense in which those balloons belonged with each other any more. When he was telling me the news about Hailsham, Roger had made a remark, saying he supposed it wouldn't make so much difference to the likes of us any more. And in certain ways, he might have been right. But it was unnerving, to think things weren't still going on back there, just as always; that people like Miss Geraldine, say, weren't leading groups of Juniors around the North Playing Field.

In the months after that talk with Roger, I kept thinking about it a lot, about Hailsham closing and all the implications. And it started to dawn on me, I suppose, that a lot of things I'd always assumed I'd plenty of time to get round to doing, I might now have to act on pretty soon or else let them go forever. It's not that I started to panic, exactly. But it definitely felt like Hailsham's going away had shifted everything around us. That's why what Laura said to me that day, about my becoming Ruth's carer, had such an impact on me, even though I'd stone-walled her at the time. It was almost like a part of me had already made that decision, and Laura's words had simply pulled away a veil that had been covering it over.

I first turned up at Ruth's recovery centre in Dover – the modern one with the white tiled walls – just a few weeks after that talk with Laura. It had been around two months since Ruth's first donation – which, as Laura had said, hadn't gone at all well. When I came into her room, she was sitting on the edge of her bed in her night-dress and gave me a big smile. She got up to give me a hug, but almost immediately sat down again. She told me I was looking better than ever, and that my hair suited me really well. I said nice things about her too, and for the next half hour or so, I think we were genuinely delighted to be with each other. We talked about all kinds of things – Hailsham, the Cottages, what we'd been doing since then – and it felt like we could talk and talk forever. In other words, it was a really encouraging start – better than I'd dared expect.

Even so, that first time, we didn't say anything about the way we'd parted. Maybe if we'd tackled it at the start, things would have played out differently, who knows? As it was, we just skipped over it, and once we'd been talking for a while, it was as if we'd agreed to pretend none of that had ever happened.

That may have been fine as far as that first meeting was concerned. But once I officially became her carer, and I began to see her regularly, the sense of something not being right grew stronger and stronger. I developed a routine of coming in three or four times a week in the late afternoon, with mineral water and a packet of her favourite biscuits, and it should have been wonderful, but at the beginning it was anything but that. We'd start talking about something, something completely innocent, and for no obvious reason we'd come to a halt. Or if we did manage to keep up a conversation, the longer we went on, the more stilted and guarded it became.

Then one afternoon, I was coming down her corridor to see her and heard someone in the shower room opposite her door. I guessed it was Ruth in there, so I let myself into her room, and was standing waiting for her, looking at the view from her window over all the rooftops. About five minutes passed, then she came in wrapped in a towel. Now to be fair, she wasn't expecting me for another hour, and I suppose we all feel a bit vulnerable after a shower with just a towel on. Even so, the look of alarm that went across her face took me aback. I have to explain this a bit. Of course, I was expecting her to be a little surprised. But the thing was, after she'd taken it in and seen it was me, there was a clear second, maybe more, when she went on looking at me if not with fear, then with a real wariness. It was like she'd been waiting and waiting for me to do something to her, and she thought the time had now come.

The look was gone the next instant and we just carried on as usual, but that incident gave us both a jolt. It made me realise Ruth didn't trust me, and for all I know, maybe she herself hadn't fully realised it until that moment. In any case, after that day, the atmosphere got even worse. It was like we'd let something out into the open, and far from clearing the air, it had made us more aware than ever of everything that had come between us. It got to the stage where before I went in to see her, I'd sit in my car for several minutes working myself up for the ordeal. After one particular session, when we did all the checks on her in stony silence, then afterwards just sat there in more silence, I was about ready to report to them that it hadn't worked out, that I should stop being Ruth's carer. But then everything changed again, and that was because of the boat.

God knows how these things work. Sometimes it's a particular joke, sometimes a rumour. It travels from centre to centre, right the way across the country in a matter of days, and suddenly every donor's talking about it. Well, this time it was to do with this boat. I'd first heard about it from a couple of my donors up in North Wales. Then a few days later, Ruth too started telling me about it. I was just relieved we'd found something to talk about, and encouraged her to go on.

'This boy on the next floor,' she said. 'His carer's actually been to see it. He says it's not far from the road, so anyone can get to it without much bother. This boat, it's just sitting there, stranded in the marshes.'

'How did it get there?' I asked.

'How do I know? Maybe they wanted to dump it, whoever owned it. Or maybe sometime, when everything was flooded, it just drifted in and got itself beached. Who knows? It's supposed to be this old fishing boat. With a little cabin for a couple of fishermen to squeeze into when it's stormy.'

The next few times I came to see her, she always managed to bring up the boat again. Then one afternoon, when she began telling me how one of the other donors at the centre had been taken by her carer to see it, I said to her:

'Look, it's not particularly near, you know. It would take an hour, maybe an hour and a half to drive.'

'I wasn't suggesting anything. I know you've got other donors to worry about.'

'But you'd like to see it. You'd like to see this boat, wouldn't you, Ruth?'

'I suppose so. I suppose I would. You spend day after day in this place. Yeah, it'd be good to see something like that.'

'And do you suppose' – I said this gently, without a hint of sarcasm – 'if we're driving all that way, we should think about calling in on Tommy? Seeing his centre's just down the road from where this boat's meant to be?'

Ruth's face didn't show anything at first. 'I suppose we could think about it,' she said. Then she laughed and added: 'Honest, Kathy, that wasn't the only reason I've been going on about the boat. I do want to see it, for its own sake. All this time in and out of hospital. Then cooped up here. Things like that matter more than they once did. But all right, I did know. I knew Tommy was at the Kingsfield centre.'

'Are you sure you want to see him?'

'Yes,' she said, no hesitation, looking straight at me. 'Yes, I do.' Then she said quietly: 'I haven't seen that boy for a long time. Not since the Cottages.'

Then, at last, we talked about Tommy. We didn't go into things in a big way and I didn't learn much I didn't know already. But I think we both felt better we'd finally brought him up. Ruth told me how, by the time she left the Cottages the autumn after me, she and Tommy had more or less drifted apart.

'Since we were going different places to do our training anyway,' she said, 'it didn't seem worth it, to split up properly. So we just stayed together until I left.'

And at that stage, we didn't say much more about it than that.

As for the trip out to see the boat, I neither agreed nor disagreed to it, that first time we discussed it. But over the next couple of weeks, Ruth kept bringing it up, and our plans somehow grew firmer, until in the end, I sent a message to Tommy's carer through a contact, saying that unless we heard from Tommy telling us not to, we'd show up at the Kingsfield on a particular afternoon the following week.

CHAPTER NINETEEN

I'd hardly ever been to the Kingsfield in those days, so Ruth and I had to consult the map a number of times on the way and we still arrived several minutes late. It's not very well-appointed as recovery centres go, and if it wasn't for the associations it now has for me, it's not somewhere I'd look forward to visiting. It's out of the way and awkward to get to, and yet when you're there, there's no real sense of peace and quiet. You can always hear traffic on the big roads beyond the fencing, and there's a general feeling they never properly finished converting the place. A lot of the donors' rooms you can't get to with a wheelchair, or else they're too stuffy or too draughty. There aren't nearly enough bathrooms and the ones there are are hard to keep clean, get freezing in winter and are generally too far from the donors' rooms. The Kingsfield, in other words, falls way short of a place like Ruth's centre in Dover, with its gleaming tiles and double-glazed windows that seal at the twist of a handle.

Later on, after the Kingsfield became the familiar and precious place it did, I was in one of the admin buildings and came across a framed black-and-white photo of the place the way it was before it was converted, when it was still a holiday camp for ordinary families. The picture was probably taken in the late fifties or early sixties, and shows a big rectangular swimming pool with all these happy people – children, parents – splashing about having a great time. It's concrete all around the pool, but people have set up deck chairs and sun loungers, and they've got large parasols to keep them in the shade. When I first saw this, it took me a while to realise I was looking at what the donors now call 'the Square' – the place where you drive in when you first arrive at the centre. Of course, the pool's filled in now, but the outline's still there, and they've left standing at one end – an example of this unfinished atmosphere – the metal frame for the high diving board. It was only when I saw the photo it occurred to me what the frame was and why it was there, and today, each time I see it, I can't help picturing a swimmer taking a dive off the top only to crash into the cement.

I might not have easily recognised the Square in the photo, except for the white bunker-like two-storey buildings in the background, on all three visible sides of the pool area. That must have been where the families had their holiday apartments, and though I'd guess the interiors have changed a lot, the outsides look much the same. In some ways, I suppose, the Square today isn't so different to what the pool was back then. It's the social hub of the place, where donors come out of their rooms for a bit of air and a chat. There are a few wooden picnic benches around the Square, but – especially when the sun's too hot, or it's raining – the donors prefer to gather under the overhanging flat roof of the recreation hall at the far end behind the old diving board frame.

That afternoon Ruth and I went to the Kingsfield, it was overcast and a bit chilly, and as we drove into the Square it was deserted except for a group of six or seven shadowy figures underneath that roof. As I brought the car to a stop somewhere over the old pool – which of course I didn't know about then – one figure detached itself from the group and came towards us, and I saw it was Tommy. He had on a faded green track-suit top and looked about a stone heavier than when I'd last seen him.

Beside me Ruth, for a second, seemed to panic. 'What do we do?' she went. 'Do we get out? No, no, let's not get out. Don't move, don't move.'

I don't know what I'd been intending to do, but when Ruth said this, for some reason, without really thinking about it, I just stepped out of the car. Ruth stayed where she was, and that was why, when Tommy came up to us, his gaze fell on me and why it was me he hugged first. I could smell a faint odour of something medical on him which I couldn't identify. Then, though we hadn't yet said anything to each other, we both sensed Ruth watching us from the car and pulled away.

There was a lot of sky reflected in the windscreen, so I couldn't make her out very well. But I got the impression Ruth had on a serious, almost frozen look, like Tommy and I were people in a play she was watching. There was something odd about the look and it made me uneasy. Then Tommy was walking past me to the car. He opened a rear door, got into the back seat, and then it was my turn to watch them, inside the car, exchanging words, then polite little kisses on the cheeks.

Across the Square, the donors under the roof were also watching, and though I felt nothing hostile about them, I suddenly wanted to get out of there quickly. But I made myself take my time getting back into the car, so that Tommy and Ruth could have a little longer to themselves.

We began by driving through narrow, twisting lanes. Then we came out into open, featureless countryside and travelled on along a near-empty road. What I remember about that part of our trip to the boat was that for the first time in ages the sun started to shine weakly through the greyness; and whenever I glanced at Ruth beside me, she had on a quiet little smile. As for what we talked about, well, my memory is that we behaved much as if we'd been seeing each other regularly, and there was no need to talk about anything other than what we had immediately in front of us. I asked Tommy if he'd been to see the boat already, and he said no, he hadn't, but a lot of the other donors at the centre had. He'd had a few opportunities, but hadn't taken them.

'I wasn't *not* wanting to go,' he said, leaning forward from the back. 'I couldn't be bothered really. I was going to go once, with a couple of others and their carers, but then I got a bit of bleeding and couldn't go any more. That was ages ago now. I don't get any trouble like that any more.'

Then a little further on, as we continued across the empty countryside, Ruth turned right round in her seat until she was facing Tommy, and just kept looking at him. She still had on her little smile, but said nothing, and I could see in my mirror Tommy looking distinctly uncomfortable. He kept looking out of the window beside him, then back at her, then back out of the window again. After a while, without taking her gaze off him, Ruth started on a rambling anecdote about someone or other, a donor at her centre, someone we'd never heard of, and all the time she kept looking at Tommy, the gentle smile never leaving her face. Perhaps because I was getting bored by her anecdote, perhaps because I wanted to help Tommy out, I interrupted after a minute or so, saying:

'Yeah, okay, we don't need to hear every last thing about her.'

I said this without any malice, and really hadn't intended anything by it. But even before Ruth paused, almost as I was still speaking, Tommy made a sudden laughing noise, a kind of explosion, a noise I'd never heard him make before. And he said:

'That's exactly what I was about to say. I lost track of it a while ago.'

My eyes were on the road, so I wasn't sure if he'd addressed me or Ruth. In any case, Ruth stopped talking and slowly turned back in her seat until she was facing the front again. She didn't seem particularly upset, but the smile had gone, and her eyes looked far away, fixed somewhere on the sky ahead of us. But I have to be honest: at that instant I wasn't really thinking about Ruth. My heart had done a little leap, because in a single stroke, with that little laugh of agreement, it felt as though Tommy and I had come close together again after all the years.

I found the turning we needed around twenty minutes after we'd set off from the Kingsfield. We went down a narrow curving road shrouded by hedges, and parked beside a clump of sycamores. I led the way to where the woods began, but then, faced with three distinct paths through the trees, had to stop to consult the sheet of directions I'd brought with me. While I stood there trying to decipher the person's handwriting, I was suddenly conscious of Ruth and Tommy standing behind me, not talking, waiting almost like children to be told which way to go.

We entered the woods, and though it was pretty easy walking, I noticed Ruth's breath coming less and less easily. Tommy, by contrast, didn't seem to be experiencing any difficulty, though there was a hint of a limp in his gait. Then we came to a barbed wire fence, which was tilted and rusted, the wire itself yanked all over the place. When Ruth saw it, she came to an abrupt halt.

'Oh no,' she said, anxiously. Then she turned to me: 'You didn't say anything about this. You didn't say we had to get past barbed wire!'

'It's not going to be difficult,' I said. 'We can go under it. We just have to hold it for each other.'

But Ruth looked really upset and didn't move. And it was then, as she stood there, her shoulders rising and falling with her breathing, that Tommy seemed to become aware for the first time just how frail she was. Maybe he'd noticed before, and hadn't wanted to take it in. But now he stared at her for a good few seconds. Then I think what happened next – though of course I can't know for certain – was that the both of us, Tommy and I, we remembered what had happened in the car, when we'd more or less ganged up on her. And almost as an instinct, we both went to her. I took an arm, Tommy supported her elbow on the other side, and we began gently guiding her towards the fence.

I let go of Ruth only to pass through the fence myself. Then I held up the wire as high as I could, and Tommy and I both helped her through. It wasn't so difficult for her in the end: it was more a confidence thing, and with us there for support, she seemed to lose her fear of the fence. On the other side, she actually made a go of helping me hold up the wire for Tommy. He came through without any bother, and Ruth said to him:

'It's only bending down like that. I'm sometimes not so clever at it.'

Tommy was looking sheepish, and I wondered if he was embarrassed by what had just happened, or if he was remembering again our ganging up on Ruth in the car. He nodded towards the trees in front of us and said:

'I suppose it's through that way. Is that right, Kath?'

I glanced at my sheet and began to lead the way again. Further into the trees, it grew quite dark and the ground became more and more marshy.

203

'Hope we don't get lost,' I heard Ruth say to Tommy with a laugh, but I could see a clearing not far away. And now with time to reflect, I realised why I was so bothered by what had happened in the car. It wasn't simply that we'd ganged up on Ruth: it was the way she'd just taken it. In the old days, it was inconceivable she'd have let something like that happen without striking back. As this point sunk in, I paused on the path, waited for Ruth and Tommy to catch up, and put my arm around Ruth's shoulders.

This didn't seem so soppy; it just looked like carer stuff, because by now there *was* something uncertain about her walk, and I wondered if I'd badly underestimated how weak she still was. Her breathing was getting quite laboured, and as we walked together, she'd now and then lurch into me. But then we were through the trees and into the clearing, and we could see the boat.

Actually, we hadn't really stepped into a clearing: it was more that the thin woods we'd come through had ended, and now in front of us there was open marshland as far as we could see. The pale sky looked vast and you could see it reflected every so often in the patches of water breaking up the land. Not so long ago, the woods must have extended further, because you could see here and there ghostly dead trunks poking out of the soil, most of them broken off only a few feet up. And beyond the dead trunks, maybe sixty yards away, was the boat, sitting beached in the marshes under the weak sun.

'Oh, it's just like my friend said it was,' Ruth said. 'It's really beautiful.'

We were surrounded by silence and when we started to move towards the boat, you could hear the squelch under our shoes. Before long I noticed my feet sinking beneath the tufts of grass, and called out: 'Okay, this is as far as we can go.'

The other two, who were behind me, raised no objection, and when I glanced over my shoulder, I saw Tommy was again holding Ruth by the arm. It was clear, though, this was just to steady her. I took long strides to the nearest dead tree trunk, where the soil was firmer, and held onto it for balance. Following my example, Tommy and Ruth made their way to another tree trunk, hollow and more emaciated than mine, a short way behind to my left. They perched on either side of it and seemed to settle. Then we gazed at the beached boat. I could now see how its paint was cracking, and how the timber frames of the little cabin were crumbling away. It had once been painted a sky blue, but now looked almost white under the sky.

'I wonder how it got here,' I said. I'd raised my voice to let it get to the others and had expected an echo. But the sound was surprisingly close, like I was in a carpeted room.

Then I heard Tommy say behind me: 'Maybe this is what Hailsham looks like now. Do you think?'

'Why would it look like this?' Ruth sounded genuinely puzzled. 'It wouldn't turn into marshland just because it's closed.'

'I suppose not. Wasn't thinking. But I always see Hailsham being like this now. No logic to it. In fact, this is pretty close to the picture in my head. Except there's no boat, of course. It wouldn't be so bad, if it's like this now.'

'That's funny,' Ruth said, 'because I was having this dream the other morning. I was dreaming I was up in Room 14. I knew the whole place had been shut down, but there I was, in Room 14, and I was looking out of the window and everything outside was flooded. Just like a giant lake. And I could see rubbish floating by under my window, empty drinks cartons, everything. But there wasn't any sense of panic or anything like that. It was nice and tranquil, just like it is here. I knew I wasn't in any danger, that it was only like that because it had closed down.'

'You know,' Tommy said, 'Meg B. was at our centre for a while. She's left now, gone up north somewhere for her third donation. I never heard how she got on. Have either of you heard?'

I shook my head, and when I didn't hear Ruth say anything, turned to look at her. At first I thought she was still staring at the boat, but then I saw her gaze was on the vapour trail of a plane in the far distance, climbing slowly into the sky. Then she said:

'I'll tell you something I heard. I heard about Chrissie. I heard she completed during her second donation.'

'I heard that as well,' said Tommy. 'It must be right. I heard exactly the same. A shame. Only her second as well. Glad that didn't happen to me.'

'I think it happens much more than they ever tell us,' Ruth said. 'My carer over there. She probably knows that's right. But she won't say.'

'There's no big conspiracy about it,' I said, turning back to the boat. 'Sometimes it happens. It was really sad about Chrissie. But that's not common. They're really careful these days.'

'I bet it happens much more than they tell us,' Ruth said again. 'That's one reason why they keep moving us around between donations.'

'I ran into Rodney once,' I said. 'It wasn't so long after Chrissie completed. I saw him in this clinic, up in North Wales. He was doing okay.'

'I bet he was cut up about Chrissie though,' said Ruth. Then to Tommy: 'They don't tell you the half of it, you see?'

'Actually,' I said, 'he wasn't too bad about it. He was sad, obviously. But he was okay. They hadn't seen each other for a couple of years anyway. He said he thought Chrissie wouldn't have minded too much. And I suppose he should know.'

'Why would he know?' Ruth said. 'How could he possibly know what Chrissie would have felt? What she would have wanted? It wasn't him on that table, trying to cling onto life. How would he know?'

This flash of anger was more like the old Ruth, and made me turn to her again. Maybe it was just the glare in her eyes, but she seemed to be looking back at me with a hard, stern expression.

'It can't be good,' Tommy said. 'Completing at the second donation. Can't be good.'

'I can't believe Rodney was okay about it,' Ruth said. 'You only spoke to him for a few minutes. How can you tell anything from that?'

'Yeah,' said Tommy, 'but if like Kath says, they'd already split up . . .'

'That wouldn't make any difference,' Ruth cut in. 'In some ways that might have made it worse.'

'I've seen a lot of people in Rodney's position,' I said. 'They do come to terms with it.'

'How would you know?' said Ruth. 'How could you possibly know? You're still a carer.'

'I get to see a lot as a carer. An awful lot.'

'She wouldn't know, would she, Tommy? Not what it's really like.'

For a moment we were both looking at Tommy, but he just went on gazing at the boat. Then he said:

'There was this guy, at my centre. Always worried he wouldn't make it past his second. Used to say he could feel it in his bones. But it all turned out fine. He's just come through his third now, and he's completely all right.' He put up a hand to shield his eyes. 'I wasn't much good as a carer. Never learnt to drive even. I think that's why the notice for my first came so early. I know it's not supposed to work that way, but I reckon that's what it was. Didn't mind really. I'm a pretty good donor, but I was a lousy carer.'

No one spoke for a while. Then Ruth said, her voice quieter now:

'I think I was a pretty decent carer. But five years felt about enough for me. I was like you, Tommy. I was pretty much ready when I became a donor. It felt right. After all, it's what we're *supposed* to be doing, isn't it?'

I wasn't sure if she expected me to respond to this. She hadn't said it in any obviously leading way, and it's perfectly possible this was a statement she'd come out with just out of habit – it was the sort of thing you hear donors say to each other all the time. When I turned to them again, Tommy still had his hand up to shade his eyes.

'Pity we can't go closer to the boat,' he said. 'One day when it's drier, maybe we could come back.'

'I'm glad to have seen it,' Ruth said, softly. 'It's really nice. But I think I want to go back now. This wind's quite chilly.'

'At least we've seen it now,' Tommy said.

*

We chatted much more freely on our walk back to the car than on the way out. Ruth and Tommy were comparing notes on their centres – the food, the towels, that kind of thing – and I was always part of the conversation because they kept asking me about other centres, if this or that was normal. Ruth's walk was much steadier now and when we came to the fence, and I held up the wire, she hardly hesitated.

We got in the car, again with Tommy in the back, and for a while there was a perfectly okay feeling between us. Maybe, looking back, there was an atmosphere of something being held back, but it's possible I'm only thinking that now because of what happened next.

The way it began, it was a bit like a repeat of earlier. We'd got back onto the long near-empty road, and Ruth made some remark about a poster we were passing. I don't even remember the poster now, it was just one of those huge advertising images on the roadside. She made the remark almost to herself, obviously not meaning much by it. She said something like: 'Oh my God, look at that one. You'd think they'd at least *try* to come up with something new.'

But Tommy said from the back: 'Actually I quite like that one. It's been in the newspapers as well. I think it's got something.'

Maybe I was wanting that feeling again, of me and Tommy being brought close together. Because although the walk to the boat had been fine in itself, I was starting to feel that apart from our first embrace, and that moment in the car earlier on, Tommy and I hadn't really had much to do with each other. Anyway, I found myself saying:

'Actually, I like it too. It takes a lot more effort than you'd think, making up these posters.'

'That's right,' Tommy said. 'Someone told me it takes weeks and weeks putting something like that together. Months even. People sometimes work all night on them, over and over, until they're just right.'

'It's too easy,' I said, 'to criticise when you're just driving by.'

'Easiest thing in the world,' Tommy said.

Ruth said nothing, and kept looking at the empty road in front of us. Then I said:

'Since we're on the subject of posters. There was one I noticed on the way out. It should be coming up again pretty soon. It'll be on our side this time. It should come up any time now.'

'What's it of?' Tommy asked.

'You'll see. It'll be coming up soon.'

I glanced at Ruth beside me. There was no anger in her eyes, just a kind of wariness. There was even a sort of hope, I thought, that when the poster appeared, it would be perfectly innocuous – something that reminded us of Hailsham, something like that. I could see all of this in her face, the way it didn't quite settle on any one expression, but hovered tentatively. All the time, her gaze remained fixed in front of her.

I slowed down the car and pulled over, bumping up onto the rough grass verge.

'Why are we stopping, Kath?' Tommy asked.

'Because you can see it best from here. Any nearer, we have to look up at it too much.'

I could hear Tommy shifting behind us, trying to get a better view. Ruth didn't move, and I wasn't even sure she was looking at the poster at all.

'Okay, it's not exactly the same,' I said after a moment. 'But it reminded me. Open-plan office, smart smiling people.'

Ruth stayed silent, but Tommy said from the back: 'I get it. You mean, like that place we went to that time.'

'Not only that,' I said. 'It's a lot like that ad. The one we found on the ground. You remember, Ruth?'

'I'm not sure I do,' she said quietly.

'Oh, come on. You remember. We found it in a magazine in some lane. Near a puddle. You were really taken by it. Don't pretend you don't remember.'

'I think I do.' Ruth's voice was now almost a whisper. A lorry went past, making our car wobble and, for a few seconds, obscuring our view of the hoarding. Ruth bowed her head, as though she hoped the lorry had removed the image forever, and when we could see it clearly again, she didn't raise her gaze.

'It's funny,' I said, 'remembering it all now. Remember how you used to go on about it? How you'd one day work in an office like that one?'

'Oh yeah, that was why we went that day,' Tommy said, like he'd only that second remembered. 'When we went to Norfolk. We went to find your possible. Working in an office.'

'Don't you sometimes think,' I said to Ruth, 'you should have looked into it more? All right, you'd have been the first. The first one any of us would have heard of getting to do something like that. But you might have done it. Don't you wonder sometimes, what might have happened if you'd tried?'

'How could I have tried?' Ruth's voice was hardly audible. 'It's just something I once dreamt about. That's all.'

'But if you'd at least looked into it. How do you know? They might have let you.'

'Yeah, Ruth,' Tommy said. 'Maybe you should at least have tried. After going on about it so much. I think Kath's got a point.'

'I didn't *go on* about it, Tommy. At least, I don't remember going on about it.'

'But Tommy's right. You should at least have tried. Then you could see a poster like that one, and remember that's what you wanted once, and that you at least looked into it . . .'

'How could I have looked into it?' For the first time, Ruth's voice had hardened, but then she let out a sigh and looked down again. Then Tommy said:

'You kept talking like you might qualify for special treatment. And for all you know, you might have done. You should have asked at least.'

'Okay,' Ruth said. 'You say I should have looked into it. How? Where would I have gone? There wasn't a way to look into it.'

'Tommy's right though,' I said. 'If you believed yourself special, you should at least have asked. You should have gone to Madame and asked.'

As soon as I said this – as soon as I mentioned Madame – I

realised I'd made a mistake. Ruth looked up at me and I saw something like triumph flash across her face. You see it in films sometimes, when one person's pointing a gun at another person, and the one with the gun's making the other one do all kinds of things. Then suddenly there's a mistake, a tussle, and the gun's with the second person. And the second person looks at the first person with a gleam, a kind of can't-believe-my-luck expression that promises all kinds of vengeance. Well, that was how suddenly Ruth was looking at me, and though I'd said nothing about deferrals, I'd mentioned Madame, and I knew we'd stumbled into some new territory altogether.

Ruth saw my panic and shifted round in her seat to face me. So I was preparing myself for her attack; busy telling myself that no matter what she came at me with, things were different now, she wouldn't get her way like she'd done in the past. I was telling myself all of this, and that's why I wasn't at all ready for what she did come out with.

'Kathy,' she said, 'I don't really expect you to forgive me ever. I can't even see why you should. But I'm going to ask you to all the same.'

I was so thrown by this, all I could find to say was a rather limp: 'Forgive you for what?'

'Forgive me for what? Well, for starters, there's the way I always lied to you about your urges. When you used to tell me, back then, how sometimes it got so you wanted to do it with virtually anyone.'

Tommy shifted again behind us, but Ruth was leaning forward now, looking straight at me, like for the moment Tommy wasn't with us in the car at all.

'I knew how it worried you,' she said. 'I should have told you. I should have said how it was the same for me too, just the way you described it. You realise all of this now, I know. But you didn't back then, and I should have said. I should have told you how even though I was with Tommy, I couldn't resist doing it with other people sometimes. At least three others when we were at the Cottages.'

She said this still without looking Tommy's way. But it wasn't so much like she was ignoring him, than that she was trying so intensely to get through to me everything else had been blurred out.

'I almost did tell you a few times,' she went on. 'But I didn't. Even then, at the time, I realised you'd look back one day and realise and blame me for it. But I still didn't say anything to you. There's no reason you should ever forgive me for that, but I want to ask now because . . .' She stopped suddenly.

'Because what?' I asked.

She laughed and said: 'Because nothing. I'd like you to forgive me, but I don't expect you to. Anyway, that's not the half of it, not even a small bit of it, actually. The main thing is, I kept you and Tommy apart.' Her voice had dropped again, almost to a whisper. 'That was the worst thing I did.'

She turned a little, taking Tommy in her gaze for the first time. Then almost immediately, she was looking just at me again, but now it was like she was talking to the both of us.

'That was the worst thing I did,' she said again. 'I'm not even asking you to forgive me about that. God, I've said all this in my head so many times, I can't believe I'm really doing it. It should have been you two. I'm not pretending I didn't always see that. Of course I did, as far back as I can remember. But I kept you apart. I'm not asking you to forgive me for that. That's not what I'm after just now. What I want is for you to put it right. Put right what I messed up for you.'

'How d'you mean, Ruth?' Tommy asked. 'How d'you mean, put it right?' His voice was gentle, full of child-like curiosity, and I think that was what started me sobbing.

'Kathy, listen,' Ruth said. 'You and Tommy, you've got to try and get a deferral. If it's you two, there's got to be a chance. A real chance.'

She'd reached out a hand and put it on my shoulder, but I shook her off roughly and glared at her through the tears.

'It's too late for that. Way too late.'

'It's not too late. Kathy, listen, it's not too late. Okay, so

Tommy's done two donations. Who says that has to make any difference?'

'It's too late for all that now.' I'd started to sob again. 'It's stupid even thinking about it. As stupid as wanting to work in that office up there. We're all way beyond that now.'

Ruth was shaking her head. 'It's not too late. Tommy, you tell her.'

I was leaning on the steering wheel, so couldn't see Tommy at all. He made a kind of puzzled humming sound, but didn't say anything.

'Look,' Ruth said, 'both of you, listen. I wanted us all to do this trip, because I wanted to say what I just said. But I also wanted it because I wanted to give you something.' She'd been rummaging in the pockets of her anorak, and now she held out a crumpled piece of paper. 'Tommy, you'd better take this. Look after it. Then when Kathy changes her mind, you'll have it.'

Tommy reached forward between the seats and took the paper. 'Thanks, Ruth,' he said, like she'd given him a chocolate bar. Then after a few seconds, he said: 'What is it? I don't get it.'

'It's Madame's address. It's like you were saying to me just now. You've at least got to try.'

'How d'you find it?' Tommy asked.

'It wasn't easy. It took me a long time, and I ran a few risks. But I got it in the end, and I got it for you two. Now it's up to you to find her and try.'

I'd stopped sobbing by now and started the engine. 'That's enough of all this,' I said. 'We've got to get Tommy back. Then we need to be getting back ourselves.'

'But you will think about it, both of you, won't you?'

'I just want to get back now,' I said.

'Tommy, you'll keep that address safe? In case Kathy comes round.'

'I'll keep it,' Tommy said. Then, much more solemnly than the last time: 'Thanks, Ruth.'

'We've seen the boat,' I said, 'but now we've got to get back. It might be over two hours back to Dover.'

I put the car on the road again, and my memory of it is that we didn't talk much more on the way back to the Kingsfield. There was still a small group of donors huddled under the roof as we came into the Square. I turned the car before letting Tommy out. Neither of us hugged or kissed him, but as he walked away towards his fellow donors, he paused and gave us a big smile and wave.

It might seem odd, but on the journey back to Ruth's centre, we didn't really discuss any of what had just happened. It was partly because Ruth was exhausted – that last conversation on the roadside seemed to have drained her. But also, I think we both sensed we'd done enough serious talking for one day, and that if we tried any more of it, things would start going wrong. I'm not sure how Ruth was feeling on that drive home, but as for me, once all the strong emotions had settled, once the night began to set in and all the lights came on along the roadside, I was feeling okay. It was like something that had been hanging over me for a long time had gone, and even if things were still far from sorted, it felt like there was now at least a door open to somewhere better. I'm not saying I was elated or anything like that. Everything between the three of us seemed really delicate and I felt tense, but it wasn't altogether a bad tension.

We didn't even discuss Tommy beyond saying how he looked okay, and wondering how much weight he'd put on. Then we spent large stretches of the journey watching the road together in silence.

It wasn't until a few days later I came to see what a difference that trip had made. All the guardedness, all the suspicions between me and Ruth evaporated, and we seemed to remember everything we'd once meant to each other. And that was the start of it, that era, with the summer coming on, and Ruth's health at least on an even keel, when I'd come in the evenings with biscuits and mineral water, and we'd sit side by side at her window, watching the sun go down over the roofs, talking about Hailsham, the Cottages, anything that drifted into our minds. When I think about Ruth now, of course, I feel sad she's gone; but I also feel really grateful for that period we had at the end.

There was, even so, one topic we never discussed properly, and that was about what she'd said to us on the roadside that day. Just every now and then, Ruth would allude to it. She'd come out with something like:

'Have you thought any more about becoming Tommy's carer? You know you could arrange it, if you wanted to.'

Soon, it was this idea – of my becoming Tommy's carer – that came to stand in for all the rest of it. I'd tell her I was thinking about it, that anyway it wasn't so simple, even for me, to arrange such a thing. Then we'd usually let the topic drop. But I could tell it was never far from Ruth's mind, and that's why, that very last time I saw her, even though she wasn't able to speak, I knew what it was she wanted to say to me.

That was three days after her second donation, when they finally let me in to see her in the small hours of the morning. She was in a room by herself, and it looked like they'd done everything they could for her. It had become obvious to me by then, from the way the doctors, the co-ordinator, the nurses were behaving, that they didn't think she was going to make it. Now I took one glance at her in that hospital bed under the dull light and recognised the look on her face, which I'd seen on donors often enough before. It was like she was willing her eyes to see right inside herself, so she could patrol and marshal all the better the separate areas of pain in her body – the way, maybe, an anxious carer might rush between three or four ailing donors in different parts of the country. She was, strictly speaking, still conscious, but she wasn't accessible to me as I stood there beside her metal bed. All the same, I pulled up a chair and sat with her hand in both of mine, squeezing whenever another flood of pain made her twist away from me.

I stayed beside her like that for as long as they let me, three hours, maybe longer. And as I say, for almost all of that time, she was far away inside herself. But just once, as she was twisting herself in a way that seemed scarily unnatural, and I was on the verge of calling the nurses for more painkillers, just for a few seconds, no more, she looked straight at me and she knew exactly who I was. It was one of those little islands of lucidity donors sometimes get to in the midst of their ghastly battles, and she looked at me, just for that moment, and although she didn't speak, I knew what her look meant. So I said to her: 'It's okay, I'm going to do it, Ruth. I'm going to become Tommy's carer as soon as I can.' I said it under my breath, because I didn't think she'd hear the words anyway, even if I shouted them. But my hope was that with our gazes locked as they were for those few seconds, she'd read my expression exactly as I'd read hers. Then the moment was over, and she was away again. Of course, I'll never know for sure, but I think she did understand. And even if she didn't, what occurs to me now is that she probably knew all along, even before I did, that I'd become Tommy's carer, and that we'd 'give it a try', just as she'd told us to in the car that day.

CHAPTER TWENTY

I became Tommy's carer almost a year to the day after that trip to see the boat. It wasn't long after Tommy's third donation, and though he was recovering well, he was still needing a lot of time to rest, and as it turned out, that wasn't a bad way at all for us to start this new phase together. Before long, I was getting used to the Kingsfield, growing to like it even.

Most donors at the Kingsfield get their own room after third donation, and Tommy was given one of the largest singles in the centre. Some people assumed afterwards I'd fixed it for him, but that wasn't the case; it was just luck, and anyway, it wasn't that great a room. I think it had been a bathroom back in the holiday camp days, because the only window had frosted glass and was really high up near the ceiling. You could only look out by standing on a chair and holding open the pane, and then you only got a view down onto the dense shrubbery. The room was L-shaped, which meant they could get in, as well as the usual bed, chair and wardrobe, a little school desk with a lift-up lid – an item that proved a real bonus, as I'll explain.

I don't want to give the wrong idea about that period at the Kingsfield. A lot of it was really relaxed, almost idyllic. My usual time to arrive was after lunch, and I'd come up to find Tommy stretched out on the narrow bed – always fully clothed because he didn't want to 'be like a patient'. I'd sit in the chair and read to him from various paperbacks I'd bring in, stuff like *The Odyssey* or *One Thousand and One Nights*. Otherwise we'd just talk, sometimes about the old days, sometimes about other things. He'd often doze off in the late afternoon, when I'd catch up on my reports over at his school desk. It was amazing really, the way the years seemed to melt away, and we were so easy with each other.

Obviously, though, not everything was like before. For a start,

Tommy and I finally started having sex. I don't know how much Tommy had thought about us having sex before we started. He was still recovering, after all, and maybe it wasn't the first thing on his mind. I wasn't wanting to force it on him, but on the other hand it had occurred to me if we left it too long, just when we were starting out together again, it would just get harder and harder to make it a natural part of us. And my other thought, I suppose, was that if our plans went along the lines Ruth had wanted, and we did find ourselves going for a deferral, it might prove a real drawback if we'd never had sex. I don't mean I thought this was necessarily something they'd ask us about. But my worry was that it would show somehow, in a kind of lack of intimacy.

So I decided to start it off one afternoon up in that room, in a way he could take or leave. He'd been lying on the bed as usual, staring at the ceiling while I read to him. When I finished, I went over, sat on the edge of the bed, and slid a hand under his T-shirt. Pretty soon I was down around his stuff, and though it took a while for him to get hard, I could tell straight away he was happy about it. That first time, we still had stitches to worry about, and anyway, after all the years of knowing each other and not having sex, it was like we needed some intermediary stage before we could get into it in a full-blown way. So after a while I just did it for him with my hands, and he just lay there not making any attempt to feel me up in return, not even making any noises, but just looking peaceful.

But even that first time, there was something there, a feeling, right there alongside our sense that this was a beginning, a gateway we were passing through. I didn't want to acknowledge it for a long time, and even when I did, I tried to persuade myself it was something that would go away along with his various aches and pains. What I mean is, right from that first time, there was something in Tommy's manner that was tinged with sadness, that seemed to say: 'Yes, we're doing this now and I'm glad we're doing it now. But what a pity we left it so late.'

And in the days that followed, when we had proper sex and we were really happy about it, even then, this same nagging feeling would always be there. I did everything to keep it away. I had us going at it all stops out, so that everything would become a delirious blur, and there'd be no room for anything else. If he was on top, I'd put my knees right up for him; whatever other position we used, I'd say anything, do anything I thought would make it better, more passionate, but it still never quite went away.

Maybe it was to do with that room, the way the sun came in through the frosted glass so that even in early summer, it felt like autumn light. Or maybe it was because the stray sounds that would occasionally reach us as we lay there were of donors milling about, going about their business around the grounds, and not of students sitting in a grassy field, arguing about novels and poetry. Or maybe it had to do with how sometimes, even after we'd done it really well and were lying in each other's arms, bits of what we'd just done still drifting through our heads, Tommy would say something like: 'I used to be able to do it twice in a row easy. But I can't any more.' Then that feeling would come right to the fore and I'd have to put my hand over his mouth, whenever he said things like that, just so we could go on lying there in peace. I'm sure Tommy felt it too, because we'd always hold each other very tight after times like that, as though that way we'd manage to keep the feeling away.

For the first few weeks after I arrived, we hardly brought up Madame or that conversation with Ruth in the car that day. But the very fact of my having become his carer served as a reminder that we weren't there to mark time. And so too, of course, did Tommy's animal drawings.

I'd often wondered about Tommy's animals over the years, and even that day we'd gone to see the boat, I'd been tempted to ask him about them. Was he still drawing them? Had he kept the ones from the Cottages? But the whole history around them had made it difficult for me to ask.

Then one afternoon, maybe about a month after I'd started, I came up to his room and found him at his school desk, carefully going over a drawing, his face nearly touching the paper. He'd called for me to come in when I'd knocked, but now he didn't raise his head or stop what he was doing, and just a glance told me he was working on one of his imaginary creatures. I stopped in the doorway, uncertain whether I should come in, but eventually he looked up and closed his notebook – which I noticed looked identical to the black books he'd got from Keffers all those years ago. I came in then and we began talking about something else entirely, and after a while he put away his notebook without us mentioning it. But after that, I'd often come in and see it left on the desk or tossed beside his pillow.

Then one day we were up in his room with several minutes to kill before we set off for some checks, and I noticed something odd coming into his manner: something coy and deliberate which made me think he was after some sex. But then he said:

'Kath, I just want you to tell me. Tell me honestly.'

Then the black notebook came out of his desk, and he showed me three separate sketches of a kind of frog – except with a long tail as though a part of it had stayed a tadpole. At least, that's what it looked like when you held it away from you. Close up, each sketch was a mass of minute detail, much like the creatures I'd seen years before.

'These two I did thinking they were made of metal,' he said. 'See, everything's got shiny surfaces. But this one here, I thought I'd try making him rubbery. You see? Almost blobby. I want to do a proper version now, a really good one, but I can't decide. Kath, be honest, what do you think?'

I can't remember what I answered. What I do remember is the strong mix of emotions that engulfed me at that moment. I realised immediately this was Tommy's way of putting behind us everything that had happened around his drawings back at the Cottages, and I felt relief, gratitude, sheer delight. But I was aware too why the animals had emerged again, and of all the possible layers behind Tommy's apparently casual query. At the least, I could see, he was showing me he hadn't forgotten, even though we'd hardly discussed anything openly; he was telling me he wasn't complacent, and that he was busy getting on with his part of the preparations.

But that wasn't all I felt looking at those peculiar frogs that day. Because it was there again, only faint and in the background at first, but growing all the while, so that afterwards it was what I kept thinking about. I couldn't help it, as I looked at those pages, the thought went through my mind, even as I tried to grab it and put it away. It came to me that Tommy's drawings weren't as fresh now. Okay, in many ways these frogs were a lot like what I'd seen back at the Cottages. But something was definitely gone, and they looked laboured, almost like they'd been copied. So that feeling came again, even though I tried to keep it out: that we were doing all of this too late; that there'd once been a time for it, but we'd let that go by, and there was something ridiculous, reprehensible even, about the way we were now thinking and planning.

Now I'm going over this again, it occurs to me that might have been another reason we were so slow to talk openly to each other about our plans. It was certainly the case that none of the other donors at the Kingsfield were ever heard talking about deferrals or anything like that, and we were probably vaguely embarrassed, almost like we shared a shameful secret. We might even have been scared of what might happen if word got out to the others.

But as I say, I don't want to paint too gloomy a view of that time at the Kingsfield. For a lot of it, especially after that day he asked me about his animals, there seemed to be no more shadows left from the past, and we really settled into each other's company. And though he never asked me again for advice about his pictures, he was happy to work on them in front of me, and we'd often spend our afternoons like that: me on the bed, maybe reading aloud; Tommy at the desk, drawing.

Perhaps we'd have been happy if things had stayed that way for a lot longer; if we could have whiled away more afternoons chatting, having sex, reading aloud and drawing. But with the summer drawing to an end, with Tommy getting stronger, and the possibility of notice for his fourth donation growing ever more distinct, we knew we couldn't keep putting things off indefinitely.

It had been an unusually busy period for me, and I'd not been to the Kingsfield for almost a week. I arrived in the morning that day, and I remember it was bucketing down. Tommy's room was almost dark, and you could hear a gutter splashing away near his window. He'd been down to the main hall for breakfast with his fellow donors, but had come back up again and was now sitting on his bed, looking vacant, not doing anything. I came in exhausted – I'd not had a proper night's sleep for ages – and just collapsed onto his narrow bed, pushing him against the wall. I lay like that for a few moments, and might easily have fallen asleep if Tommy hadn't kept prodding my knees with a toe. Then finally I sat up beside him and said:

'I saw Madame yesterday, Tommy. I never spoke to her or anything. But I saw her.'

He looked at me, but stayed quiet.

'I saw her come up the street and go into her house. Ruth got it right. The right address, right door, everything.'

Then I described to him how the previous day, since I was down on the south coast anyway, I'd gone to Littlehampton in the late afternoon, and just as I'd done the last two times, walked down that long street near the seafront, past rows of terraced houses with names like 'Wavecrest' and 'Sea View', until I'd come to the public bench beside the phone box. And I'd sat down and waited – again, the way I'd done before – with my eyes fixed on the house over the street.

'It was just like detective stuff. The previous times, I'd sat there for over half an hour each go, and nothing, absolutely nothing. But something told me I'd be lucky this time.'

I'd been so tired, I'd nearly nodded off right there on the bench. But then I'd looked up and she was there, coming down the street towards me.

'It was really spooky,' I said, 'because she looked exactly the same. Maybe her face was slightly older. But otherwise, there was no real difference. Same clothes even. That smart grey suit.'

'It couldn't *literally* have been the same suit.'

'I don't know. It looked like it was.'

'So you didn't try and speak to her?'

'Of course not, stupid. Just one step at a time. She was never exactly nice to us, remember.'

I told him how she'd walked right past me on the opposite side, never glancing over to me; how for a second I thought she would also go past the door I'd been watching – that Ruth had got the wrong address. But Madame had turned sharply at the gate, covered the tiny front path in two or three steps and vanished inside.

After I'd finished, Tommy stayed quiet for some time. Then he said:

'You sure you won't get into trouble? Always driving out to places you're not supposed to be?'

'Why do you think I'm so tired? I've been working all kinds of hours to get everything in. But at least we've found her now.'

The rain kept splashing outside. Tommy turned onto his side and put his head on my shoulder.

'Ruth did well for us,' he said, softly. 'She got it right.'

'Yeah, she did well. But now it's up to us.'

'So what's the plan, Kath? Have we got one?'

'We just go there. We just go there and ask her. Next week, when I take you for the lab tests. I'll get you signed out for the whole day. Then we can go to Littlehampton on the way back.'

Tommy gave a sigh and put his head deeper into my shoulder. Someone watching might have thought he was being unenthusiastic, but I knew what he was feeling. We'd been thinking about the deferrals, the theory about the Gallery, all of it, for so long – and now, suddenly, here we were. It was definitely a bit scary.

'If we get this,' he said, eventually. 'Just suppose we do. Suppose she lets us have three years, say, just to ourselves. What do we do exactly? See what I mean, Kath? Where do we go? We can't stay here, this is a centre.'

'I don't know, Tommy. Maybe she'll tell us to go back to the

Cottages. But it'd be better somewhere else. The White Mansion, maybe. Or perhaps they've got some other place. Somewhere separate for people like us. We'll just have to see what she says.'

We lay quietly on the bed for a few more minutes, listening to the rain. At some stage, I began prodding him with a foot, the way he'd been doing to me earlier. Eventually he retaliated and pushed my feet off the bed altogether.

'If we're really going,' he said, 'we'll have to decide about the animals. You know, choose the best ones to take along. Maybe six or seven. We'll have to do it quite carefully.'

'Okay,' I said. Then I stood up and stretched out my arms. 'Maybe we'll take more. Fifteen, twenty even. Yeah, we'll go and see her. What can she do to us? We'll go and talk to her.'

CHAPTER TWENTY-ONE

From days before we went, I'd had in my mind this picture of me and Tommy standing in front of that door, working up the nerve to press the bell, then having to wait there with hearts thumping. The way it turned out, though, we got lucky and were spared that particular ordeal.

We deserved a bit of luck by then, because the day hadn't been going at all well. The car had played up on the journey out and we were an hour late for Tommy's tests. Then a mix-up at the clinic had meant Tommy having to re-do three of the tests. This had left him feeling pretty woozy, so when we finally set off for Littlehampton towards the end of the afternoon, he began to feel carsick and we had to keep stopping to let him walk it off.

We finally arrived just before six o'clock. We parked the car behind the bingo hall, took out from the boot the sports bag containing Tommy's notebooks, then set off towards the town centre. It had been a fine day and though the shops were all closing, a lot of people were hanging about outside the pubs, talking and drinking. Tommy began to feel better the more we walked, until eventually he remembered how he'd had to miss lunch because of the tests, and declared he'd have to eat before facing what was in front of us. So we were searching for some place to buy a take-away sandwich, when he suddenly grabbed my arm, so hard I thought he was having some sort of attack. But then he said quietly into my ear:

'That's her, Kath. Look. Going past the hairdressers.'

And sure enough there she was, moving along the opposite pavement, dressed in her neat grey suit, just like the ones she'd always worn.

We set off after Madame at a reasonable distance, first through the pedestrian precinct, then along the near-deserted High Street.

I think we were both reminded of that day we'd followed Ruth's possible through another town. But this time things proved far simpler, because pretty soon she'd led us onto that long seafront street.

Because the road was completely straight, and because the setting sun was falling on it all the way down to the end, we found we could let Madame get quite a way ahead – till she wasn't much more than a dot – and there'd still be no danger of losing her. In fact, we never even stopped hearing the echo of her heels, and the rhythmic thudding of Tommy's bag against his leg seemed to be a kind of answer.

We went on like that for a long time, past the rows of identical houses. Then the houses on the opposite pavement ran out, areas of flat lawn appeared in their place, and you could see, beyond the lawns, the tops of the beach huts lining the seafront. The water itself wasn't visible, but you could tell it was there, just from the big sky and the seagull noises.

But the houses on our side continued without a change, and after a while I said to Tommy:

'It's not long now. See that bench over there? That's the one I sit on. The house is just over from it.'

Until I said this, Tommy had been pretty calm. But now something seemed to get into him, and he began to walk much faster, like he wanted to catch up with her. But now there was no one between Madame and us, and as Tommy kept closing the gap, I had to grab his arm to slow him down. I was all the time afraid she'd turn and look at us, but she didn't, and then she was going in through her little gateway. She paused at her door to find her keys in her handbag, and then there we were, standing by her gate, watching her. She still didn't turn, and I had an idea that she'd been aware of us all along and was deliberately ignoring us. I thought too that Tommy was about to shout something to her, and that it would be the wrong thing. That was why I called from the gate, so quickly and without hesitation.

It was only a polite 'Excuse me!' but she spun round like I'd thrown something at her. And as her gaze fell on us, a chill passed through me, much like the one I'd felt years ago that time we'd waylaid her outside the main house. Her eyes were as cold, and her face maybe even more severe than I remembered. I don't know if she recognised us at that point; but without doubt, she saw and decided in a second *what we were*, because you could see her stiffen – as if a pair of large spiders was set to crawl towards her.

Then something changed in her expression. It didn't become warmer exactly. But that revulsion got put away somewhere, and she studied us carefully, squinting in the setting sun.

'Madame,' I said, leaning over the gate. 'We don't want to shock you or anything. But we were at Hailsham. I'm Kathy H., maybe you remember. And this is Tommy D. We haven't come to give you any trouble.'

She came a few steps back towards us. 'From Hailsham,' she said, and a small smile actually went across her face. 'Well, this is a surprise. If you aren't here to give me trouble, then why are you here?'

Suddenly Tommy said: 'We have to talk with you. I've brought some things' – he raised his bag – 'some things you might want for your gallery. We've got to talk with you.'

Madame went on standing there, hardly moving in the low sun, her head tilted as though listening for some sound from the seafront. Then she smiled again, though the smile didn't seem to be for us, but just herself.

'Very well then. Come inside. Then we'll see what it is you wish to talk about.'

As we went in, I noticed the front door had coloured glass panels, and once Tommy closed it behind us, everything got pretty dark. We were in a hallway so narrow you felt you'd be able to touch the walls on either side just by stretching out your elbows. Madame had stopped in front of us, and was standing still, her back to us, again like she was listening. Peering past her, I saw that the hallway, narrow as it was, divided further: to the left was a staircase going upstairs; to the right, an even narrower passage leading deeper into the house.

Following Madame's example, I listened too, but there was only silence in the house. Then, maybe from somewhere upstairs, there was a faint thump. That small noise seemed to signify something to her, because she now turned to us and pointing into the darkness of the passage, said:

'Go in there and wait for me. I'll be down shortly.'

She began to climb the stairs, then seeing our hesitation, leaned over the banister and pointed again into the dark.

'In there,' she said, then vanished upstairs.

Tommy and I wandered forward and found ourselves in what must have been the front room of the house. It was like a servant of some sort had got the place ready for the night-time, then left: the curtains were closed and there were dim table lamps switched on. I could smell the old furniture, which was probably Victorian. The fireplace had been sealed off with a board, and where the fire would have been, there was a picture, woven like a tapestry, of a strange owl-like bird staring out at you. Tommy touched my arm and pointed to a framed picture hanging in a corner over a little round table.

'It's Hailsham,' he whispered.

We went up to it, but then I wasn't so sure. I could see it was a pretty nice watercolour, but the table lamp beneath it had a crooked shade covered with cobweb traces, and instead of lighting up the picture, it just put a shine over the murky glass, so you could hardly make it out at all.

'It's the bit round the back of the duck pond,' Tommy said.

'What do you mean?' I whispered back. 'There's no pond. It's just a bit of countryside.'

'No, the pond's behind you.' Tommy seemed surprisingly irritated. 'You must be able to remember. If you're round the back with the pond behind you, and you're looking over towards the North Playing Field . . .'

We went silent again because we could hear voices somewhere in the house. It sounded like a man's voice, maybe coming from upstairs. Then we heard what was definitely Madame's voice coming down the stairs, saying: 'Yes, you're quite right. Quite right.'

We waited for Madame to come in, but her footsteps went past the door and to the back of the house. It flashed through my mind she was going to prepare tea and scones and bring it all in on a trolley, but then I decided that was rubbish, that she'd just as likely forgotten about us, and now she'd suddenly remember, come in and tell us to leave. Then a gruff male voice called something from upstairs, so muffled it might have been two floors up. Madame's footsteps came back into the hallway, then she called up: 'I've told you what to do. Just do as I explained.'

Tommy and I waited several more minutes. Then the wall at the back of the room began to move. I saw almost immediately it wasn't really a wall, but a pair of sliding doors which you could use to section off the front half of what was otherwise one long room. Madame had rolled back the doors just part of the way, and she was now standing there staring at us. I tried to see past her, but it was just darkness. I thought maybe she was waiting for us to explain why we were there, but in the end, she said:

'You told me you were Kathy H. and Tommy D. Am I correct? And you were at Hailsham how long ago?'

I told her, but there was no way of telling if she remembered us or not. She just went on standing there at the threshold, as though hesitating to come in. But now Tommy spoke again:

'We don't want to keep you long. But there's something we have to talk to you about.'

'So you say. Well then. You'd better make yourselves comfortable.'

She reached out and put her hands on the backs of two matching armchairs just in front of her. There was something odd about her manner, like she hadn't really invited us to sit down. I felt that if we did as she was suggesting and sat on those chairs, she'd just go on standing behind us, not even taking her hands away from the backs. But when we made a move towards her, she too came forwards, and – perhaps I imagined it – tucked her shoulders in tightly as she passed between us. When we turned to sit down, she was over by the windows, in front of the heavy velvet curtains, holding us in a glare, like we were in a class and she was a teacher. At least, that's the way it looked to me at that moment. Tommy, afterwards, said he thought she was about to burst into song, and that those curtains behind her would open, and instead of the street and the flat grassy expanse leading to the seafront, there'd be this big stage set, like the ones we'd had at Hailsham, with even a chorus line to back her up. It was funny, when he said that afterwards, and I could see her again then, hands clasped, elbows out, sure enough like she was getting ready to sing. But I doubt if Tommy was really thinking anything like that at the time. I remember noticing how tense he'd got, and worrying he'd blurt out something completely daft. That was why, when she asked us, not unkindly, what it was we wanted, I stepped in quickly.

It probably came out pretty muddled at first, but after a while, as I became more confident she'd hear me out, I calmed down and got a lot clearer. I'd been turning over in my mind for weeks and weeks just what I'd say to her. I'd gone over it during those long car journeys, and while sitting at quiet tables in service-station cafés. It had seemed so difficult then, and I'd eventually resorted to a plan: I'd memorised word for word a few key lines, then drawn a mental map of how I'd go from one point to the next. But now she was there in front of me, most of what I'd prepared seemed either unnecessary or completely wrong. The strange thing was – and Tommy agreed when we discussed it afterwards – although at Hailsham she'd been like this hostile stranger from the outside, now that we were facing her again, even though she hadn't said or done anything to suggest any warmth towards us, Madame now appeared to me like an intimate, someone much closer to us than anyone new we'd met over the recent years. That's why suddenly all the things I'd been preparing in my head just went, and I spoke to her honestly and simply, almost as I might have done years ago to a guardian. I told her what we'd heard, the rumours about Hailsham students and deferrals; how we realised the rumours might not be accurate, and that we weren't banking on anything.

'And even if it *is* true,' I said, 'we know you must get tired of it, all these couples coming to you, claiming to be in love. Tommy and me, we never would have come and bothered you if we weren't really sure.'

'Sure?' It was the first time she'd spoken for ages and we both jolted back a bit in surprise. 'You say you're *sure*? Sure that you're in love? How can you know it? You think love is so simple? So you are in love. Deeply in love. Is that what you're saying to me?'

Her voice sounded almost sarcastic, but then I saw, with a kind of shock, little tears in her eyes as she looked from one to the other of us.

'You believe this? That you're deeply in love? And therefore you've come to me for this . . . this deferral? Why? Why did you come to me?'

If she'd asked this in a certain way, like the whole idea was completely crazy, then I'm sure I'd have felt pretty devastated. But she hadn't quite said it like that. She'd asked it almost like it was a test question she knew the answer to; as if, even, she'd taken other couples through an identical routine many times before. That was what kept me hopeful. But Tommy must have got anxious, because he suddenly burst in:

'We came to see you because of your gallery. We think we know what your gallery's for.'

'My gallery?' She leaned back on the window ledge, causing the curtains to sway behind her, and took a slow breath. 'My gallery. You must mean my collection. All those paintings, poems, all those things of yours I gathered over the years. It was hard work for me, but I believed in it, we all did in those days. So you think you know what it was for, why we did it. Well, that would be most interesting to hear. Because I have to say, it's a question I ask myself all the time.' She suddenly switched her gaze from Tommy to me. 'Do I go too far?' she asked.

I didn't know what to say, so just replied: 'No, no.'

'I go too far,' she said. 'I'm sorry. I often go too far on this subject. Forget what I just said. Young man, you were going to tell me about my gallery. Please, let me hear.'

'It's so you could tell,' Tommy said. 'So you'd have something to go on. Otherwise how would you know when students came to you and said they were in love?'

Madame's gaze had drifted over to me again, but I had the feeling she was staring at something on my arm. I actually looked down to see if there was birdshit or something on my sleeve. Then I heard her say:

'And this is why you think I gathered all those things of yours. My *gallery*, as all of you always called it. I laughed when I first heard that's what you were calling it. But in time, I too came to think of it as that. My gallery. Now why, young man, explain it to me. Why would my gallery help in telling which of you were really in love?'

'Because it would help show you what we were like,' Tommy said. 'Because . . .'

'Because of course' – Madame cut in suddenly – 'your art will reveal your inner selves! That's it, isn't it? Because your art will display your *souls*!' Then suddenly she turned to me again and said: 'I go too far?'

She'd said this before, and I again had the impression she was staring at a spot on my sleeve. But by this point a faint suspicion I'd had ever since the first time she'd asked 'I go too far?' had started to grow. I looked at Madame carefully, but she seemed to sense my scrutiny and she turned back to Tommy.

'All right,' she said. 'Let us continue. What was it you were telling me?'

'The trouble is,' Tommy said, 'I was a bit mixed up in those days.'

'You were saying something about your art. How art bares the soul of the artist.'

'Well, what I'm trying to say,' Tommy persisted, 'is that I was so mixed up in those days, I didn't really do any art. I didn't do anything. I know now I should have done, but I was mixed up. So you haven't got anything of mine in your gallery. I know that's my fault, and I know it's probably way too late, but I've brought some things with me now.' He raised his bag, then began to unzip it. 'Some of it was done recently, but some of it's from quite a long

232

time ago. You should have Kath's stuff already. She got plenty into the Gallery. Didn't you, Kath?'

For a moment they were both looking at me. Then Madame said, barely audibly:

'Poor creatures. What did we do to you? With all our schemes and plans?' She let that hang, and I thought I could see tears in her eyes again. Then she turned to me and asked: 'Do we continue with this talk? You wish to go on?'

It was when she said this that the vague idea I'd had before became something more substantial. 'Do I go too far?' And now: 'Do we continue?' I realised, with a little chill, that these questions had never been for me, or for Tommy, but for someone else – someone listening behind us in the darkened half of the room.

I turned round quite slowly and looked into the darkness. I couldn't see anything, but I heard a sound, a mechanical one, surprisingly far away – the house seemed to go much further back into the dark than I'd guessed. Then I could make out a shape moving towards us, and a woman's voice said: 'Yes, Marie-Claude. Let us carry on.'

I was still looking into the darkness when I heard Madame let out a kind of snort, and she came striding past us and on into the dark. Then there were more mechanical sounds, and Madame emerged pushing a figure in a wheelchair. She passed between us again, and for a moment longer, because Madame's back was blocking the view, I couldn't see the person in the wheelchair. But then Madame steered it around to face us and said:

'You speak to them. It's you they've come to speak to.'

'I suppose it is.'

The figure in the wheelchair was frail and contorted, and it was the voice more than anything that helped me recognise her.

'Miss Emily,' Tommy said, quite softly.

'You speak to them,' Madame said, as though washing her hands of everything. But she remained standing behind the wheelchair, her eyes blazing towards us.

CHAPTER TWENTY-TWO

'Marie-Claude is correct,' Miss Emily said. 'I'm the one to whom you should be speaking. Marie-Claude worked hard for our project. And the way it all ended has left her feeling somewhat disillusioned. As for myself, whatever the disappointments, I don't feel so badly about it. I think what we achieved merits some respect. Look at the two of you. You've turned out well. I'm sure you have much you could tell me to make me proud. What did you say your names were? No, no, wait. I think I shall remember. You're the boy with the bad temper. A bad temper, but a big heart. Tommy. Am I right? And you, of course, are Kathy H. You've done well as a carer. We've heard a lot about you. I remember, you see. I dare say I can remember you all.'

'What good does it do you or them?' Madame asked, then strode away from the wheelchair, past the two of us and into the darkness, for all I know to occupy the space Miss Emily had been in before.

'Miss Emily,' I said, 'it's very nice to see you again.'

'How kind of you to say so. I recognised you, but you may well not have recognised me. In fact, Kathy H., once not so long ago, I passed you sitting on that bench out there, and you certainly didn't recognise me then. You glanced at George, the big Nigerian man pushing me. Oh yes, you had quite a good look at him, and he at you. I didn't say a word, and you didn't know it was me. But tonight, in context, as it were, we know each other. You both look rather shocked at the sight of me. I've not been well recently, but I'm hoping this contraption isn't a permanent fixture. Unfortunately, my dears, I won't be able to entertain you for as long as I'd like just now, because in a short while some men are coming to take away my bedside cabinet. It's a quite wonderful object. George has put protective padding around it, but I've

234

insisted I'll accompany it myself all the same. You never know with these men. They handle it roughly, hurl it around their vehicle, then their employer claims it was like that from the start. It happened to us before, so this time, I've insisted on going along with it. It's a beautiful object, I had it with me at Hailsham, so I'm determined to get a fair price. So when they come, I'm afraid that's when I shall have to leave you. But I can see, my dears, you've come on a mission close to your hearts. I must say, it does cheer me to see you. And it cheers Marie-Claude too, even though you'd never know it to look at her. Isn't that so, darling? Oh, she pretends it's not so, but it is. She's touched that you've come to find us. Oh, she's in a sulk, ignore her, students, ignore her. Now, I'll try and answer your questions the best I can. I've heard this rumour countless times. When we still had Hailsham, we'd get two or three couples each year, trying to get in to talk to us. One even wrote to us. I suppose it's not so hard to find a large estate like that if you mean to break the rules. So you see, it's been there, this rumour, from long before your time.'

She stopped, so I said: 'What we want to know now, Miss Emily, is if the rumour's true or not.'

She went on gazing at us for a moment, then took a deep breath. 'Within Hailsham itself, whenever this talk started up, I made sure to stamp it out good and proper. But as for what students said after they'd left us, what could I do? In the end, I came to believe – and Marie-Claude believes this too, don't you, darling? – I came to believe that this rumour, it's not just a single rumour. What I mean is, I think it's one that gets created from scratch over and over. You go to the source, stamp it out, you'll not stop it starting again elsewhere. I came to this conclusion and ceased to worry about it. Marie-Claude never did worry about it. Her view was: "If they're so foolish, let them believe it." Oh yes, don't show me that sour face of yours. That's been your view of it from the beginning. After many years of it, I came not exactly to the same viewpoint. But I began to think, well, perhaps I shouldn't worry. It's not my doing, after all. And for the few couples who get disappointed, the rest will never put it to the test anyway. It's something for them to

235

dream about, a little fantasy. What harm is there? But for the two of you, I can see this doesn't apply. You are serious. You've thought carefully. You've *hoped* carefully. For students like you, I do feel regret. It gives me no pleasure at all to disappoint you. But there it is.'

I didn't want to look at Tommy. I felt surprisingly calm, and even though Miss Emily's words should have crushed us, there was an aspect to them that implied something further, something being held back, that suggested we hadn't yet got to the bottom of things. There was even the possibility she wasn't telling the truth. So I asked:

'Is it the case, then, that deferrals don't exist? There's nothing you can do?'

She shook her head slowly from side to side. 'There's no truth in the rumour. I'm sorry. I truly am.'

Suddenly Tommy asked: 'Was it true once though? Before Hailsham closed?'

Miss Emily went on shaking her head. 'It was never true. Even before the Morningdale scandal, even back when Hailsham was considered a shining beacon, an example of how we might move to a more humane and better way of doing things, even then, it wasn't true. It's best to be clear about this. A wishful rumour. That's all it ever was. Oh dear, is that the men come for the cabinet?'

The doorbell had gone, and footsteps came down the stairs to answer it. There were men's voices out in the narrow hall, and Madame came out of the darkness behind us, crossed the room and went out. Miss Emily leaned forward in the wheelchair, listening intently. Then she said:

'It's not them. It's that awful man from the decorating company again. Marie-Claude will see to it. So, my dears, we have a few minutes more. Was there something else you wished to talk to me about? This is all strictly against regulations, of course, and Marie-Claude should never have asked you in. And naturally, I should have turned you out the second I knew you were here. But Marie-Claude doesn't care much for their regulations these days, and I must say, neither do I. So if you wish to stay a little longer, you're very welcome.'

'If the rumour was never true,' Tommy said, 'then why did you take all our art stuff away? Didn't the Gallery exist either?'

'The Gallery? Well, that rumour *did* have some truth to it. There *was* a gallery. And after a fashion, there still is. These days it's here, in this house. I had to prune it down, which I regret. But there wasn't room for all of it in here. But why did we take your work away? That's what you're asking, isn't it?'

'Not just that,' I said quietly. 'Why did we do all of that work in the first place? Why train us, encourage us, make us produce all of that? If we're just going to give donations anyway, then die, why all those lessons? Why all those books and discussions?'

'Why Hailsham at all?' Madame had said this from the hall-way. She came past us again and back into the darkened section of the room. 'It's a good question for you to ask.'

Miss Emily's gaze followed her, and for a moment, remained fixed behind us. I felt like turning to see what looks were being exchanged, but it was almost like we were back at Hailsham, and we had to keep facing the front with complete attention. Then Miss Emily said:

'Yes, why Hailsham at all? Marie-Claude likes to ask that a lot these days. But not so long ago, before the Morningdale scandal, she wouldn't have dreamt of asking a question like that. It wouldn't have entered her head. You know that's right, don't look at me like that! There was only one person in those days who would ask a question like that, and that was me. Long before Morningdale, right from the very beginning, I asked that. And that made it easy for the rest of them, Marie-Claude, all the rest of them, they could all carry on without a care. All you students too. I did all the worrying and questioning for the lot of you. And as long as I was steadfast, then no doubts ever crossed your minds, any of you. But you asked your questions, dear boy. Let's answer the simplest one, and perhaps it will answer all the rest. Why did we take your artwork? Why did we do that? You said an interest-ing thing earlier, Tommy. When you were discussing this with

Marie-Claude. You said it was because your art would reveal what you were like. What you were like inside. That's what you said, wasn't it? Well, you weren't far wrong about that. We took away your art because we thought it would reveal your souls. Or to put it more finely, we did it to *prove you had souls at all*.'

She paused, and Tommy and I exchanged glances for the first time in ages. Then I asked:

'Why did you have to prove a thing like that, Miss Emily? Did someone think we didn't have souls?'

A thin smile appeared on her face. 'It's touching, Kathy, to see you so taken aback. It demonstrates, in a way, that we did our job well. As you say, why would anyone doubt you had a soul? But I have to tell you, my dear, it wasn't something commonly held when we first set out all those years ago. And though we've come a long way since then, it's still not a notion universally held, even today. You Hailsham students, even after you've been out in the world like this, you still don't know the half of it. All around the country, at this very moment, there are students being reared in deplorable conditions, conditions you Hailsham students could hardly imagine. And now we're no more, things will only get worse.'

She paused again, and for a moment she seemed to be inspecting us carefully through narrowed eyes. Finally she went on:

'Whatever else, we at least saw to it that all of you in our care, you grew up in wonderful surroundings. And we saw to it too, after you left us, you were kept away from the worst of those horrors. We were able to do that much for you at least. But this dream of yours, this dream of being able to *defer*. Such a thing would always have been beyond us to grant, even at the height of our influence. I'm sorry, I can see what I'm saying won't be welcome to you. But you mustn't be dejected. I hope you can appreciate how much we *were* able to secure for you. Look at you both now! You've had good lives, you're educated and cultured. I'm sorry we couldn't secure more for you than we did, but you must realise how much worse things once were. When Marie-Claude and I started out, there were no places like Hailsham in existence.

238

We were the first, along with Glenmorgan House. Then a few years later came the Saunders Trust. Together, we became a small but very vocal movement, and we challenged the entire way the donations programme was being run. Most importantly, we demonstrated to the world that if students were reared in humane, cultivated environments, it was possible for them to grow to be as sensitive and intelligent as any ordinary human being. Before that, all clones – or *students*, as we preferred to call you – existed only to supply medical science. In the early days, after the war, that's largely all you were to most people. Shadowy objects in test tubes. Wouldn't you agree, Marie-Claude? She's being very quiet. Usually you can't get her to shut up on this subject. Your presence, my dears, appears to have tied her tongue. Very well. So to answer your question, Tommy. That was why we collected your art. We selected the best of it and put on special exhibitions. In the late seventies, at the height of our influence, we were organising large events all around the country. There'd be cabinet ministers, bishops, all sorts of famous people coming to attend. There were speeches, large funds pledged. "There, look!" we could say. "Look at this art! How dare you claim these children are anything less than fully human?" Oh yes, there was a lot of support for our movement back then, the tide was with us.'

For the next few minutes, Miss Emily went on reminiscing about different events from those days, mentioning a lot of people whose names meant nothing to us. In fact, for a moment, it was almost like we were listening to her again at one of her morning assemblies as she drifted off on tangents none of us could follow. She seemed to enjoy herself, though, and a gentle smile settled around her eyes. Then suddenly she came out of it and said in a new tone:

'But we never quite lost touch with reality, did we, Marie-Claude? Not like our colleagues at the Saunders Trust. Even during the best of times, we always knew what a difficult battle we were engaged in. And sure enough, the Morningdale business came along, then one or two other things, and before we knew it all our hard work had come undone.'

'But what I don't understand,' I said, 'is why people would want students treated so badly in the first place.'

'From your perspective today, Kathy, your bemusement is perfectly reasonable. But you must try and see it historically. After the war, in the early fifties, when the great breakthroughs in science followed one after the other so rapidly, there wasn't time to take stock, to ask the sensible questions. Suddenly there were all these new possibilities laid before us, all these ways to cure so many previously incurable conditions. This was what the world noticed the most, wanted the most. And for a long time, people preferred to believe these organs appeared from nowhere, or at most that they grew in a kind of vacuum. Yes, there *were* arguments. But by the time people became concerned about . . . about *students*, by the time they came to consider just how you were reared, whether you should have been brought into existence at all, well by then it was too late. There was no way to reverse the process. How can you ask a world that has come to regard cancer as curable, how can you ask such a world to put away that cure, to go back to the dark days? There was no going back. However uncomfortable people were about your existence, their overwhelming concern was that their own children, their spouses, their parents, their friends, did not die from cancer, motor neurone disease, heart disease. So for a long time you were kept in the shadows, and people did their best not to think about you. And if they did, they tried to convince themselves you weren't really like us. That you were less than human, so it didn't matter. And that was how things stood until our little movement came along. But do you see what we were up against? We were virtually attempting to square the circle. Here was the world, requiring students to donate. While that remained the case, there would always be a barrier against seeing you as properly human. Well, we fought that battle for many years, and what we won for you, at least, were many improvements, though of course, you were only a select few. But then came the Morningdale scandal, then other things, and before we knew it, the climate had quite changed. No one wanted to be seen supporting us any more, and our little movement, Hailsham, Glenmorgan, the Saunders Trust, we were all of us swept away.'

'What was this Morningdale scandal you keep mentioning, Miss Emily?' I asked. 'You'll have to tell us, because we don't know about it.'

'Well, I suppose there's no reason why you should. It was never such a large matter in the wider world. It concerned a scientist called James Morningdale, quite talented in his way. He carried on his work in a remote part of Scotland, where I suppose he thought he'd attract less attention. What he wanted was to offer people the possibility of having children with enhanced characteristics. Superior intelligence, superior athleticism, that sort of thing. Of course, there'd been others with similar ambitions, but this Morningdale fellow, he'd taken his research much further than anyone before him, far beyond legal boundaries. Well, he was discovered, they put an end to his work and that seemed to be that. Except, of course, it wasn't, not for us. As I say, it never became an enormous matter. But it did create a certain atmosphere, you see. It reminded people, reminded them of a fear they'd always had. It's one thing to create students, such as yourselves, for the donation programme. But a generation of created children who'd take their place in society? Children demonstrably *superior* to the rest of us? Oh no. That frightened people. They recoiled from that.'

'But Miss Emily,' I said, 'what did any of that have to do with us? Why did Hailsham have to close because of something like that?'

'We didn't see an obvious connection either, Kathy. Not at first. And I often think now, we were culpable not to do so. Had we been more alert, less absorbed with ourselves, if we'd worked very hard at that stage when the news about Morningdale first broke, we might have been able to avert it. Oh, Marie-Claude disagrees. She thinks it would have happened no matter what we did, and she might have a point. After all, it wasn't just Morningdale. There were other things at that time. That awful television series, for instance. All these things contributed, contributed to the turning of the tide. But I suppose when it comes down to it, the central flaw was this. Our little movement, we were always too fragile, always too dependent on the whims of our supporters. So long as the climate was in our favour, so long as a corporation or a politician could see a benefit in supporting us, then we were able to keep afloat. But it had always been a struggle, and after Morningdale, after the climate changed, we had no chance. The world didn't want to be reminded how the donation programme really worked. They didn't want to think about you students, or about the conditions you were brought up in. In other words, my dears, they wanted you back in the shadows. Back in the shadows where you'd been before the likes of Marie-Claude and myself ever came along. And all those influential people who'd once been so keen to help us, well of course, they all vanished. We lost our sponsors, one after the other, in a matter of just over a year. We kept going for as long as we could, we went on for two years more than Glenmorgan. But in the end, as you know, we were obliged to close, and today there's hardly a trace left of the work we did. You won't find anything like Hailsham anywhere in the country now. All you'll find, as ever, are those vast government "homes", and even if they're somewhat better than they once were, let me tell you, my dears, you'd not sleep for days if you saw what still goes on in some of those places. And as for Marie-Claude and me, here we are, we've retreated to this house, and upstairs we have a mountain of your work. That's what we have to remind us of what we did. And a mountain of debt too, though that's not nearly so welcome. And the memories, I suppose, of all of you. And the knowledge that we've given you better lives than you would have had otherwise.'

'Don't try and ask them to thank you,' Madame's voice said from behind us. 'Why should they be grateful? They came here looking for something much more. What we gave them, all the years, all the fighting we did on their behalf, what do they know of that? They think it's God-given. Until they came here, they knew nothing of it. All they feel now is disappointment, because we haven't given them everything possible.'

Nobody spoke for a while. Then there was a noise outside and the doorbell rang again. Madame came out of the darkness and went out into the hall.

'This time it *must* be the men,' Miss Emily said. 'I shall have to get ready. But you can stay a little longer. The men have to bring the thing down two flights of stairs. Marie-Claude will see they don't damage it.'

Tommy and I couldn't quite believe that was the end of it. We neither of us stood up, and anyway, there was no sign of anyone helping Miss Emily out of her wheelchair. I wondered for a moment if she was going to try and get up by herself, but she remained still, leaning forward as before, listening intently. Then Tommy said:

'So there's definitely nothing. No deferral, nothing like that.'

'Tommy,' I murmured, and glared at him. But Miss Emily said gently:

'No, Tommy. There's nothing like that. Your life must now run the course that's been set for it.'

'So, what you're saying, Miss,' Tommy said, 'is that everything we did, all the lessons, everything. It was all about what you just told us? There was nothing more to it than that?'

'I can see,' Miss Emily said, 'that it might look as though you were simply pawns in a game. It can certainly be looked at like that. But think of it. You were lucky pawns. There was a certain climate and now it's gone. You have to accept that sometimes that's how things happen in this world. People's opinions, their feelings, they go one way, then the other. It just so happens you grew up at a certain point in this process.'

'It might be just some trend that came and went,' I said. 'But for us, it's our life.'

'Yes, that's true. But think of it. You were better off than many who came before you. And who knows what those who come after you will have to face. I'm sorry, students, but I must leave you now. George! George!'

There had been a lot of noise out in the hallway, and perhaps this had stopped George from hearing, because there was no response. Tommy asked suddenly:

'Is that why Miss Lucy left?'

For a while I thought Miss Emily, whose attention was on what was going on in the hallway, hadn't heard him. She leaned back in her wheelchair and began moving it gradually towards the door. There were so many little coffee tables and chairs there didn't seem a way through. I was about to get up and clear a path, when she stopped suddenly.

'Lucy Wainright,' she said. 'Ah yes. We had a little trouble with her.' She paused, then adjusted her wheelchair back to face Tommy. 'Yes, we had a little trouble with her. A disagreement. But to answer your question, Tommy. The disagreement with Lucy Wainright wasn't to do with what I've just been telling you. Not directly, anyway. No, that was more, shall we say, an internal matter.'

I thought she was going to leave it at that, so I asked: 'Miss Emily, if it's all right, we'd like to know about it, about what happened with Miss Lucy.'

Miss Emily raised her eyebrows. 'Lucy Wainright? She was important to you? Forgive me, dear students, I'm forgetting again. Lucy wasn't with us for long, so for us she's just a peripheral figure in our memory of Hailsham. And not an altogether happy one. But I appreciate, if you were there during just those years . . .' She laughed to herself and seemed to be remembering something. In the hall, Madame was telling the men off really loudly, but Miss Emily now seemed to have lost interest. She was going through her memories with a look of concentration. Finally she said: 'She was a nice enough girl, Lucy Wainright. But after she'd been with us for a while, she began to have these ideas. She thought you students had to be made more aware. More aware of what lay ahead of you, who you were, what you were for. She believed you should be given as full a picture as possible. That to do anything less would be somehow to cheat you. We considered her view and concluded she was mistaken.'

'Why?' Tommy asked. 'Why did you think that?'

'Why? She meant well, I'm sure of that. I can see you were fond of her. She had the makings of an excellent guardian. But what she was wanting to do, it was too *theoretical*. We had run Hailsham for many years, we had a sense of what could work, what was best for the students in the long run, beyond Hailsham. Lucy Wainright was idealistic, nothing wrong with that. But she had no grasp of practicalities. You see, we were able to give you something, something which even now no one will ever take from you, and we were able to do that principally by *sheltering* you. Hailsham would not have been Hailsham if we hadn't. Very well, sometimes that meant we kept things from you, lied to you. Yes, in many ways we *fooled* you. I suppose you could even call it that. But we sheltered you during those years, and we gave you your childhoods. Lucy was well-meaning enough. But if she'd had her way, your happiness at Hailsham would have been shattered. Look at you both now! I'm so proud to see you both. You built your lives on what we gave you. You wouldn't be who you are today if we'd not protected you. You wouldn't have become absorbed in your lessons, you wouldn't have lost yourselves in your art and your writing. Why should you have done, knowing what lay in store for each of you? You would have told us it was all pointless, and how could we have argued with you? So she had to go.'

We could hear Madame now shouting at the men. She hadn't lost her temper exactly, but her voice was frighteningly stern, and the men's voices, which until this point had been arguing with her, fell silent.

'Perhaps it's just as well I've remained in here with you,' Miss Emily said. 'Marie-Claude does this sort of thing so much more efficiently.'

I don't know what made me say it. Maybe it was because I knew the visit would have to finish pretty soon; maybe I was getting curious to know how exactly Miss Emily and Madame felt about each other. Anyway, I said to her, lowering my voice and nodding towards the doorway:

'Madame never liked us. She's always been afraid of us. In the way people are afraid of spiders and things.'

I waited to see if Miss Emily would get angry, no longer caring much if she did. Sure enough, she turned to me sharply, as if I'd thrown a ball of paper at her, and her eyes flashed in a way that reminded me of her Hailsham days. But her voice was even and soft when she replied:

'Marie-Claude has given *everything* for you. She has worked and worked and worked. Make no mistake about it, my child, Marie-Claude is on your side and will always be on your side. Is she afraid of you? We're *all* afraid of you. I myself had to fight back my dread of you all almost every day I was at Hailsham. There were times I'd look down at you all from my study window and I'd feel such revulsion . . .' She stopped, then something in her eyes flashed again. 'But I was determined not to let such feelings stop me doing what was right. I fought those feelings and I won. Now, if you'd be so good as to help me out of here, George should be waiting with my crutches.'

With us at each elbow, she walked carefully into the hall, where a large man in a nursing uniform started with alarm and quickly produced a pair of crutches.

The front door was open to the street and I was surprised to see there was still daylight left. Madame's voice was coming from outside, talking more calmly now to the men. It felt like time for Tommy and me to slip away, but the George man was helping Miss Emily with her coat, while she stood steadily between her crutches; there was no way we could get past, so we just waited. I suppose, too, we were waiting to say goodbye to Miss Emily; maybe, after everything else, we wanted to thank her, I'm not sure. But she was now preoccupied with her cabinet. She began to make some urgent point to the men outside, then left with George, not looking back at us.

Tommy and I stayed in the hall for a while longer, not sure what to do. When we did eventually wander outside, I noticed the lamps had come on all the way down the long street, even though the sky wasn't yet dark. A white van was starting up its engine. Right behind was a big old Volvo with Miss Emily in the passenger seat. Madame was crouching by the window, nodding to something Miss Emily was saying, while George closed up the boot and moved round to the driver's door. Then the white van moved off, and Miss Emily's car followed.

Madame watched the departing vehicles for a long time. Then she turned as though to go back into the house, and seeing us there on the pavement, stopped abruptly, almost shrinking back.

'We're going now,' I said. 'Thank you for talking to us. Please say goodbye to Miss Emily for us.'

I could see her studying me in the fading light. Then she said:

'Kathy H. I remember you. Yes, I remember.' She fell silent, but went on looking at me.

'I think I know what you're thinking about,' I said, in the end. 'I think I can guess.'

'Very well.' Her voice was dreamy and her gaze had slightly lost focus. 'Very well. You are a mind-reader. Tell me.'

'There was a time you saw me once, one afternoon, in the dormitories. There was no one else around, and I was playing this tape, this music. I was sort of dancing with my eyes closed and you saw me.'

'That's very good. A mind-reader. You should be on the stage. I only recognised you just now. But yes, I remember that occasion. I still think about it from time to time.'

'That's funny. So do I.'

'I see.'

We could have ended the conversation there. We could have said goodbye and left. But she stepped closer to us, looking into my face all the time.

'You were much younger then,' she said. 'But yes, it's you.'

'You don't have to answer this if you don't want to,' I said. 'But it's always puzzled me. May I ask you?'

'You read my mind. But I cannot read yours.'

'Well, you were . . . upset that day. You were watching me, and when I realised, and I opened my eyes, you were watching me

247

and I think you were crying. In fact, I know you were. You were watching me and crying. Why was that?'

Madame's expression didn't change and she kept staring into my face. 'I was weeping,' she said eventually, very quietly, as though afraid the neighbours were listening, 'because when I came in, I heard your music. I thought some foolish student had left the music on. But when I came into your dormitory, I saw you, by yourself, a little girl, dancing. As you say, eyes closed, far away, a look of yearning. You were dancing so very sympathetically. And the music, the song. There was something in the words. It was full of sadness.'

'The song,' I said, 'it was called "Never Let Me Go".' Then I sang a couple of lines quietly under my breath for her. *'Never let me go. Oh, baby, baby. Never let me go . . .'*

She nodded as though in agreement. 'Yes, it was that song. I've heard it once or twice since then. On the radio, on the television. And it's taken me back to that little girl, dancing by herself.'

'You say you're not a mind-reader,' I said. 'But maybe you were that day. Maybe that's why you started to cry when you saw me. Because whatever the song was really about, in my head, when I was dancing, I had my own version. You see, I imagined it was about this woman who'd been told she couldn't have babies. But then she'd had one, and she was so pleased, and she was holding it ever so tightly to her breast, really afraid something might separate them, and she's going baby, baby, never let me go. That's not what the song's about at all, but that's what I had in my head that time. Maybe you read my mind, and that's why you found it so sad. I didn't think it was so sad at the time, but now, when I think back, it does feel a bit sad.'

I'd spoken to Madame, but I could sense Tommy shifting next to me, and was aware of the texture of his clothes, of everything about him. Then Madame said:

'That's most interesting. But I was no more a mind-reader then than today. I was weeping for an altogether different reason. When I watched you dancing that day, I saw something else. I saw a new world coming rapidly. More scientific, efficient, yes.

More cures for the old sicknesses. Very good. But a harsh, cruel world. And I saw a little girl, her eyes tightly closed, holding to her breast the old kind world, one that she knew in her heart could not remain, and she was holding it and pleading, never to let her go. That is what I saw. It wasn't really you, what you were doing, I know that. But I saw you and it broke my heart. And I've never forgotten.'

Then she came forward until she was only a step or two from us. 'Your stories this evening, they touched me too.' She looked now to Tommy, then back at me. 'Poor creatures. I wish I could help you. But now you're by yourselves.'

She reached out her hand, all the while staring into my face, and placed it on my cheek. I could feel a trembling go all through her body, but she kept her hand where it was, and I could see again tears appearing in her eyes.

'You poor creatures,' she repeated, almost in a whisper. Then she turned and went back into her house.

We hardly discussed our meeting with Miss Emily and Madame on the journey back. Or if we did, we talked only about the less important things, like how much we thought they'd aged, or the stuff in their house.

I kept us on the most obscure back roads I knew, where only our headlights disturbed the darkness. We'd occasionally encounter other headlights, and then I'd get the feeling they belonged to other carers, driving home alone, or maybe like me, with a donor beside them. I realised, of course, that other people used these roads; but that night, it seemed to me these dark byways of the country existed just for the likes of us, while the big glittering motorways with their huge signs and super cafés were for everyone else. I don't know if Tommy was thinking something similar. Maybe he was, because at one point, he remarked:

'Kath, you really know some weird roads.'

He did a little laugh as he said this, but then he seemed to fall deep into thought. Then as we were going down a particularly dark lane in the back of nowhere, he said suddenly:

'I think Miss Lucy was right. Not Miss Emily.'

I can't remember if I said anything to that. If I did, it certainly wasn't anything very profound. But that was the moment I first noticed it, something in his voice, or maybe his manner, that set off distant alarm bells. I remember taking my eyes off the twisting road to glance at him, but he was just sitting there quietly, gazing straight ahead into the night.

A few minutes later, he said suddenly: 'Kath, can we stop? I'm sorry, I need to get out a minute.'

Thinking he was feeling sick again, I pulled up almost immediately, hard against a hedge. The spot was completely unlit, and even with the car lights on, I was nervous another vehicle might come round the curve and run into us. That's why, when Tommy got out and disappeared into the blackness, I didn't go with him. Also, there'd been something purposeful about the way he'd got out that suggested even if he was feeling ill, he'd prefer to cope with it on his own. Anyway, that's why I was still in the car, wondering whether to move it a little further up the hill, when I heard the first scream.

At first I didn't even think it was him, but some maniac who'd been lurking in the bushes. I was already out of the car when the second and third screams came, and by then I knew it was Tommy, though that hardly lessened my urgency. In fact, for a moment, I was probably close to panic, not having a clue where he was. I couldn't really see anything, and when I tried to go towards the screams, I was stopped by an impenetrable thicket. Then I found an opening, and stepping through a ditch, came up to a fence. I managed to climb over it and I landed in soft mud.

I could now see my surroundings much better. I was in a field that sloped down steeply not far in front of me, and I could see the lights of some village way below in the valley. The wind here was really powerful, and a gust pulled at me so hard, I had to reach for the fence post. The moon wasn't quite full, but it was bright enough, and I could make out in the mid-distance, near where the field began to fall away, Tommy's figure, raging, shouting, flinging his fists and kicking out.

I tried to run to him, but the mud sucked my feet down. The mud was impeding him too, because one time, when he kicked out, he slipped and fell out of view into the blackness. But his jumbled swear-words continued uninterrupted, and I was able to reach him just as he was getting to his feet again. I caught a glimpse of his face in the moonlight, caked in mud and distorted with fury, then I reached for his flailing arms and held on tight. He tried to shake me off, but I kept holding on, until he stopped shouting and I felt the fight go out of him. Then I realised he too had his arms around me. And so we stood together like that, at the top of that field, for what seemed like ages, not saying anything, just holding each other, while the wind kept blowing and blowing at us, tugging our clothes, and for a moment, it seemed like we were holding onto each other because that was the only way to stop us being swept away into the night.

When at last we pulled apart, he muttered: 'I'm really sorry, Kath.' Then he gave a shaky laugh and added: 'Good job there weren't cows in the field. They'd have got a fright.'

I could see he was doing his best to reassure me it was all okay now, but his chest was still heaving and his legs shaking. We walked together back towards the car, trying not to slip.

'You stink of cow poo,' I said, finally.

'Oh God, Kath. How do I explain this? We'll have to sneak in round the back.'

'You'll still have to sign in.'

'Oh God,' he said, and laughed again.

I found some rags in the car and we got the worst of the muck off. But I'd taken out of the boot, just while I was searching for the rags, the sports bag containing his animal pictures, and when we set off again, I noticed Tommy brought it inside with him.

We travelled some way, not saying much, the bag on his lap. I was waiting for him to say something about the pictures; it even occurred to me he was working up to another rage, when he'd throw all the pictures out of the window. But he held the bag protectively with both hands and kept staring at the dark road unfolding before us. After a long period of silence, he said:

'I'm sorry about just now, Kath. I really am. I'm a real idiot.' Then he added: 'What are you thinking, Kath?'

'I was thinking,' I said, 'about back then, at Hailsham, when you used to go bonkers like that, and we couldn't understand it. We couldn't understand how you could ever get like that. And I was just having this idea, just a thought really. I was thinking maybe the reason you used to get like that was because at some level you always *knew*.'

Tommy thought about this, then shook his head. 'Don't think so, Kath. No, it was always just me. Me being an idiot. That's all it ever was.' Then after a moment, he did a small laugh and said: 'But that's a funny idea. Maybe I did know, somewhere deep down. Something the rest of you didn't.'

CHAPTER TWENTY-THREE

Nothing seemed to change much in the week or so after that trip. I didn't expect it to stay that way though, and sure enough, by the start of October, I started noticing little differences. For one thing, though Tommy carried on with his animal pictures, he became cagey about doing them in my presence. We weren't quite back to how it was when I'd first become his carer and all the Cottages stuff was still hanging over us. But it was like he'd thought about it and come to a decision: that he'd continue with the animals as the mood took him, but if I came in, he'd stop and put them away. I wasn't that hurt by this. In fact, in many ways, it was a relief: those animals staring us in the face when we were together would have only made things more awkward.

But there were other changes I found less easy. I don't mean we weren't still having some good times up in his room. We were even having sex every now and then. But what I couldn't help noticing was how, more and more, Tommy tended to identify himself with the other donors at the centre. If, for instance, the two of us were reminiscing about old Hailsham people, he'd sooner or later move the conversation round to one of his current donor friends who'd maybe said or done something similar to what we were recalling. There was one time in particular, when I drove into the Kingsfield after a long journey and stepped out of the car. The Square was looking a bit like that time I'd come to the centre with Ruth the day we'd gone to see the boat. It was an overcast autumn afternoon, and there was no one about except for a group of donors clustered under the overhanging roof of the recreation building. I saw Tommy was with them – he was standing with a shoulder against a post – and was listening to a donor who was sitting crouched on the entrance steps. I came towards them a little way, then stopped and waited, there in the open, under the grey sky. But Tommy, though he'd seen me, went on listening to his friend, and eventually he and all the others burst out laughing. Even then, he carried on listening and smiling. He claimed afterwards he'd signalled to me to come over, but if he had, it hadn't been at all obvious. All I registered was him smiling vaguely in my direction, then going back to what his friend was saying. Okay, he was in the middle of something, and after a minute or so, he did come away, and the two of us went up to his room. But it was quite different to the way things would have happened before. And it wasn't just that he'd kept me waiting out in the Square. I wouldn't have minded that so much. It was more that I sensed for the first time that day something close to resentment on his part at having to come away with me, and once we were up in his room, the atmosphere between us wasn't so great.

To be fair, a lot of it might have been down to me as much as him. Because as I'd stood there watching them all talking and laughing, I'd felt an unexpected little tug; because there was something about the way these donors had arranged themselves in a rough semi-circle, something about their poses, almost studiedly relaxed, whether standing or sitting, as though to announce to the world how much each one of them was savouring the company, that reminded me of the way our little gang used to sit around our pavilion together. That comparison, as I say, tugged something inside me, and so maybe, once we were up in his room, it was as much me feeling resentful as the other way round.

I'd feel a similar little prickle of resentment each time he told me I didn't understand something or other because I wasn't yet a donor. But apart from one particular time, which I'll come to in a moment, a little prickle was all it was. Usually he'd say these things to me half-jokingly, almost affectionately. And even when there was something more to it, like the time he told me to stop taking his dirty washing to the laundry because he could do it himself, it hardly amounted to a row. That time, I'd asked him:

'What difference does it make, which one of us takes the towels down? I'm going out that way anyway.'

To which he'd shaken his head and said: 'Look, Kath, I'll sort out my own things. If you were a donor, you'd see.'

Okay, it did niggle, but it was something I could forget easily enough. But as I say, there was this one time he brought it up, about my not being a donor, that really riled me.

It happened about a week after the notice came for his fourth donation. We'd been expecting it and had already talked it through a lot. In fact, we'd had some of our most intimate conversations since the Littlehampton trip discussing the fourth donation. I've known donors to react in all sorts of ways to their fourth donation. Some want to talk about it all the time, endlessly and pointlessly. Others will only joke about it, while others refuse to discuss it at all. And then there's this odd tendency among donors to treat a fourth donation as something worthy of congratulations. A donor 'on a fourth', even one who's been pretty unpopular up till then, is treated with special respect. Even the doctors and nurses play up to this: a donor on a fourth will go in for a check and be greeted by whitecoats smiling and shaking their hand. Well, Tommy and I, we talked about all of this, sometimes jokingly, other times seriously and carefully. We discussed all the different ways people tried to handle it, and which ways made the best sense. Once, lying side by side on the bed with the dark coming on, he said:

'You know why it is, Kath, why everyone worries so much about the fourth? It's because they're not sure they'll really complete. If you knew for certain you'd complete, it would be easier. But they never tell us for sure.'

I'd been wondering for a while if this would come up, and I'd been thinking about how I'd respond. But when it did, I couldn't find much to say. So I just said: 'It's just a lot of rubbish, Tommy. Just talk, wild talk. It's not even worth thinking about.'

But Tommy would have known I had nothing to back up my words. He'd have known, too, he was raising questions to which even the doctors had no certain answers. You'll have heard the same talk. How maybe, after the fourth donation, even if you've technically completed, you're still conscious in some sort of way;

255

how then you find there are more donations, plenty of them, on the other side of that line; how there are no more recovery centres, no carers, no friends; how there's nothing to do except watch your remaining donations until they switch you off. It's horror movie stuff, and most of the time people don't want to think about it. Not the whitecoats, not the carers – and usually not the donors. But now and again, a donor will bring it up, as Tommy did that evening, and I wish now we'd talked about it. As it was, after I dismissed it as rubbish, we both shrank back from the whole territory. At least, though, I knew it was on Tommy's mind after that, and I was glad he'd at least confided in me that far. What I'm saying is that all in all I was under the impression we were dealing with the fourth donation pretty well together, and that's why I was so knocked off balance by what he came out with that day we walked around the field.

The Kingsfield doesn't have much in the way of grounds. The Square's the obvious congregating point and the few bits behind the buildings look more like wasteland. The largest chunk, which the donors call 'the field', is a rectangle of overgrown weeds and thistles held in by wire-mesh fences. There's always been talk of turning it into a proper lawn for the donors, but they haven't done it yet, even now. It might not be so peaceful even if they did get round to it, because of the big road nearby. All the same, when donors get restless and need to walk it off, that's where they tend to go, scraping through all the nettles and brambles. The particular morning I'm talking about, it was really foggy, and I knew the field would be soaking, but Tommy had been insistent we go there for a walk. Not surprisingly, we were the only ones there – which probably suited Tommy fine. After crashing about the thickets for a few minutes, he stopped next to the fence and stared at the blank fog on the other side. Then he said:

'Kath, I don't want you to take this the wrong way. But I've been thinking it over a lot. Kath, I think I ought to get a different carer.'

In the few seconds after he said this, I realised I wasn't surprised by it at all; that in some funny way I'd been waiting for it. But I was angry all the same and didn't say anything.

'It's not just because the fourth donation's coming up,' he went on. 'It's not just about that. It's because of stuff like what happened last week. When I had all that kidney trouble. There's going to be much more stuff like that coming.'

'That's why I came and found you,' I said. 'That's exactly why I came to help you. For what's starting now. And it's what Ruth wanted too.'

'Ruth wanted that other thing for us,' Tommy said. 'She wouldn't necessarily have wanted you to be my carer through this last bit.'

'Tommy,' I said, and I suppose by now I was furious, but I kept my voice quiet and under control, 'I'm the one to help you. That's why I came and found you again.'

'Ruth wanted the other thing for us,' Tommy repeated. 'All this is something else. Kath, I don't want to be that way in front of you.'

He was looking down at the ground, a palm pressed against the wire-mesh fence, and for a moment he looked like he was listening intently to the sound of the traffic somewhere beyond the fog. And that was when he said it, shaking his head slightly:

'Ruth would have understood. She was a donor, so she would have understood. I'm not saying she'd necessarily have wanted the same thing for herself. If she'd been able to, maybe she'd have wanted you as her carer right to the end. But she'd have understood, about me wanting to do it differently. Kath, sometimes you just don't see it. You don't see it because you're not a donor.'

It was when he came out with this that I turned and walked off. As I said, I'd been almost prepared for the bit about not wanting me any more as his carer. But what had really stung, coming after all those other little things, like when he'd kept me standing in the Square, was what he'd said then, the way he'd divided me off yet again, not just from all the other donors, but from him and Ruth.

This never turned into a huge fight though. When I stalked off, there wasn't much else I could do other than go back up to his room, and then he came up himself several minutes later. I'd cooled down by then and so had he, and we were able to have a better conversation about it. It was a bit stiff, but we made peace, and even got into some of the practicalities of changing carers. Then, as we were sitting in the dull light, side by side on the edge of his bed, he said to me:

'I don't want us to fight again, Kath. But I've been wanting to ask you this a lot. I mean, don't you get tired of being a carer? All the rest of us, we became donors ages ago. You've been doing it for years. Don't you sometimes wish, Kath, they'd hurry up and send you your notice?'

I shrugged. 'I don't mind. Anyway, it's important there are good carers. And I'm a good carer.'

'But is it really that important? Okay, it's really nice to have a good carer. But in the end, is it really so important? The donors will all donate, just the same, and then they'll complete.'

'Of course it's important. A good carer makes a big difference to what a donor's life's actually like.'

'But all this rushing about you do. All this getting exhausted and being by yourself. I've been watching you. It's wearing you out. You must do, Kath, you must sometimes wish they'd tell you you can stop. I don't know why you don't have a word with them, ask them why it's been so long.' Then when I kept quiet, he said: 'I'm just saying, that's all. Let's not fight again.'

I put my head on his shoulder and said: 'Yeah, well. Maybe it won't be for much longer anyway. But for now, I have to keep going. Even if you don't want me around, there are others who do.'

'I suppose you're right, Kath. You *are* a really good carer. You'd be the perfect one for me too if you weren't you.' He did a laugh and put his arm round me, though we kept sitting side by side. Then he said: 'I keep thinking about this river somewhere, with the water moving really fast. And these two people in the water, trying to hold onto each other, holding on as hard as they can, but in the end it's just too much. The current's too strong. They've got to let go, drift apart. That's how I think it is with us. It's a shame, Kath, because we've loved each other all our lives. But in the end, we can't stay together forever.'

When he said this, I remembered the way I'd held onto him that night in the wind-swept field on the way back from Little-hampton. I don't know if he was thinking about that too, or if he was still thinking about his rivers and strong currents. In any case, we went on sitting like that on the side of the bed for a long time, lost in our thoughts. Then in the end I said to him:

'I'm sorry I blew up at you earlier. I'll talk to them. I'll try and see to it you get someone really good.'

'It's a shame, Kath,' he said again. And I don't think we talked any more about it that morning.

I remember the few weeks that came after that – the last few weeks before the new carer took over - as being surprisingly tran-quil. Maybe Tommy and I were making a special effort to be nice to each other, but the time seemed to slip by in an almost carefree way. You might think there would have been an air of unreality about us being like that, but it didn't seem strange at the time. I was quite busy with a couple of my other donors in North Wales and that kept me from the Kingsfield more than I'd have wanted, but I still managed to come in three or four times a week. The weather grew colder, but stayed dry and often sunny, and we whiled away the hours in his room, sometimes having sex, more often just talking, or with Tommy listening to me read. Once or twice, Tommy even brought out his notebook and doodled away for new animal ideas while I read from the bed.

Then I came in one day and it was the last time. I arrived just after one o'clock on a crisp December afternoon. I went up to his room, half expecting some change – I don't know what. Maybe I thought he'd have put up decorations in his room or some-thing. But of course, everything was as normal, and all in all, that was a relief. Tommy didn't look any different either, but when we started talking, it was hard to pretend this was just another visit. Then again, we'd talked over so much in the previous weeks, it wasn't as though we had anything in particular we *had* to get through. And I think we were reluctant to start any new conversation we'd regret not being able to finish properly. That's why there was a kind of emptiness to our talk that day.

Just once, though, after I'd been wandering aimlessly around his room for a while, I did ask him:

'Tommy, are you glad Ruth completed before finding out everything we did in the end?'

He was lying on the bed, and went on staring at the ceiling for a while before saying: 'Funny, because I was thinking about the same thing the other day. What you've got to remember about Ruth, when it came to things like that, she was always different to us. You and me, right from the start, even when we were little, we were always trying to find things out. Remember, Kath, all those secret talks we used to have? But Ruth wasn't like that. She always wanted to believe in things. That was Ruth. So yeah, in a way, I think it's best the way it happened.' Then he added: 'Of course, what we found out, Miss Emily, all of that, it doesn't change anything about Ruth. She wanted the best for us at the end. She really wanted the best for us.'

I didn't want to get into a big discussion about Ruth at that stage, so I just agreed with him. But now I've had more time to think about it, I'm not so sure how I feel. A part of me keeps wishing we'd somehow been able to share everything we discovered with Ruth. Okay, maybe it would have made her feel bad; made her see whatever damage she'd once done to us couldn't be repaired as easily as she'd hoped. And maybe, if I'm honest, that's a small part of my wishing she knew it all before she completed. But in the end, I think it's about something else, something much more than my feeling vengeful and mean-spirited. Because as Tommy said, she wanted the best for us at the end, and though she said that day in the car I'd never forgive her, she was wrong about that. I've got no anger left for her now. When I say I wish she'd found out the whole score, it's more because I feel sad at the idea of her finishing up different from me and Tommy. The way it is, it's like there's a line with us on one side and Ruth on the other, and when all's said and done, I feel sad about that, and I think she would too if she could see it.

Tommy and I, we didn't do any big farewell number that day. When it was time, he came down the stairs with me, which he didn't usually do, and we walked across the Square together to the car. Because of the time of year, the sun was already setting behind the buildings. There were a few shadowy figures, as usual, under the overhanging roof, but the Square itself was empty. Tommy was silent all the way to the car. Then he did a little laugh and said:

'You know, Kath, when I used to play football back at Hailsham. I had this secret thing I did. When I scored a goal, I'd turn round like this' – he raised both arms up in triumph – 'and I'd run back to my mates. I never went mad or anything, just ran back with my arms up, like this.' He paused for a moment, his arms still in the air. Then he lowered them and smiled. 'In my head, Kath, when I was running back, I always imagined I was splashing through water. Nothing deep, just up to the ankles at the most. That's what I used to imagine, every time. Splash, splash, splash.' He put his arms up again. 'It felt really good. You've just scored, you turn, and then, splash, splash, splash.' He looked at me and did another little laugh. 'All this time, I never told a single soul.'

I laughed too and said: 'You crazy kid, Tommy.'

After that, we kissed – just a small kiss – then I got into the car. Tommy kept standing there while I turned the thing round. Then as I pulled away, he smiled and waved. I watched him in my rearview, and he was standing there almost till the last moment. Right at the end, I saw him raise his hand again vaguely and turn away towards the overhanging roof. Then the Square had gone from the mirror.

I was talking to one of my donors a few days ago who was complaining about how memories, even your most precious ones, fade surprisingly quickly. But I don't go along with that. The memories I value most, I don't see them ever fading. I lost Ruth, then I lost Tommy, but I won't lose my memories of them.

I suppose I lost Hailsham too. You still hear stories about some ex-Hailsham student trying to find it, or rather the place where it used to be. And the odd rumour will go round sometimes about what Hailsham's become these days – a hotel, a school, a ruin. Myself, for all the driving I do, I've never tried to find it. I'm not really interested in seeing it, whatever way it is now.

Mind you, though I say I never go looking for Hailsham, what I find is that sometimes, when I'm driving around, I suddenly think I've spotted some bit of it. I see a sports pavilion in the distance and I'm sure it's ours. Or a row of poplars on the horizon next to a big woolly oak, and I'm convinced for a second I'm coming up to the South Playing Field from the other side. Once, on a grey morning, on a long stretch of road in Gloucestershire, I passed a broken-down car in a lay-by, and I was sure the girl standing in front of it, gazing emptily out towards the on-coming vehicles, was Susanna C., who'd been a couple of years above us and one of the Sales monitors. These moments hit me when I'm least expecting it, when I'm driving with something else entirely in my mind. So maybe at some level, I *am* on the lookout for Hailsham.

But as I say, I don't go searching for it, and anyway, by the end of the year, I won't be driving around like this any more. So the chances are I won't ever come across it now, and on reflection, I'm glad that's the way it'll be. It's like with my memories of Tommy and of Ruth. Once I'm able to have a quieter life, in whichever centre they send me to, I'll have Hailsham with me, safely in my head, and that'll be something no one can take away.

The only indulgent thing I did, just once, was a couple of weeks after I heard Tommy had completed, when I drove up to Norfolk, even though I had no real need to. I wasn't after anything in particular and I didn't go up as far as the coast. Maybe I just felt like looking at all those flat fields of nothing and the huge grey skies. At one stage I found myself on a road I'd never been on, and for about half an hour I didn't know where I was and didn't care. I went past field after flat, featureless field, with virtually no change except when occasionally a flock of birds, hearing my engine, flew up out of the furrows. Then at last I spotted a few trees in the distance, not far from the roadside, so I drove up to them, stopped and got out.

I found I was standing before acres of ploughed earth. There was a fence keeping me from stepping into the field, with two lines of barbed wire, and I could see how this fence and the cluster of three or four trees above me were the only things breaking the wind for miles. All along the fence, especially along the lower line of wire, all sorts of rubbish had caught and tangled. It was like the debris you get on a sea-shore: the wind must have carried some of it for miles and miles before finally coming up against these trees and these two lines of wire. Up in the branches of the trees, too, I could see, flapping about, torn plastic sheeting and bits of old carrier bags. That was the only time, as I stood there, looking at that strange rubbish, feeling the wind coming across those empty fields, that I started to imagine just a little fantasy thing, because this was Norfolk after all, and it was only a couple of weeks since I'd lost him. I was thinking about the rubbish, the flapping plastic in the branches, the shore-line of odd stuff caught along the fencing, and I half-closed my eyes and imagined this was the spot where everything I'd ever lost since my childhood had washed up, and I was now standing here in front of it, and if I waited long enough, a tiny figure would appear on the horizon across the field, and gradually get larger until I'd see it was Tommy, and he'd wave, maybe even call. The fantasy never got beyond that – I didn't let it – and though the tears rolled down my face, I wasn't sobbing or out of control. I just waited a bit, then turned back to the car, to drive off to wherever it was I was supposed to be.